Little Doves

Little Doves

Sara Ennis

Good Girl Charlie

DEDICATION

The things I inherited from my parents are love of story and an ability to identify mental health issues at a glance, so it seems only fitting that I put those skills to good use.

DEDICATION

Prologue

Something is wrong with her eyes. She can't see anything, but there are shadows.

Her nose is trying to help, presenting a flood of smells, none good: sweat, dank and oniony. There's something earthy, but not the good kind of earthy, like camping. This is a sweet, musty, sour scent. Rusty. Metallic. And under all of it, old pee.

She tries to sit up. She can't. Her body isn't working. She tries to raise a hand, but it stays on the floor, rough, damp concrete under her fingertips. She tries to roll onto her back, and a shriek of intense pain lights her body like fireworks. She stops moving.

Did she scream? She must have. If she didn't, she should. Someone needs to know how much it hurts. She breathes in and reaches down into her depths, trying to express the intensity of the pain gripping her, but nothing comes, not even a whisper.

She's probably dead. No one could be alive and hurt this bad.

Images flash, like a movie, through her head. Her mind recoils, and her brain clicks away as if she's changed the channel on the TV. She's not where she's supposed to be. She was in the parking lot of The Madalena. There were happy voices. Girls laughing. Boys goofing around and showing off. Parents yelling at their kids to hurry up. When was that? A few minutes ago? A few hours ago? Days? When?

There are no happy sounds here. It's quiet. Too quiet. Creepy. She hears soft shuffling noises, tiny feet, noses sniffing the air. The sound stops, then starts again. Her brain tells her what the sound is, but she denies what her heart knows to be true. It's definitely not rats. No, definitely not.

1

Somewhere close, the click...click...click of liquid hitting metal. It's going to drive her crazy if she focuses on it. Is this what Chinese Water Torture is?

Her brain feels so foggy. Is she sleeping? Yes, she must be. It feels like she's waking up from a bad dream, the kind you have when you're really sick. Maybe that's what's happening. Maybe she's got a bad flu, so bad she doesn't even realize. That would explain why she doesn't understand anything. But why can't she see? What's wrong with her eyes? And why does her body hurt so very much? The answer to both of those questions seems important.

If she's sick, she should be at home, or if she's really sick, she should be in a hospital. She should not be on a concrete floor, and the concrete under her is the one thing she's absolutely sure of. She's cold. Why is she so cold? It's summer. She should be hot, not cold. She tries to move her hand again, and this time it cooperates, although it seems like she's moving in slow motion. She rubs her arm to warm herself. Her arm is bare. Her legs, too. All of her. She's naked. Why is she naked? Why is she naked?

She tries to pull herself away, somewhere else, somewhere safe. Fear washes over her. Thin memories try to push through, but she fights them back. There's nowhere to hide, and even if there was, her muscles and bones aren't capable of that much activity. The best she manages is a small wiggle that sends more shooting pain through her hips and belly. Her flailing arm smacks against something hard, metal, and cold, causing ripples of pain to roar through her. Every nerve is on fire.

Her brain insists on pressing the truth at her. She's not in a hospital. She's not sick. She's not where she's supposed to be. She's scared. Very scared. Tears start, and they burn. She touches her eyelid and finds wet, sticky... blood. Her eyelid is cut, sliced open just under the eyebrow in

2

the crease. The flesh around it is thick and swollen. She makes herself open her eyes, ignoring the terrible pain.

Don't cry, don't cry, don't cry, and that makes her cry harder. *Get up. Get up and run.*

But her body won't cooperate. Everything is… fuzzy. Fuzzy and disconnected and slow, and dear God, it hurts so bad.

God. God will help. Dear God, whatever I need to do to make it all right, I will do it. I'll be a better daughter, a better sister. I won't argue with my parents. I'll do extra English homework even though Ms. Scott always assigns boring books. I'll volunteer to pick up trash on the side of the highway. Anything. Anything to make this a terrible dream and let me wake up.

A new sound, a terrifying sound, makes her suck in a breath and hold it, as if her breathing is so loud it will drown out the part of her brain she needs to think. Footsteps. Slow. Coming toward her. Closer. Closer. Here.

The footsteps stop. She can't tell exactly where, but they're too close. If the owner of the feet was kind, they'd be speaking, asking if she's all right, asking why she's naked on a concrete floor. But the person isn't speaking. They're looking, right? They must be. That's what they're doing if they've stopped moving and aren't talking? They're staring at the naked girl on the floor. But they're not trying to help her.

Thoughts are trying to break through, but part of her is holding them back, refusing to let her hear them, to understand.

Another sound. A click. The shadows change, and light hurts her eyes, which are screaming, "Shut! Shut! Shut!" Part of her thinks maybe the person didn't see her before! Maybe now they will, with the lights on.

She tries to say, "Help," but the word comes out a grunt.

"Hello, little dove." He says it the way a mother would speak to her beloved baby. Only she's not beloved to him.

Now she remembers. It's one of the voices that brings pain. Cruelty. Terror. This voice makes her wish she was dead if she can't be home with Mama, Dad, and Stasia.

"Please..." she whispers, but it is only a weak hiss. Her mouth hurts, and she runs her tongue around. It feels as though a crocodile crawled inside and died. Her tastebuds, hard and stiff, are rough against the roof of her mouth. She musters up moisture, just a tiny bit, then touches her tongue to her teeth. Except where her teeth should be solid and strong, sharp bits threaten to cut if she's not careful.

She slowly brings her hand to her mouth. Her lips are torn, raw, and crusty with blood. Her teeth are broken.

She sobs.

"Please..." she whispers again.

The voice answers this time, and she fights to see him through hurting eyes. There's only the vague shape of a man. The form is coming closer. Closer. She wants to get away from him, but she can't. Her body doesn't work.

When he squats next to her, she cries out. All the memories flood back, and her heart pounds so hard in her chest that it might explode through her skin. Fear pushes her brain against her skull, tight and floaty at the same time.

"Oh, little dove, you're scared. I know. I'm going to do something for you. Give you a chance to save yourself." He puts his hands on her and moves her to a sitting position. She screams because the pain is so intense, the fear so deep. He doesn't care. He laughs.

"You may not be able to see it, but I have a gun in my hand. It's a Ruger, a very nice gun, simple, but that's really all we need for this." Shadows move.

A new fear takes root, cold and deep.

"There are six chambers in the cylinder of this gun. One of those six chambers holds a bullet. You've learned about odds in school, right? The odds of pulling the trigger and a bullet coming out are one in six, or seventeen percent. Better than nothing, right?" The man says, so cheerful. There's a metallic sound. "Here's what I'm going to do. I'm going to put the gun in your hand. You get to make a choice. You can point the gun at me, pull the trigger, and hope there's a bullet in the chamber, and that bullet kills me. Or, you can point the gun at yourself, pull the trigger, and hope you kill yourself. Of course, in either of those cases, you might pull the trigger and find yourself with one of the empty chambers, and nothing at all will happen. But the choice is up to you where to aim."

He forces her aching fingers open, then closes them around the gun. He adjusts her index finger so it's on the trigger. "I've pulled back the hammer, so you don't have to worry about that."

She has no idea what a hammer is. She's never held a gun. Never wanted to.

"Okay! You're ready! What choice will you make?" The man demands. She sees his shadow just in front of her now. He's either sitting on the ground or squatting. He's low, like her. "I promise I won't try to stop you, whatever you decide. This one chance is entirely yours. Make your decision, and pull. You have until I count to ten."

One.

Her brain is foggy, and she can't think.

Two.

Can she kill someone? Somewhere in the back of her mind, she understands that if she doesn't, he will kill her. But first, there will be more pain. Much more pain.

Three.

If she misses, then what? Then it was all for nothing.

5

Four.

Memories flash through her mind, reminding her why she is in such pain.

Five.

Better to die now, of her own choice, and stop the pain. Yes. Yes, that's the choice she will make.

Six.

She raises the gun to her head, ignoring screams of agony from her elbow, and pushes the gun's tip against her right temple.

Seven.

"Good choice!" The man sounds happy when he says,

Eight.

She tries to pull the trigger, but the part of her that wants to live resists.

Nine.

His tone reminds her this is her only chance. Screaming, she tightens her finger on the trigger and sends up a prayer to her family, "I love you."

Click.

She's still alive.

The man laughs.

Chapter 1

DAY 0

STASIA

I'd bet a thousand dollars none of my coworkers or patients have a clue Dr. Stasia King is having a shitty day. Not the man who fell down the stairs of his brownstone, not the little girl having a severe asthma attack, not the woman miscarrying a child she hadn't known existed. I saw nearly forty patients during my nine-hour shift, and I can confidently say none of them were aware of my sadness.

Every year around this date I wonder how it's possible that life goes on as if nothing happened, nothing changed. If there is justice, the world should pause in honor of Natasha King's short life. There should be no music. No laughter. No children giggling. Everything and everyone should recognize the terrible anniversary of my sister's death.

That's what my heart says. Intellectually, I know tomorrow will be the same as any other day. The world will continue spinning, people will fall in love, puppies will romp, joy will be had. And as I've done each year for the last twenty years, I will try to carry on as if my heart isn't broken, my soul freshly torn.

The emergency room will still be full of people who need help, and I will give them care to the best of my ability. I'll hit the gym before my morning shift, as I do every day. Officially, I could go home at seven, except my calendar reminds me there's a birthday celebration at the Happy Amigos. Dreaded anniversary or not, I would never miss a nurse's birthday. I make it a point to be there for the important stuff; you never know when it will be the last time you see someone.

Besides, as a shrink advised me many years ago, living in the now can help keep my mind off things. Things like the memory of Mama's panicked face when she got home from work and realized that even though it was nearly dark, her fourteen-year-old daughter wasn't on the couch watching TV. Or my father's blank, beer-glazed stare when Mama asked why he hadn't called Tasha's boss, her friends, or the police. Or the two uniformed patrol officers who eventually arrived to ask stupid, irrelevant questions. "Did you have a fight?" "Fourteen-year-old girls are emotional. Has she run away before?" "Does she have a boyfriend? A girlfriend?" *No, no, no.*

Maybe tequila will keep my mind off the next day when volunteers walked our neighborhood, looking for any signs of the smiling girl whose face was printed on hundreds of flyers. The flyers made Natasha King seem very one-dimensional. She was so much more than that. She just hadn't had time to fully blossom into her potential.

I hate that photo. That flyer. And it never leaves the back of my mind. Every time I meet a stranger—and being an ER doc, I meet a lot of strangers—my weird little brain puts their face next to Tasha's. It's not like she's missing. She's not going to turn up in my emergency room needing a tetanus shot. I don't know why I do it. But I can't stop.

Maybe nachos will keep me from thinking about the reporters who showed up out of obligation rather than actual interest. And the second day, when Mama and Dad had a huge fight, which turned out to be the beginning of their end.

I know nothing will keep my mind off the fourteen days between when she went missing, and the day she was found.

Honestly, it feels like this should all be easier by now. Twenty years have flown by. Plenty of time to "get over it." Yet here I am, still waiting for the hurt to fade from sharp, unexpected jabs to a persistent dull ache.

Instead of living a full life, I'm curled up on the sofa in my condo with the small TV on for company. Not for the first time, I recognize how bland my life is. Although my living room is beautiful with its white walls, dark wood floor, and historic built-ins surrounding the plaster fireplace, the few items in the room are strictly functional: a gray couch, a basic faux oak build-it-yourself entertainment cabinet, and a matching square coffee table. There is no wood in the fireplace. There are no flowers, no art, no color.

The small but functional kitchen is equally dull. Boxes of cereal and pasta, canned tomatoes, tuna, and soup take up less than half a shelf in one cabinet. The others are mostly empty except for four plates, four bowls, four glasses, and a couple pots and pans. There are four of each because that's how they're sold at Target. I don't need four. I've never had company, not even Mama.

A gray bathmat and coordinating towels break up the white in the bathroom. They, too, were sold as a set, along with a matching plastic garbage can.

The smaller of the two bedrooms is my office, with a cheap desk and chair, my laptop, and a collection of medical texts. Everything is organized and put away. It looks like a photo in a catalogue rather than a real human's space.

The sheer white drapes at each window were here when I bought the place. If I'm honest, there was more style and personality when the realtor staged the apartment years ago.

The only hobby I have is rollerblading, limited by time and weather. I don't volunteer. I don't date. I rarely socialize with colleagues. Even working 60 to 80 hours a week, there are gaps that need to be filled, and for me, books fill the need. They're my friends, my lovers, my therapist. Since I read on my tablet or listen to audio, there aren't even colorful books on the bookshelf.

I'm aware I'm a very boring human being. The only place I come alive, and allow myself to feel, is at the hospital. I'm good at my job. Not just the medicine part, but the people and the organization.

It's after midnight, and I have to be up early. I should go to bed, try for sleep. Instead, I stay tucked into the sofa, stroking the sterling silver ballerina pendant that hangs from my neck as I try to focus on a documentary on the wildlife of South America.

What would twelve-year-old Stasia—Anastasia, to Mama, and no one else—think of thirty-four-year-old Stasia? Without a DNA test, it would be hard to prove we're the same person. Young Stasia dreamed of being a landscape architect, making the world beautiful and tackling environmental challenges. Grown-up Stasia is a doctor, exhausted by and thriving in the chaotic world of emergency medicine. Young Stasia was social, although never cool. She had friends and enjoyed meeting new people. She loved noise, and color, and adventure. Adult Stasia works hard simply to exist in the world around her.

The fact is the person who obliterated Natasha King obliterated me, too. That's a conscious choice rather than a certainty, but I can't seem to muster the energy to change. Maybe next year.

I open the calendar app again and click the plus sign to add a reminder. "Call Mama."

My gut rumbles, and I hurry to the bathroom. No surprise that my belly is the barometer of my mental health. Once the contents of my belly are purged, I crawl into bed. And as I have done this time every year, I assure myself our sisterly argument was not a fight.

As I allow myself to be sucked down into anxious sleep, fingers wrapped around the ballerina as she lays on my chest, I hazily think, time travel exists. The problem is, once I'm at my destination, all I can do is watch. I can't change the past.

My phone pings an email alert. I read the email, then read it again because, surprisingly, it's good news. It's not good enough to erase the bad, but it's good enough.

Each summer, I attend a medical conference. I spend two weeks driving across the country, visiting presidential grave sites and exploring parks and points of interest along the way. In my head it keeps Tasha with me since it's something we did together when we were kids. I look forward to it. Each year, I try to persuade Mama to come with me. I haven't been successful yet.

This year, I registered for an emergency medicine conference in Seattle. The conference producers just offered me a seat on a panel. It's an incredible honor.

There's a small smile on my lips as I settle in to sleep.

JUNE 2, 2002

STASIA

Tasha was being a selfish jerk. A friend had invited Stasia to go to Mount Vernon on Saturday, but Mama said she could only go if Tasha went, too, because there would be a couple of hours where the parents couldn't supervise. Polly's parents were happy to include Tasha, but Tasha refused to take one stupid day off from her job at the dumb country club.

Now, Stasia refused to speak to her older sister. She ignored Tasha while she dressed in her work uniform of khaki shorts and white blouse. She ignored her when Tasha dug her white sneakers out from under the nightstand between their beds. She ignored her when she slipped lip gloss, her house key, and a pack of gum into her mini backpack.

"Don't be such a baby, Stas," Tasha said, adding insult to injury.

Stasia threw a Backstreet Boys pillow at Tasha's head as she ducked out of their bedroom. "You're such a jerk! I hate you! I'm never speaking to you again, Natasha King."

"Good. It will be nice to have some quiet for a change."

Stasia swung her legs over the side of her bed. Tasha's beloved ballerina jewelry box sat open on the shelf above Tasha's desk. Stasia stomped over to it and flicked the little ballerina repeatedly with her middle finger, muttering "I hate you, hate you, hate you" with each flick.

Eventually the ballerina tipped and stayed in a bent position. Stasia gasped in dismay, anger quickly replaced by guilt.

She tried to puff herself up with righteousness, but it didn't work. She hadn't meant to break it. Tasha loved the ballerina. It was a gift from their Ukrainian grandmother, who died a year after her last visit. Stasia would look for glue later and try to fix it.

Because it was summer, and because George and Olena King couldn't afford to send her to camp, Stasia spent the day shooting hoops in her driveway, walking her neighbor's dog, Buddy, and watching TV with her father. He barely said a handful of words to her all afternoon, as usual. Tasha was his favorite and Stasia was Mama's, although Mama loved both her daughters. Stasia wasn't sure her father would even notice if Stasia was gone.

At six-thirty Stasia set the table. Mama would be home by seven. Mama had set the crockpot on this morning, and the small house smelled insanely good, even though beef stew wasn't something Stasia would normally think to eat during the hot days of summer. But Mama got a chuck roast cheap and whatever was on sale was what they ate, since Dad wasn't working.

Tasha was late; normally she'd already be on the couch telling Dad stories about the weird people at The Madalena Club, chatting with him about local news and talking about what she was looking forward to at space camp.

When Mama walked in the door at 7:05, there was still no sign of Tasha. "George, did Tasha say when she'd be home?"

"Haven't talked to her." He grunted from his recliner. His eyes were half-closed.

"It's after 7. She's two hours late. You didn't think to try to find your daughter?" Mama stood in the doorway between the small dining room and the living room, a potholder in her hand. When Mama was angry her Ukrainian accent was front-and-center.

"Haven't talked to her, I said. It's not that late. Girl's fine. One of those rich assholes probably paid her extra to stay and entertain their brat." George muttered.

"I'm going to call The Madalena," Mama announced, tossing the potholder at him. He didn't notice.

They had two phones: a wall-mounted yellow one in the kitchen, and a white princess-style in her parent's bedroom. The one in the kitchen had a cord long enough Mama could use it from the dining table.

Stasia turned the crock pot to 'warm' and got out the container of sour cream Mama liked to serve with stew. She needed to stay busy. Something was wrong. She could feel it in her gut.

"Yes, hello. This is Olena King. I'm looking for my daughter, Natasha King. She works in the daycare center. Usually she's home by now, but she hasn't arrived. Do you know if she was asked to stay late?" Mama was saying into the phone, her voice calm, even though she was pale. Whoever she was talking to said something, and Mama's voice notched up a bit. Stasia's gut clenched hard. "Are you sure? Absolutely sure? Can you check? Please?"

Check? "Check what?" Stasia didn't realize she'd asked the question out loud until Mama looked at her and mouthed, "Check to be sure she's left."

Stasia nodded and sat in her chair at the table. She realized she was twisting the red checked napkin in her hands, and set it aside, then picked it up again. If Tasha had left, why wasn't she home? The club was a forty-five-minute bike ride from their house, most of it on bike paths. Tasha was super responsible and boringly cautious. She wouldn't do something dumb like ride on the streets in traffic. If she'd been in an accident, the police would have called them, wouldn't they?

"Thank you for checking." Mama hung up without saying goodbye and looked at Stasia, then the back of George's head. She raised her voice to compete with the television. She was no longer calm. "Tasha left at her usual time. She should have been home two hours ago. Something is wrong. Something is very wrong."

***

It took almost an hour for the two bored-looking officers to arrive. The officers took Mama and Dad into separate parts of the house to ask questions. Stasia heard her father answer belligerently when asked about trouble at home. Stasia couldn't hear Mama—or at least couldn't understand the actual words. When Mama was upset, her accent was thicker. The female officer and Mama finished first, then the officer took Stasia into the dining room to 'chat.' Her questions made Stasia want to scream. Were Mama and Dad fighting? A little or a lot? Did it ever get physical? Did anyone in the family hit anyone, an adult or a kid? Were there money troubles Stasia knew of? Did Tasha get along with her parents? Did Tasha and Stasia get along? Did Tasha have a secret crush? Had Tasha complained about anyone at work? Did Tasha drink or do drugs? The questions went on and on and on, and while Stasia understood they were important, she wanted to tell her, "Stop asking stupid questions and go find my sister!"

Eventually, the police decided this was a 'legitimate' missing person's case and put out a report. More police showed up to canvass the neighborhood, even though it was almost nine at night. Stasia heard one officer say another group of police were 'walking The Madalena' since that was the last place anyone saw Tasha. Still others checked the bike path Tasha took to get to and from work.

It would be fine, Stasia told herself. It had to be fine. Bad things happened on TV and in movies, but not to real people. Not to her family. The police would find Tasha, sitting somewhere with a scraped up knee and a flat tire. When she came home Mama would make her cabbage rolls, and Dad would smile and tell her about something funny he saw on the news.

Stasia thought maybe if she could fix the broken ballerina, that would bring Tasha home, so she went into the garage and found a bottle of Superglue in a pile with her father's tools. While the cops talked to each other and her parents, she sat at the desk and tried to unbend and unbreak the sad doll. It didn't work. No matter what she did, the little lady would not stand up on her pointe shoes. I really did a number on her. Stasia wiped tears from her eyes and hid the jewelry box under her bed.

She tried to be helpful, offering to make hot chocolate while they waited. Dad called her stupid for thinking hot chocolate would make anyone feel better.

Mama told Stasia to "Go to bed, get some rest. No point sitting up and worrying. I'm sure Tasha will be home soon. Maybe she went to a movie and forgot to call." They both knew she was lying. Stasia tried to argue, but in the end, as always, Mama won.

Stasia curled into a ball and stared at the empty bed across from her. The hum of voices outside her door finally carried her into a dark sleep, but it wasn't restful and didn't last long.

In her dreams, Tasha was a ballerina, dancing joyfully across the floor of a large performance hall. Suddenly a giant hand reached down and bent her in half. When Stasia saw the face of the ballerina killer, she realized she herself was the monster, and she had broken her sister.

Stasia woke with a gasp. No more sleeping. No more dreams.

It was after midnight, but she would stay awake no matter what. She pressed her back against the headboard, dragged the covers to her chin, and hugged her stuffed dog. First, she recited the state capitols. Next, she ran through multiplication tables. Then she listed the United States presidents in order. She caught herself dozing and pinched her thigh to stay awake.

It was going to be a long night.

Please, Tasha, come home. I'm sorry I broke your ballerina.

Chapter 2

DAY ONE

STASIA

During my lunch break, I prop my iPhone against a stack of books and arrange my face into a smile. Time-travel might not be a thing, but FaceTime is. I swallow a small laugh as Mama struggles to adjust her laptop camera, first capturing the midsection of her shirt, then the kitchen ceiling, and finally, her face. A Ukrainian curse accompanies each lopsided position.

My Mama, Olena Popov King, is an attractive woman, despite herself. Her thick red hair is streaked with white around her face and at the crown, and somehow it looks glamorous rather than old. Despite being sixty-two, her pale skin is nearly flawless, with no age spots, deep lines, or even noticeable wrinkles. Long, thick lashes frame her brown eyes. The deep shadows under those eyes are the only thing that betrays her age. She doesn't bother with makeup, preferring tinted sunscreen and a stick of lip balm applied obsessively many times per day. It's one of her self-soothing tics.

Mama rarely looks happy, but today, on the 20th anniversary of her daughter's disappearance, she seems especially unhappy, and her Ukrainian accent is more pronounced. "My Anastasia. How is life in the big city?"

"Things are fine, Mama. How are you? How's work?"

A year after Tasha's death, Mama left her husband—I struggle to think of him as my father after everything that happened—and then her job as a bookkeeper for a manufacturing company. She went to work at an accounting firm and seems to enjoy it as much as she enjoys anything. She did not replace my father.

"Work is fine. But... something bad has happened." Mama pushes air between her lips, then takes in a deep breath. "A girl has gone missing."

The blood drains from my face, and I reach for the ballerina pendant. My fingers rub the cold metal like worry beads. "Oh, no. How old? Do they know anything yet?" She wouldn't be telling me if there wasn't something different

21

about this. Sadly, girls go missing all the time. Many are runaways. Some are parental custody fights. Stranger abductions like Tasha's are uncommon.

Mama shakes her head. "She's the child of my coworker. She's just thirteen. Elspeth was attending a summer volleyball clinic. All was fine for the first two weeks, and then suddenly, yesterday, poof! At the end of the day, she never got on the bus back to her school." She adds, almost whispering, "It's too much. Too close."

My heart pounds violently under my navy scrub shirt. I focus on calming myself. A panic attack won't be good for either of us. "She's a friend of yours? I mean, the child of a friend?"

Mama nods. "Patrick Bridges. We work together. He and his wife, Anna, are absolutely distraught, of course. Patrick knows what happened to Natasha, so he asked me to come and help him and Anna through the process."

I want to blurt, "Be careful!" but force myself to hold back the words.

"I cannot refuse. That would be too cruel, but I will admit it is very difficult. I spent the night with them and came home this morning to change. I can't go back," Mama's voice breaks into a whimper, "but of course, I must."

It would be difficult for anyone but on the anniversary of her own child's abduction? *Cruel* isn't dreadful enough. "I have to work tomorrow, but I'll drive down right after my shift ends."

Mama wants to object, to say she's okay. I see it on her face. In the end, Mama doesn't resist. She attempts a smile, but it falls flat. "Thank you, Anastasia."

We won't talk about Tasha now, none of the usual reminiscing about the funny way she clapped, how she couldn't tell a joke properly because she always messed up the punch line or the ongoing battle over the right way to fold bath towels. Instead, we sit together quietly for a few moments, Mama wiping tears she'd deny, me counting the seconds until I can hop off and press my face into my arm and scream.

XANDER

To the outside world, we're just two men, each enjoying breakfast in a diner, seated fifteen feet apart, with an invisible line between us.

Recently retired Chief of Police Jim Gifford is the man who announced my father was the person who killed Natasha King. I knew he was wrong, but I was a kid. Nobody would listen to me, no matter how loud or long I yelled. They decided Army Sergeant Homer Williams was responsible for a fourteen-year-old girl's rape, torture, and murder, and I had nothing tangible to prove otherwise. But I've done some digging as an adult, and the evidence they had back then was so thin you could blow it away like the head of a damned dandelion. Chief Gifford and his cronies were looking for a way to close the case quickly, and a homeless man living under a bridge was an easy way to do that. Never mind that homeless man served his country for six years and saw things those pussy ass law enforcement idiots couldn't imagine. Never mind that the government abandoned him—and so many others—when he returned home. He tried to rejoin his family and become a good citizen. He did everything he could do. But he needed help beyond what Mom and Willow and I could provide, and time after time the government that sent him places that broke him rejected his requests for assistance to get put back together.

Then it was too late.

Seeing Chief Gifford enjoying his breakfast has ruined my appetite. I drop a twenty on the table and navigate between chairs until I'm at Gifford's right hand. I'm not in the mood to go to jail, so instead of doing what I want to do—shove the bastard's ugly face into his corned beef and eggs—I snarl, "Who are you going to frame when this new girl turns up dead?"

Gifford recognizes me but can't place where or why we've met. He puffs up with the bluster of someone who thinks they rule the world. "I'm not sure what you're babbling about, son, but I suggest you move on." He gives me what he considers a stern look and flips the front of his jacket aside to show off the gun in a shoulder holster.

I give him a look that lets him know I'm not intimidated. "There will come a time, asshole, when you're called to account for your crimes. And I, for one, will be in the front row cheering it on."

Common sense overrides my emotions for a change and I leave the diner before I do something I regret.

Every time I encounter one of the motherfuckers in the real world, and it happens far too often, what little common sense I have flies right out the goddamn window. I can be in the best mood ever, then I'll see Judge Miller or Chief Gifford, and suddenly I'm Bruce Banner trying to keep the Hulk in check.

Today my emotional dial is turned all the way up with news of another missing girl. It's not that a girl is missing; if I went out of my mind every time a girl disappeared, I'd have exploded long ago. But this time, this girl, it's ringing bells. There are too many similarities to another girl twenty years ago. The girl who is the reason my father is dead.

Natasha King.

This new girl, Elizabeth or Elspeth—I think that's her name—is about the same age Natasha was back then. One day has passed, and there's the same dread in the air. Everybody knows the longer a kid is missing, the less likely they will be found alive.

When a kid goes missing, people are eager to help. They hand out flyers door-to-door and form human chains to walk fields and woods. It's not passive, the way it is if a twenty-something woman doesn't show up for work. When it's a kid, everyone is on edge.

The bizarre thing about this new girl is that her parents are friends of Olena King. I about spit out my coffee when I saw the kid's mom clinging to Olena at the press conference. I don't think Olena has anything to do with it. My memory of her is a basic mom who works at a job, shows up at her kids' school events, and goes home and watches TV. That doesn't make it any less strange. What are the odds in a metro of hundreds of thousands of people that two young girls would disappear from the same place, on almost the same day twenty years apart, and their parents freaking know each other? Pretty small, me thinks.

My nerves are wound tight as guitar strings. Every year, right about now, I miss my sister Willow. When I was fifteen, she up and left town. She couldn't take it anymore, and I don't blame her—now. I used to resent the hell out of her. If I had a choice, I'd have done the same; but it didn't feel right to leave Mom all alone without a daughter, without a son and without a husband. And if I'm brutally honest, I became a bit of a fuckup after Dad's death. I'm still a bit of a fuckup, so it's better to do the fucking up around home where I have support if things go really wrong.

APRIL 2002

XANDER

Willow's bedroom door slammed, and Xander tried not to roll his eyes. She was two years older but sometimes acted five years younger. Were all girls dramatic, or did he luck out? He wasn't sure he wanted to know.

"Just let her go." Xander caught his mom by the arm to keep her from going after Willow, who was in a full-blown huff. Family therapy did not go well. The counselor, a well-meaning lady too young to have been out of school long, was doing her best to help Dad battle the demons controlling him. But getting those nasty demons to coexist with family life wasn't going great, particularly for Willow.

"I'll get dinner started." Mom went into the kitchen, and Xander parked in front of the TV. The new issue of *Outdoor Life* had come in the mail, and Mom tossed it on the couch for him. Not long ago, he couldn't wait for the magazine to arrive to flip through its pages and plan trips for after Dad returned. He missed long weekends in the country, camping in a tent or a rented cabin, hunting or fishing, or just exploring nature. God, he missed it. But there hadn't been a single trip since Dad got back six months ago. The last time they went camping, Xander was eight. He was twelve now. Four years of missing his dad, and now he was back, and Xander still missed him, maybe even more than when he was in another country.

"You okay, kiddo?" Mom sat next to him, still in her nurse's scrubs. She'd gone straight from work to the VA. Xander and Will took the bus. He wasn't sure how Dad got there. Probably a bus, too, since his car was parked out front in the driveway. Mom had Xander start it once a week to keep the battery alive.

"Yeah, sure," Xander nodded and bumped her arm with his. She returned the bump, kissed his forehead, then moved a chunk of his hair away. Xander laughed and pushed her hand. "It's supposed to do that."

"Uh, huh. I like seeing your eyes." He was pretty sure that phrase came in the official Mom's handbook. She got quiet, pretending to watch TV. Eventually, she said, "How's school?"

"Fine." As fine as seventh grade could be, anyway. He couldn't wait to get to high school. He was convinced it would be a lot more fun and a lot more interesting than middle school.

"How's Will? Has she said anything? She won't talk to me at all. I feel so—disconnected." She caught him in a gentle choke hold and whispered, trying to be funny, "Don't you ever disconnect from me. I couldn't stand it." The crack in her voice gave her away.

"She's fine, Mom. We learned all about it in health class," Xander said. "You see, when a young woman reaches a certain age—" he said in the serious professorial tone their teacher had used and laughed when Mom smacked him.

"Dinner will be ready in about five minutes. Wash your hands and see if you can persuade the rebel to come out of her room."

Xander stopped at Willow's closed door before heading to the bathroom. He put his ear to the hollow core and listened. She wasn't crying and wasn't talking to anyone on the cordless phone, which was missing from its base in the hallway. No music. He took a breath and knocked on the door but didn't wait before he pushed it open, half expecting it to be locked. "Hey."

Willow was lying on the unmade bed, on her stomach, her brown hair a curtain hiding half of her face. A diary-type notebook was open in front of her. She didn't look up but said, "Hey."

"Dinner's ready."

She nodded. "I want to finish this, and then I'll be there."

"Okay. Do me a favor and go easier on Mom, would ya? She didn't do anything. Nobody did. It's just—what happens to vets, I guess." Xander leaned against the door frame and tried to get a peek at the book.

"I know, I do. I'm just so freaking frustrated by that stupid therapist. She asks the dumbest questions, and everyone tries to make her happy, saying what she wants to hear. She's not helping him. Dad still looks like a stranger. I don't think it's working. It just makes me mad and Mom sad."

"Mom is sad about the whole thing. The therapist isn't affecting that one way or another."

Will shrugged, "Yeah. You're right."

"Not to sound like the therapist, but is there anything I can do to help?" he smiled.

Will stared at him for a minute, then laughed. "Yeah, you can kiss my big, round, denim-covered ass, sir. Get out of my room. I'll be there in a minute, and I'll try to be nicer to Mom. Promise."

Xander pushed his lips together exaggeratedly and made kissing noises. "Thanks, sis!"

She threw a pillow at him, and he closed the door. She'd be okay. They'd all be okay. They just needed to give it some time, and let Dad find his way back to them.

***

Willow made a double batch of 'Homer-style' chocolate chip cookies, which included pecans and Rice Krispies, and packaged them up in a zip-lock bag. "Take these to Dad."

Xander often took his dad a care package of essentials. He didn't want him to worry they didn't love him or think about him. His mother was an 'essentials hoarder'—buying personal care items in bulk, so it was easy to find things to take.

Xander found a large reusable shopping bag and added toothpaste, a toothbrush, deodorant, and wet wipes. He went into his parents' bedroom and slid the closet door open. Mom hadn't touched Dad's clothes; she still had hope. Xander grabbed a pair of jeans, a couple of T-shirts, and a hoodie since it was still cool overnight. He shoved them into the bag on top of the toiletries, then added the cookies on top.

Homer spent most of his time in a three-block square about a mile from their house, in the opposite direction from the middle and high schools, so his kids didn't have to see him—or so he didn't have to see his kids? In a way, Xander was grateful. This whole mess sucked bad enough without people he knew seeing Homer, who was usually dirty and smelly.

Sometimes his friends who had known Homer before would ask about him. Xander lied and said he was fine. Once, he said he was out of town and wouldn't be back for a while. It hurt to admit, even to himself, that he was embarrassed by his father. That embarrassment is what caused him to start thinking of his father as 'Homer' instead of Dad—to soften the intense emotions attached to the title.

He found Homer hunkered down outside a ripped tent near the underpass. To even find the small patch of dirt in the center of a ring of scrub trees, you had to notice and follow a narrow dirt path that pushed between prickly shrubs and weeds. The only way Xander knew to look was because he'd followed him here once before, after spotting Homer outside a convenience store.

Homer never seemed to join up with the other homeless people; he kept as much distance as possible between him and the world to avoid hurting someone during one of his bad moments. Xander hated that he was involved in the incident that caused his father to remove himself from their family. If he'd only understood more about PTSD, and how Homer's subconscious played tricks on him, he would have been more careful around his father when he was sleeping. The fact that Homer nearly hit Xander when he was startled out of sleep was the one and only lesson Homer needed to convince himself he wasn't safe to be around.

When Homer saw him now, he tried to smile, but it was more of a grimace. Homer's face was a reddish brown from the sun and dirt, the whites around his blue eyes the only brightness. He was in his thirties but looked closer to sixty. His hair was matted and peppered with leaves.

Xander tried to hide his misery seeing his father this way. "Hey, Dad." He dropped to the ground next to Homer and held out the overly full bag. "Will made you cookies. I grabbed some clothes and other stuff."

Homer dunked his head in a nod, and the side of his mouth curved into a half-smile. "Thanks."

Xander wasn't sure what to say next. Sometimes, when he made these visits, they'd just sit together in silence until Xander finally stood and said, "I guess I'll see ya later." Once in a while, Homer would take part in a brief chat, though that never lasted long. Today, Xander brought a conversation starter: the *Outdoor Life* magazine. He pulled it from his back pocket, where he'd carried it rolled into a tube. "Remember these? We used to love reading them, figuring out where we wanted to go." He worked at straightening it out, but the curves fought him. "Look. This is that cabin we stayed at when I was like six or seven." He flipped to the page, turned the magazine upside down, and showed it to his father.

Homer was silent, his eyes glued to the photos. He traced the cabin with a dirty finger. Another half-smile.

"That was so fun. I wish—I mean, I hope, we can do that again some-time," Xander waved a hand to say Homer should keep the magazine. Homer held it in his hands and continued to stare at the cabin. His face made Xander wonder whether the magazine was a good idea. Xander hadn't thought it through. He just wanted to remind him of the good times and give him some hope. Maybe it was rubbing salt in a wound, reminding Homer what had been, what could have been, if he hadn't come back from the war broken. Now Xander wanted to jump up and run home and pretend he hadn't made such a terrible mistake. "Hey, well, I gotta go. But I'll come to visit soon. Unless you—" he almost said, *unless you want to come home*, but that would just make Homer tense up like it always did. "Unless you need something. You can call anytime." There. That was a good second-best.

Homer gave him another half-smile.

Xander pushed to his feet and started back down the little dirt path. Before he was entirely out of sight, he paused and looked back.

Homer was staring at him. He said, "I love you, kiddo. I'm sorry."

Stinging tears filled Xander's eyes, and he twisted away, whispering, "I love you too."

AVA

This is the opportunity of a lifetime for the girls sitting across from me. To me, it's like rewatching a favorite *Friends* episode again: I know every line, every laugh, and it's still satisfying. I've had this same conversation, so many times I can run through it half asleep.

"Here's to a wonderful summer, having fun and seeing the world!" I raise my champagne flute in a toast. We're enjoying a warm Atlanta day on the patio of a Midtown restaurant popular with the rich and famous when they're in town. Landscaping between the terrace and the sidewalk offers glimpses into the space inside, a tease. *You can't have this, but you can dream about it.*

Until today, my companions have only been on the other side. They're trying to act cool, but they're dazed. They're here, as guests, in this place where celebrities and sports stars and musicians and artists and very rich people come to eat and drink and, most importantly, be seen. No one will hand them a tray or tell them to clean up a spill. They're not serving; they're being served. They're being treated as if they matter.

It's a giddy feeling when you've always been on the outside, looking in.

Amber tries to seem confident but comes across as arrogant. That isn't a problem. I've been through this before, and I'll help her work through it. She's an excellent find, with her heart-shaped face, enormous blue eyes, and naturally blond hair. She's 5'10" and slim, with long legs and large breasts. She just turned eighteen last week, so technically, the champagne is off limits, but we ignore those silly rules inside these walls.

Holly is quiet and at ease with how awestruck she feels. At first glance, she's not as attractive as Amber, but I'm an artist; I see what's hidden inside the clay. A good cut and color will control her dark curly hair. She'll soon outshine her new friend with a few makeup tips and time with the David James University stylist. Even better: Holly can easily pass for seventeen, maybe even sixteen, with the proper styling. She'll be popular with my friends.

"This is seriously legit?" Holly's southern drawl is pronounced. She gapes at the French toast bananas foster our server deposits in front of her, but I know that's not what she's asking about.

I smile. "Seriously legit. Do a web search for David James University. All your expenses are paid, including first-class travel and hotels. We'll take care of your clothes, makeup, hair, and personal care. You'll have comportment classes to teach you the ins and outs of being part of this world. And you'll get a weekly allowance. We don't call it a salary; it's more like a stipend. No pesky taxes to deal with."

Amber shovels grits into her mouth like she's never eaten and doesn't finish swallowing before she asks, "And for all this magical stuff, we just have to be nice to people? Like, hostesses?" She's skeptical but not put off.

"That's exactly right. You'll ensure the guests are comfortable and have a good time. But unlike a server or a shop girl, you won't be separate from the guests. You're right there with them, enjoying and experiencing it all." I dip my fork into shakshuka eggs, drawing the rich orange yolk through the bright red tomato sauce. I'm craving a grilled cheese or PB&J. As soon as I'm back in Virginia, I'll make time for some self-care. There are two more day trips to complete first.

"We don't have to have sex with anyone, do we?" Holly whispers. She won't meet my eyes.

I shake my head. "No, nothing like that. If you like someone, and they like you, there's no rule against exploring your attraction. But you'll never be forced to do anything against your will." That is true enough.

"Have any of the girls married a guest?" Amber asks, hopeful. I'm not concerned about the dollar signs in her eyes. Only people born with money judge someone else for wanting it.

"Married? Not that I know of. There are some long-term relationships. And just as valuable, it's a good steppingstone to your future. One girl is getting her

Ph.D. in physics. Another is launching her own fashion brand in LA." I reach into my purse and extract two plump envelopes. "Here's the plan. Go home, take care of what you need to take care of, pack a bag—don't bring a lot, because we'll be doing some major shopping and the house is already stocked with things like shampoo and toothpaste. I'm guessing you live with roommates?"

The girls nod.

I slide one envelope to each of them. "There's enough cash to pay your next month's rent, so you don't have to worry about giving notice. Anything left is yours. Get yourselves to the private hangar at Hartfield-Jackson and ask for me. Our flight is leaving tomorrow morning at 10, with or without you. If you decide this isn't for you, no worries. Keep the money and do something good with it. Think of it as a blessing," I deliver this with my well-practiced warm smile. Not one girl has missed a flight in the years I've been doing this. I stand and retrieve my Fendi bag. I don't particularly like Fendi, but it's easy to recognize for people who aspire to greater things. "The check is taken care of, but have another cocktail if you'd like. I have a quick meeting before we leave Atlanta, so I need to run. I hope to see you in the morning! Adventures await!"

Chapter 3

DAY TWO

NICK

Is my phone buzzing, or are the dog farts strong enough to wake me? Both the buzz and the smell are solid possibilities. I swim my way out of sleep, groggy and disoriented. I reach for the phone and discover I'm not lying in bed like a normal person. I'm stretched from corner to opposite corner. The nightstand is nowhere within reach. I pat around and feel three furry bodies in the space to my left and one warm, hairless body to my right. I want to pull the smooth body close and go back to sleep.

"Your phone. Answer," grunts the smooth body. Not a morning person, my Angel.

"I'm trying. Nope won't move her sausage self," I mutter. Thick curtains keep the room pitch black, and I don't want to kick Asa or put a hand down on Cat. I love these creatures—all four of them because until she's had coffee, Angel is most definitely a creature—but they are oblivious.

Finally, I slither my way out between the two dogs, somehow avoid jabbing the cat, and only elbow Angel once. She rewards me with a sleepy kick that comes dangerously close to important bits. My feet hit the floor, and one foot lands on a hard rubber dog toy. My ankle twinges. I finally find my phone on the floor, not the nightstand where I'm sure I left it. I hobble into the living room and quietly close the bedroom door to keep the canines with Angel. They'll demand food and a trip outside if they think I'm doing more than hitting the head.

I feel like I've run a marathon, and it's not even five am.

There's a voicemail.

"Hey, Nick, it's Wayne. Jameson. From the FBI." As if I could forget who Wayne is or where he works. "We have a case here in Virginia that might be something you should check into, you and that Koboremi group you're with now." *Komo-rebi, Wayne. Not whatever you just said.* "Two days ago, a thirteen-year-old girl never got back on her bus. She's not a runaway. Anyway, if you're interested, give me a buzz."

Thirteen. Damn. I tap out a message to the crew at Komorebi, then hit the return call button to reach Wayne.

This never gets easier.

THE SURGEON

Everything is laid out on the bed: blue scrub pants and long-sleeved shirt, face mask, face shield, gloves, cap. Next to the clothing is a large plastic case with tools fitted into slots and pockets and pouches: scalpels, razor, clamps, forceps, spreaders, retractors, needle holders, hooks, saws, curette, hand drill, bone file, scissors, speculums, suction tubes, dilatator, debreeder, drains, tourniquets, dressing, sutures, sponges, dishes. It's amazing what you can buy and have delivered overnight.

I am strangely calm. I should feel anxious. I'm going to intentionally maim and kill people. For years, I've kept a wall between myself and the past, yet everything has been building to this moment. It's hard to believe it's finally here. So much will become clear in the coming days. Not just to me, but to the world. There will be no more lies, no more secrets. No more hiding, or denying the truth.

There will be confession. There will be accountability.

There will be justice.

For some, there will finally be closure.

It's been long enough. Time to get started.

AVA

If I took bets based on whether girls will show up, I'd make lots of money. Amber is a few minutes early, while Holly comes skidding in with just a minute to spare. Based on their personalities, some might assume it would be the other way around, but I know why Holly is the one who waited until the last minute to walk in the door. She's nervous and didn't want to have time to change her mind.

They've been quiet most of the two hours it takes to fly to New York, eyes wide as they take in all the physical and philosophical details of traveling in a private Gulfstream. Beauty—that's the jet's name—will do that to you.

I don't feel the need to chat them up. Champagne and a beautifully decorated cabin have a tranquilizing effect. In a way, I'm a bit envious. I lost their sense of awe and disbelief years ago. Now it's just a practical benefit I appreciate but don't think much about. I may be jaded, but it doesn't mean I take anything for granted; I know all of this could disappear in the blink of an eye.

I flip through the latest issue of *Vogue Italia*, but my thoughts are all over the place. What is Jamie, the love of my life and my partner in crime, doing right now? Do I need to make any changes to my sources in Oklahoma City and Birmingham? Neither has had a good track record lately. There's a text from Mercedes, the housemother at DJU, with the latest news of a missing young girl in Virginia. Like me, she's a true crime junkie. That catches my attention and sends my mind on a tangent.

Most people have a hobby, and true crime is mine, especially missing girls and women. Give me a name, and I can tell you where the girl lived when she disappeared, what she was doing immediately before, and what the current theory is. I listen to many podcasts when I'm alone in hotel suites. I'm a lurker on true crime chat boards, under a different name, of course. If I was another version of myself, living a different life, I might well be an FBI agent.

There are a number of theories about why women find true crime fascinating. One is that just being female in this world puts you at risk, and that fact gives us empathy. That empathy makes us interested in not just the victims, but the motivations of the perpetrator. Maybe we hope that by being able to recognize and understand evil we can see it coming and avoid it.

Another theory is that true crime gives women a safe outlet to entertain our aggressive impulses. That rings true, too.

I'm aware some might think it odd that a woman who recruits other women into a world focused on physical attributes might find this hypocritical. I would disagree. DJU empowers girls—that's what they are, when they first come to us, although Mercedes insists we call them 'women'—by giving them the knowledge and resources to use their assets to their own benefit. Too many women go through life as passengers. We put them in the driver's seat.

The first time Jamie caught me watching a crime show, he half-jokingly pointed out, "You live in a multimillion-dollar home with the best security available. There are weapons throughout the house and in our vehicles. You're always protected, doll."

I gave him a wink. "I don't watch because I'm afraid, sweetheart. I watch to learn."

Our flight attendant announces we're approaching the city. I raise my glass in another toast. "Welcome to New York, and welcome to your new lives."

AVA

After handing the girls safely off to Mercedes at the DJU residence, I take a helicopter from the Manhattan heliport to Dulles. An hour and fifteen minutes flying over our nation's capital is much more bearable than four hours sitting in traffic. Just another perk of my job.

My employer is David James University, or DJU, an entity known vaguely to the public. DJU is a sort of finishing school. Some people say it's a prostitution ring. I strongly disagree, and not just because I'm the primary recruiter. We invite young women to DJU with the understanding they'll receive all the things I told Holly and Amber about: clothes, beauty and hair care, medical care, education in etiquette, comportment, dance, food, and drink, plus a generous allowance. In exchange, they socialize with David James Ellington's friends and colleagues. "Socialize" does not mean having sex. They are escorts in the purest sense of the word. If a guest proposes additional activities, it is entirely up to the woman whether she accepts or declines.

The girls get the same care and stipend regardless of whether they choose to be intimate with guests. If there's a "but" hanging over that, it's that they must maintain a positive review score, and reviews are provided by the guests. If someone doesn't maintain a positive review score, we release them from the program. They leave with clothes, the education they've received, and all the money they've saved.

Oh, and a bulletproof forty-page non-disclosure agreement.

While that's the official DJU rules, and I stand by them 100%, David James has a taste for young women. Very young women. If it wasn't illegal, he'd date girls just starting high school... maybe younger. But it is illegal, thank God. If he privately pursues extracurricular activities, he keeps them away from DJU.

David James spends a lot of time and money to keep his private life private. All the public knows about him is that he is the head of the David James Group, which is one of the largest, if not *the* largest, private real estate developers in the United States. People find him fascinating, in part because of his rags-to-riches story, and in part because he keeps company with so many beautiful women. Their opinions are based solely on photos and the occasional news story, both of which are controlled by his PR team.

He started the DJ Group when he was twenty-two years old, his only assets an idea and a boatload of charisma. Forty years later, DJ Group owns apartment buildings, commercial buildings, hotels, golf courses, a theater chain, a couple of restaurant groups, and a company that sells timeshares in private jets and helicopters. Which is how I avoid mass transportation.

The truth is, David James built a good foundation, but Jamie Ellington, his son and my love, is the one who has navigated the organization through its significant growth in recent years. David James and his chief of staff, Bishop Oliver, keep busy traveling the world enjoying what Jamie and I privately call their 'extracurriculars.' It's very important to me that there's a giant separation between DJU and whatever else they're into. While I respect David James as my employer and my partner's father, his moral code is very different than mine. Some might ask why I continue if I feel that way. I have my reasons. And I won't stay forever.

Do I feel dirty bringing girls into DJU? No. There are great success stories from our alums. Actresses, musicians, writers, artists, and a couple of fashion designers. There are two doctors and at least one actual rocket scientist. As I told Amber and Holly, some of the girls have long-standing relationships with friends they made at DJU.

I was one of them twenty years ago. Jamie and I have been together for fifteen years, which is longer than most marriages. There's a lot to be gained if you're smart and strategic and have patience. And it doesn't hurt if you fall in love.

STASIA

I've driven to Fredericksburg at least four times a year since leaving home for college at John Hopkins: Thanksgiving, Christmas, Mama's birthday, and the anniversary of Tasha's recovery. From Manhattan, it's five and a half hours, more if traffic is bad. I always stop at the same truck stop in Elkton, Maryland, for an Auntie Anne's pretzel and to stretch my legs. If I'm not alone with my thoughts, it's a pleasant enough drive. Podcasts and audiobooks are my best friends. Routine is calming. Being in control is soothing.

I packed last night and threw my bag into my CRV before work so I could head out as soon as my shift ended at noon. Mama is usually in bed by eight, but since I'm coming, she'll wait up. I'll be shocked if there aren't potato pancakes and Ukrainian cabbage rolls waiting.

Last night, Mama stayed with Patrick and Anna. I'm afraid she'll go back. I desperately wish she wouldn't. I'm concerned about the impact this will have on her. I remember the toll Tasha's abduction, and eventual recovery, took on her physical and emotional health. There was a lot that was never shared with me because I was so young, and it's been twenty years since our family went through this, but I still remember a lot of it. Some bits are vague, but none of it is good.

It sounds as though there hasn't been much progress finding Elspeth Bridges. With each hour that passes, the chances of finding her alive grow slimmer. Mama knows this, but she's undoubtedly reassuring her friends that there's still plenty of hope. That's what the police told us in 2002, and I'm sure that's exactly what they're telling the Bridges now.

The closer I get to Fredericksburg, the less I can focus on Karin Slaughter's most recent audiobook. Twice I reverse to a place I recognize and eventually I give up and give in to the thoughts. *Get your shit together, Stasia. You can handle this. This isn't Tasha. They will find Elspeth. Maybe even alive.*

I try to ignore the same little voice adding, *Except you know that's bullshit.*

JUNE 16, 2002

STASIA

Stasia knew it was bad news when she saw two patrol cars pull into their driveway. She started to go to the living room but changed her mind. If she was wrong, she'd just get mad, again, that they hadn't found Tasha. If she was right...well, unless somehow Tasha was alive and afraid to come home because she'd be in trouble, Stasia was pretty sure she didn't want to know the details.

After a while, the police left with the same lack of fanfare with which they'd arrived. Stasia stayed in her room, pretending she hadn't heard Mama make that keening sound or her father's roaring sobs. She knew, of course, she knew, but if she hid in here, she could pretend for a few minutes more. It wouldn't be true until she heard the words.

Eventually she had no choice but to leave her room, and Mama pulled her into her arms and gently explained that Natasha had been found, and that "she has gone to join Baba in heaven." She didn't offer details. What little information Stasia had came from the news. Tasha hadn't had an accident. She hadn't become suddenly sick and pulled off the bike path. She had been killed, by someone, intentionally. If anyone knew why, they weren't telling Stasia.

Stasia's whole body hurt, as if she'd been pummeled. But her heart hurt especially. It literally ached, felt squeezed and sore. Her eyes burned from crying so many tears. She was glad it was summer, and not school, because she couldn't imagine trying to act normal. She wasn't sure she could ever feel normal again.

The following days were a blur. The media hounded them for a bit, then left when some other family's torment called to them. Friends came by with casseroles. Arrangements had to be made, but they could do nothing until the coroner released Tasha's body. Mama seemed stoic, except at night when Stasia heard her crying in her car in the driveway.

Dad was silent, anger dripping off him like rain. He ignored Stasia when Tasha passed, or worse, looked at her in a way that told her he wished she was the one who had died. The only thing he seemed to interact with was the ever-present bottle of whiskey, which he didn't bother to hide. Stasia knew things were bad because Mama and Dad didn't fight anymore. They floated around and passed each other like ghosts.

Mama arranged for Stasia to see 'someone'—she knew it was a shrink—to talk about her feelings and find a healthy way to grieve. Stasia didn't tell them she'd broken Tasha's ballerina in a pique of anger the morning her sister disappeared. She didn't tell them much of anything. She just wanted to sleep until the pain faded.

AVA

Hendrix is waiting for me at the private terminal at Dulles. Now, Hendrix is Jamie's head of security; he's always been Jamie's best friend. Before I can ask why he's here instead of a DJ Group regular driver, he tells me Jamie is flying back from Los Angeles. Hendrix has news and thought playing driver would kill two birds with the same stone.

I was in Beauty, so Jamie took Beast. Beast is a Dassault Falcon and can fly from New York to Asia without refueling. It's an impressive piece of technology and hardware, but Beauty is always my first choice among the family fleet. Her interior is more feminine and more welcoming. Beast reminds me of a Wall Street frat bro.

Instead of waiting in the lounge in the Fredericksburg Jet Center, I slip into the back of the SUV. I want to read more about the missing girl. Elspeth Bridges, age thirteen. There are a lot of photos because she's strikingly beautiful. Face round with baby fat doesn't diminish her good looks. She has enormous blue eyes framed by thick dark lashes and honey-brown hair streaked with gold. Her skin has a healthy natural glow. As an avid soccer and volleyball player, she spends a lot of time outdoors. According to her parents, she's outgoing, confident, and serious about her sports. She loves her family and idolizes her big sister. The Bridges were meant to be spending this weekend at Virginia Beach to celebrate the older sister's birthday.

Elspeth disappeared from The Madalena. I'm familiar with the Madalena; it's part of David James lore. It's the country club where he worked as a teenage caddy, building relationships that would help him grow his empire in later years. His eventual membership helped turn it into one of the most desirable golf and country clubs on the east coast.

It was also connected to Natasha King's disappearance twenty years ago.

The SUV door swings open, and Jamie slides in. Before Hendrix can close the door behind him, Jamie is playfully dipping me into a theatrical kiss. He covers my face with small pecks and nuzzles; it tickles, and I can't fight off the giggles.

Hendrix grins into the rear-view mirror at us. "I think I'd better put the privacy window up, for everyone's sake."

"Aww, Hendrix, you know we're better behaved than that," I laugh, and we are. Our sex life is plenty hot, but we're both hyper-aware of how being impulsive can take you to bad places.

"I promise we won't embarrass you, Hen, but I haven't touched this woman in five days," Jamie declares, pulling me onto his lap and wrapping me in his arms. "I need some old-fashioned making out."

Hendrix laughs and turns the sound system to modern jazz to provide some white noise between us.

"How was your trip?" Jamie asks, resting his head against my chest.

"Successful. Two new students." I run a hand through his thick, dark hair. "How was yours? This was the planned community project in Oregon?"

He nods against me. "It went well. We break ground next spring."

"Let's retire there! What do you think?" I'm only half-joking. The idea of living in a structured community where the excitement comes from the 4th of July parades and excursions to the beach sounds like the perfect next phase. Jamie is thirty-nine, and I'm thirty-seven, so it'll be a while.

"You, me, and three or four dogs. No security. No meetings. Hendrix in board shorts with a puka shell necklace around his neck. Just lazy mornings, lots of good books, hiking the woods, perfecting our tans." Jamie mutters. "We can let our hair go gray and get pleasantly plump!"

It's such a lovely dream. And like many dreams, it hangs just out of reach.

STASIA

I make good time, and get home before eight. Mama pulls me into a tight hug that lasts more than a minute. Neither of us makes a sound; we simply cling to one another. Alicia, the black cat that joined our family my last year of high school, weaves between our feet. Finally, Mama kicks the door shut behind me and takes my bag. She nods toward the small dining room where I spent much of my childhood. "Eat."

While I devour cabbage rolls and potato pancakes, Mama strokes Alicia's soft fur and catches me up. "Even with all the cameras in the world these days, there's still nothing. Elspeth did well in the clinic and was excited about a weekend trip to the beach. None of her friends noticed anything unusual."

I take a sip of what we jokingly call the house wine because Mama buys a dozen bottles at a time at Trader Joe's. Despite her Slavic heritage, Mama is not a vodka drinker. "Is the clinic at a school?"

Mama shakes her head, and something in her expression makes me pause. "They hold the clinic at The Madalena."

I chew my upper lip. The Madalena. The golf and country club where Tasha worked until she disappeared. Thoughts come and go—disjointed, unrelated, mostly incomplete. Finally, one flashes like a gigantic neon sign: *Again.*

Mama's hand covers mine. "Yes." So much in that word. *Yes, it's terrible, strange, impossible, and true.*

"Have the police—are they investigating whether there's a connection to Tasha?" There will be no more cabbage or pancakes tonight. My always angry stomach threatens violence. I wonder if I'll ever be free of the demons that run wild in my digestive system.

"How can there be a connection? Homer Williams is long dead."

Army vet Homer Williams. Crazy Homer, who lived under the bridge. Crazy Homer, who came back from overseas physically intact but mentally broken.

Crazy Homer, who couldn't live with his wife and two kids because of his PTSD.

"It's not a coincidence," I say forcefully. Maybe no one else would connect the two, but I absolutely *know* there is a connection.

"There's one—interesting?—thing. Remember that news anchor Peter Baden? After his daughter was abducted, he created an organization that helps the families of people taken by strangers. They're working with Patrick and Anna. And they sent an investigator. He used to be with the FBI, and apparently, he's brilliant. I met him briefly, but Patrick said he'd like to speak with both of us if we're willing." Mama frowns, even though this seems like good news. Maybe she's wishing there had been something similar twenty years ago.

"I'm happy to meet with him." *Happy* isn't the right word, but I'm too tired, too emotionally worn, to wordsmith myself. "Are you staying home tonight? Or going back to stay with them?" I try not to let resentment color the word 'them' but am only mildly successful.

Mama offers a rueful smile. "I'm going back if you'll be okay sleeping here alone. Anna isn't doing well. She has no family. Patrick's parents are in Washington state and are too frail to travel. They have no one who understands."

I knew before I asked, and there's no point trying to persuade her to stay, so I nod and try to fake a smile of my own. "I'm glad they have you." There was no one to help us in 2002 other than a young police officer who wasn't trained or suited to support a terrified family through such a tragedy.

"How long will you stay?" Mama busies herself, putting away leftover pancakes and cabbage rolls. She leaves the bottle of wine on the counter for me, and I fully intend to finish it. I'm not much of a drinker, but tonight I don't want to give my mind room to dream.

"Only until tomorrow late afternoon." I wrap my arms tight around her. She's four inches taller than me. The women on my father's side of the family are short, and both Tasha and I inherited the King family's lack of height.

Then she drops a bombshell. "I know it's late, but will you come see the Bridges with me? You don't need to stay long. I think it would be good for Margot, their other daughter, to meet you."

It was shortsighted of me not to anticipate she'd suggest this. I want to scream, "No!" but I don't. Mama is so strong. I wish she'd stop being tested. I'm not as tough as she is, at least not this way, but I can't deny her simple request.

"Let's go."

JUNE 17, 2002

STASIA

Stasia heard about Homer Williams from a breaking news alert that interrupted Jeopardy. Her mother was still at work. Her father had moved out and was living in a by-the-week motel. He hadn't called her, and Stasia hadn't visited him.

The reporter couldn't seem to decide whether to keep her signature smile or try to look sad as she read from the teleprompter.

News no one was hoping for. A tip to the Crime Hotline lead police to find the body of Natasha King, who has been missing for two weeks.

This morning Natasha's body was discovered under a bypass near a homeless camp. During the investigation, officers identified Homer Williams as a person of interest. The 36-year-old has since been charged with first-degree intentional homicide, first-degree sexual assault, and first-degree sexual assault resulting in great bodily harm. Chief Jim Gifford said more charges might come.

"This was an aggravated assault on an innocent child and a very disturbing incident, one of the worst of my career. Responding officers will need counseling." Chief Gifford said. "Although we were all hoping for a different outcome, we are glad we can offer the family some closure."

Officials said records show Williams was recently discharged from the Army and has had trouble readjusting to civilian life. He has been receiving counseling at the VA.

The Fredericksburg Gazette says Spotsylvania County District Court Judge Wesley Miller III set the man's cash bail at $1 million on Wednesday after prosecutors expressed concern he might be a flight risk.

District Attorney Damien Simpson told the judge that Williams seemed to be in an altered state of mind when police found him near the body, and he did not resist when they put him into handcuffs to prevent him from leaving.

In the days after Natasha's disappearance, police and community volunteers have spent dozens of hours canvassing both the neighborhood where Natasha lived and the area around The Madalena, where she worked as a summer daycare assistant. Police found no viable leads before the anonymous tip that lead to Williams' arrest.

It's going to be a sunny weekend! Ben Bradley will join us after the break—

The following day, Stasia rode her bike to a convenience store and bought a newspaper. She stared at the photo of Homer Williams on the front page. She'd seen him hanging around a liquor store near her house. She remembered thinking he was probably a veteran because of his Army shirt. He didn't ask for money or yell at anyone. He hadn't scared her at all. He just sat on a brick wall minding his own business.

But according to the paper, he was the man who had "abducted, raped, and killed fourteen-year-old Natasha King." That's how Stasia learned her sister had been raped. None of the adults would tell her the details.

She understood, in general, what rape was. She knew it meant someone, usually a man, forced a woman to have sex with him. All she knew about sex was what she'd seen in movies, which wasn't much. Mama was very strict about what films they could watch. This year she'd been allowed to go to the movies exactly twice. Once to see *The Parent Trap*, and then to see *Mulan*. Neither had even a whisper of sex, as far as she knew. Even without understanding specifics, she recognized it was terrible and understood it caused physical and emotional pain. Knowing Tasha had been hurt before she died made the agony of losing her sister all that much worse.

In the days before they found Tasha's body, the police came to the house to talk to the Kings, and twice, they would go as a family to the police station, although Stasia was always left in the hallway while Mama and Dad spoke with the officers. Stasia was grateful for the police finding her sister's killer, but she didn't like them, or trust them. While she was waiting for her parents during those visits, she sometimes heard the uniformed officers saying things that weren't very nice about victims of crimes.

In the year between Tasha's death and Homer Williams' trial, Stasia learned much too much about sex. It was shocking how much joy some of her classmates found taunting her about her sister's death. Not everyone, but enough to make school even harder. For a few weeks, someone left crude, hand-drawn images in Stasia's locker of what they said had been done to Tasha. One of them said, "Maybe she liked it!" The downright cruelty of it all built a cynical wall around Stasia's heart. If kids who hadn't spent a minute in the real world were already this anxious to hurt other people, what would they be like as adults? She didn't want to know.

Stasia wasn't a physically violent person, but she was quick with verbal retorts, and that seemed to make her fun to battle with. Most of the time, she didn't care. Unless it was Willow Williams, daughter of Homer Williams. Then she cared. She cared quite a bit.

Willow was a sophomore, and her brother Xander was a freshman like Stasia. They attended the same school because they lived in the same neighborhood. Before Tasha's murder, Willow had been one of the cool kids, and a nice one at that. But after the murder, Willow seemed to have an urgent need to poke Stasia's buttons. After the first few times, when Willow and Stasia nearly came to blows in school hallways, the administration got together and figured out a plan to keep the girls separate. For a while, it worked.

STASIA

I realize it's selfish of me but the last thing I want to do is meet the Bridges family. While Mama has jumped with both feet into the role of caretaker and comfort-provider, the only emotion I seem able to muster is a mild case of resentment. And that makes me feel guilty. My emotions are a mess, and that is, of course, making my gut hurt.

Because it matters so much to Mama, I follow in my own car when she returns to the Bridges. Another wave of guilt hits as I realize I'm comparing our family to theirs.

While Mama was stoic and strong when Tasha went missing, Anna Bridges is a walking zombie. She's tall and slender, very attractive in better circumstances, I would imagine. Her blonde hair is oily and the long layers fall in clumps around her shoulders. Her green eyes are red-rimmed and swollen. She's wearing a suit skirt and a cream-colored V neck sweater that is no longer looking fresh. I wonder if this is what she was wearing the day Elspeth disappeared, and she hasn't been bothered to change. That would make sense. I've seen people in the emergency room become zombies when their loved one is injured. Similar, I suppose.

Patrick, Mama's coworker, seems to be doing a little bit better. He's wearing jeans and a University of Virginia sweatshirt. He's handsome, and I imagine he and Anna make an attractive couple under different circumstances. He has dark hair, cut short but not too short, and a neatly-kept beard and mustache that are brown except for a small grayish patch on his chin. He's got laugh lines at the edges of his blue eyes, but there are no smiles now. Comparing him to my own father is trying to compare apples to giraffes.

Mama is eager for me to meet their older daughter, Margot. I'm just as eager to avoid her. This is all too much for me—overwhelmingly familiar, and at the same time too different. *I have my own pain, I don't want to carry yours.* That makes me an ass, I know. But I suck it up for Mama's sake, put on my best doctor's face, and go with Margot into the family room while her parents and Mama and the law enforcement folks talk in the formal dining room.

"How are you?" I ask as one does, until I remember as clearly as if I were watching myself on a monitor how I felt when people asked me that question twenty years ago. I correct myself. "Nevermind, that was a stupid question. Forget I asked."

Margot, about to turn fifteen, sucks in a deep breath and then forcefully expels it, blowing her blonde bangs off her forehead. She looks a lot like her mother with the same prep school cheerleader appeal. Elspeth is attractive, too, but in a much more interesting way. I wonder if Margot ever feels jealous of her beautiful baby sister. "Mom said your sister was kidnapped, too. And she never came back."

Well, shit. Come out with the big guns. "Yeah. Twenty years ago yesterday."

"Weird." Margot notes.

Agreed. "They're two different situations, though. Just because Tasha didn't come home doesn't mean Elspeth won't."

Margot nods, but I can tell she's unsure.

"It's awkward having people everywhere, isn't it," I mutter as yet another uniformed officer comes into the house as if he lives there.

"Oh my God, yes. They're seriously everywhere!" She whisper-hisses. "This morning I was in my bathroom washing my face and all of a sudden the door opens, and this woman walks in! She seemed surprised to see me. Where the heck did she think that door went to? It's upstairs so it was either a bathroom or a bedroom." Margot shakes her head.

I remember how it felt, and our house isn't as big as the Bridges residence. We literally couldn't turn around without bumping into some stranger. The memories are threatening to overwhelm me, so I grasp for anything that might be safe to talk about for both of us. "I hear you were planning to go to the beach for your birthday. Sucks that you'll have to wait a bit, but it'll be fun when you get to go."

Margot smiles at that. "Yeah. Happy birthday to me!" she sings it, but quietly. She doesn't want to upset her parents, but realizes it's okay to be real with me.

"Yeah, this is a pretty crappy party," I grin. Sometimes humor is the best way to deal with misery.

"I half expect someone to bring me a really ugly birthday cake. Or drop off a box of gift wrapped dog sh...crap." It's clear she wanted to say 'shit' but sees me as an adult who might disapprove.

"That would be very shitty," I can't stop the smile that forms, and it's contagious. Margot giggles, and then we both start laughing, and then we're laughing so hard tears are streaming from our eyes. Not because any of it was funny; it's just a release of emotions we've been holding, a dam breaking, and in this case, it's coming out in the form of laughter. We both know it's inappropriate and try to stop, but that makes it even harder.

One of the uniforms pops his head around the corner to check on us. That sends us off into another round, and this time I can't breathe. I'm gasping for air, and Margot slides off the sofa and onto the floor, hugging a pillow to her chest, her face shoved into the fabric.

I slide down onto the floor next to her and rest my hand on my raised knee. She grasps it and squeezes, and we sit together, quietly, wiping tears from our eyes.

At 10:30, Margot is ready to go to bed and so am I, but I have a bit of a drive back to our home. I find Mama and give her a kiss on the cheek. "I'm going." I whisper it, so as not to disturb the others, who are hunched over a map on the dining room table.

Mama plants kisses on my hair and rubs my back like I'm still a kid. Maybe I am. "Anastasia, this is a terrible time, but we will survive. It will be okay. Someday." She gives me one more kiss on the forehead, instructs me to engage all four locks on the front door once I'm home, and heads off to care for her friends.

Chapter 4

DAY THREE

NICK

It's been a few months since I've had boots on the ground in an abduction case, and I've been okay with that. More often than not, the victim is found quickly, and there's no need for me to travel. That's the best possible outcome. Sometimes the victim isn't brought home, but they're known to be with their non-custodial parent. Komorebi doesn't get involved with those. And then there are the cases that are recovery, rather than rescue.

I landed in Arlington yesterday afternoon and spent the evening with the Bridges family. Patrick is an executive for an accounting firm. Anna is a full-time mom. Older sister Margot turns fifteen this weekend. There's a cat named Patches and a Yorkie named Tigger. They live in a nicely-kept brick ranch in the Lake of the Woods, a gated community. Mature trees and older homes make it feel safe from the dangers of big city life. No one in this neighborhood would expect to be a victim of violence.

Patrick Bridges is forty-something, moderately successful, not used to anything more stressful than car trouble or a work crisis. He's friendly, despite his current situation, and welcomes me into their home. The local law enforcement team has determined he is likely not involved in his daughter's disappearance. He's trying to keep it together, as if his emotional state will have bearing on whether his child is found safe. He tells me, "None of this makes sense. We're the most boring family in America. We have some money but not kidnapping kind of money. I'd sell everything I own to get my baby back."

This is the exact kind of case Komorebi was created for. Our mission is to help the loved ones of people who are taken by strangers navigate the practical and emotional waters and to help after they're found. My cohorts at Komorebi have set the family up with a PR pro and an attorney. The PR pro will help navigate the media so the press is used as effectively as possible. They'll also build a media kit and get it out through their well-developed relationships. The local press often shows up to get the story, finds a thread to pull that adds a little more 'oomph' to get readers to click, and then leaves the family to deal with the repercussions. Our PR folks help the families control the conversation. We connect them with national media. We make the story so loud it can't be ignored. And we help them avoid land mines—because there are many. The attorney will help them navigate their interactions with the police, and if there turns out to be a ransom, they'll help with that too.

I've visited ten families in the fourteen months I've been an official Komorebi team member. Some victims were young, like Elspeth. Others were older, in their later teens, twenties, or even thirties. All but one were female. Three are still missing. Two were reunited with their families. Five were body recoveries. I hate these numbers. I want 100% found alive.

I hate that there are people who can treat other humans as a commodity, theirs to take and use and then throw away like trash. Although I miss the FBI sometimes, I appreciate having the freedom to feel my feelings now that I'm a civilian. There's room for gray. That's not territory I ever thought I'd be comfortable in, but I'm good now that I've 'lived' with it for a while.

Before I reached Virginia soil, I was put in contact with lead Detective Carl "Call me Rass" Rasmussen. Sometimes I get cooperation from the locals, sometimes, I get resistance, but I always get respect. Not just because of my years as an FBI agent who worked some of the best known cases in the country, but because I'm part of Komorebi. We've quietly grown our reputation with each case and each year.

Detective Rasmussen had no objection sharing what little they have so far.

Whenever we're working a new case, we do a quick dive into the community. That's how I found out about Natasha King. An Army vet named Homer Williams was found guilty of her abduction, rape, and murder and was sentenced to death. He died by suicide a year into his stay at Sussex State Prison before his first appeal. According to the records, he slit his throat with a piece of glass.

Now, I'm headed to a neighborhood southeast of the Bridges to see Olena and Anastasia King, the victim's mother, and sister, mainly to satisfy my curiosity. Although kidnapping for ransom hasn't been ruled out for Elspeth Bridges, it doesn't feel right. Something about the idea that two girls roughly the same age would go missing from the same location twenty years apart *and* that their parents would know each other is even less likely.

Olena King and I already met in passing. She was heading home when I arrived at the Bridges residence. I took the opportunity to offer her access to Komorebi. "It means 'the light between the trees.' I've already connected the Bridges with the resources we can offer, but I think you and your daughter would also maybe get some benefit. I'd be more than happy to put you in touch with the team. It has been a lifesaver for many."

I can almost hear her wondering where Komo was in 2002.

Her surviving daughter, an emergency room physician from New York, is in town. I'm unsure whether she comes each year on the anniversary of her sister's abduction or if this is a one-off. That will be one of my questions.

This neighborhood is working class. The older houses are packed in tight. The King home is a white ranch with an attached single-car garage. The front yard is equal parts creeping Charlie and grass with visible bald patches, but it's mowed, and the edges are trimmed. There's a planter of bright flowers on the concrete stoop. Curtains keep prying eyes out while allowing light in. There are two cars in the driveway: a newish blue Honda CRV and an older white Ford Taurus behind it. I pull my rental sedan to the curb and step out.

Angel has helped me find a happy compromise between a stodgy FBI agent (her words) and a professional but approachable investigator. Gone are the navy suits and button-down shirts. Now my work 'uniform' is khakis or jeans, solid-colored plain T-shirts, and a denim or leather jacket, depending on the weather. My hair is longer than it ever would have been at the Bureau. Honestly, I couldn't care less about what I wear, but if Angel says this look is more friendly, I'm all for it.

I step up and prepare to ring the bell, then I quickly step back when the door swings open before I have a chance. Two women study me. Olena is the taller of the two. The younger woman is smaller, plainly dressed in jeans and a white hoodie with a hospital logo on the front. She could be a knockout with different clothes or even a smile. There's no smile now, just pain.

"Nick, hello again. Please come in," Olena says, stepping back so I can navigate the screen door. She waves a hand toward the table in a dining nook between the living room and kitchen. The house is spotless, the furniture older but cared for. It smells vaguely like cabbage. Framed photos take up most of the wall space I can see in the living and dining room. "This is my daughter, Dr. Anastasia King." A moment of pride, well-deserved.

"Call me Stasia." The young woman forces a smile that doesn't reach her eyes and pulls out a chair at the table. She sits with one leg tucked under her. She has a bow-shaped mouth and a button nose that somehow makes her look like she's in her mid-twenties rather than thirty-four. Her almond-shaped eyes are like Olena's—a deep brown flecked with copper, framed by thick lashes. There's a small scar in the crescent shape of a fingernail at the outer corner of her left eye, just under the brow bone.

Olena brings a pot of coffee to the table and sets it on a trivet. There are already cups, real cream, and sugar. She goes back into the kitchen and returns with cookies. I'm sure they're home-baked. "Please, help yourself." She sits at the table's head, and I sit opposite Stasia.

"It's kind of you to help the Bridges family. I can't imagine it's been easy." I say to Olena and pour a cup of black coffee.

Olena dips her head in acknowledgment. "All the feelings come back. The fear. The anger. The frustration. The hope. And the dread."

Stasia is silent, watching. Evaluating. A black cat with bright green eyes leaps from the floor into her lap and snuggles down.

"Anna told me she doesn't think she could get through this without you. They appreciate your efforts. She and Patrick are meeting with a public relations specialist now and will make several television appearances in the next 24 hours. My job," I notch up the corner of my lip in a half-smile, "is to poke around people and places the police aren't always welcome or don't think to go."

That gets Stasia's attention. "Is that legal?"

"It's not *il*legal." I shrug. She approves of that answer. I can see it in her eyes.

"How can we help you, Nick?" Olena takes a cookie from the tray and breaks off small pieces over a napkin. She doesn't eat.

"Well..." I feel dirty asking, but I need to know. "I'm sorry. Can you tell me what you remember about the day Natasha went missing?"

Stasia sucks in a breath but says nothing. Olena gives her a soft look and touches Stasia's hand in a soothing gesture.

"It's simple. Tasha never came home. She went to work in the morning and never. came. home." Stasia says. Her tone is angry and cold.

"Her work. She had a summer job at The Madalena. Is that correct? In the daycare center?"

Olena nods. "Yes. She wanted to go to Space Academy. You know, the science program in Alabama. We didn't have the money." She looks embarrassed, and I wish I could wipe that look away. There's nothing to be embarrassed about. "So she got herself a job. She was close, too. I found the money she'd saved in her nightstand drawer."

"Did she like her job? The work? Her coworkers?"

Olena nods again. "Tasha wasn't a very outgoing girl, not a social butterfly, but she was friendly in her quiet way and a hard worker. She got along with everyone. Even the bratty kids liked her."

"That day, she left work at the usual time?" I already know the answer because I've read the report, but I'd like to hear the story from them directly.

"Her supervisor said Tasha left at five o'clock, the same as every day. She rode her bike, even though it was nearly an hour in each direction. She was careful. Most of the way, she could take bike paths. She had to ride on the street just at the very beginning and the very end." Olena's hand releases Stasia's and returns to play with the cookie again.

"The day she went missing, they didn't find her bike. It was like she disappeared, poof, off the face of the earth." Stasia says, her expression softening, before it turns hard again. "They—the police—tried to say she ran away. Went off with some boy. That wasn't Tasha. She didn't date, didn't have a boyfriend. She was shy. She wanted to be an astronaut. She had dreams; she was happy." I get the impression Stasia is not a fan of the police when it comes to the abduction of her sister.

"My understanding is there were no solid clues until Natasha was found two weeks later. Is that right?"

Stasia is angry again. "First, they thought she'd run away, even though we told them she hadn't. They didn't try very hard."

Olena doesn't try to soothe Stasia this time. I can tell from her expression she agrees. The cat must agree, too, because it transfers from Stasia's lap to Olena's. "There was absolutely nothing until the day they found Natasha, without her bike, near an overpass near one of the bike trails. Then they moved quickly, thank God. They had Homer in custody the same day."

"I'm very sorry to make you relive this. I know it's hard." I've seen the photos from Tasha's file. Her naked body was literally destroyed. Broken legs, broken arms, chunks of flesh removed, face smashed, eye sockets shattered, vaginal and anal openings shredded. The autopsy report said she'd been raped in every orifice by human appendages and other items. She'd been beaten, burned, and water-boarded. Everything done to her was done intentionally and maliciously. The ultimate cause of death was internal bleeding, which is a painful way to die. I've seen very few bodies damaged as extensively as hers. According to the coroner's report, she was alive through most of the torture, aware, in unimaginable pain. I don't want to think about that, and I'm sorry I've forced her mother and sister to revisit it.

Stasia's eyes glisten with angry tears, but she doesn't let them dampen her cheeks. She has control. Olena just looks numb. The cat is now purring so loudly I can hear it from feet away. I make a mental note to tell Angel about their emotional support kitty.

"Had you ever met Homer Williams before he was arrested for Natasha's murder?" I ask. Both women shake their heads, no. But something is different about Stasia's reaction, although I can't put my finger on what, exactly. Olena takes a deep breath and closes her eyes. I continue quietly, "Obviously, these two crimes cannot possibly be connected since Homer has been dead for more than twenty years. But there are similarities. The last known location, for one. Their ages. That neither had a reason to run away. Their positive family dynamics. Of course, it's a sad fact kids disappear every day. They run away or go to a friend's house without telling their parents. But there have only been two Caucasian girls between twelve and fourteen who have gone missing like this in Virginia in two decades: Natasha and Elspeth. Both were last seen at or near The Madalena."

Again, I see a glint of something in Stasia's face, but then it's gone. She asks, "Are you meeting with the Williams family, too?"

I hadn't thought to, but now that she's planted the idea, I think I will. "Are they still in town? Do you know?"

"Cindy Williams, Homer's wife, is," Olena says. "I've seen her once or twice at the grocery."

"And Xander works at a bar, last I heard." Stasia adds.

"Isn't there a daughter, too?" I know there is.

"I heard she left town years ago." Stasia says. She pushes back from the table. "Is there anything else we can tell you?"

I'm being dismissed. She may be petite of body but Stasia King is tough of spirit. I smile. "Could I take a quick peek at her bedroom?"

STASIA

One of the shittiest parts of my childhood was sleeping in the bedroom Tasha and I shared after she was gone. Even now, when I sleep in my old bed, I sometimes wake in the middle of the night expecting to hear her snore. Her half of the room is the same as it was the day she disappeared. The bed is made, and the bright pink comforter is smooth and clean. I wonder if Mama washes it? She must not; it still smells like Tasha. At least that's what my heart says; my scientific mind points out there's no way a smell would linger for twenty years.

Nick stands in the doorway and takes it in. Two twin beds, one on each wall, the window in between, with a large dresser underneath. Closet door on the right-hand side, desk on the left. Shelves on the wall above each bed. Mine holds an award for a science project and a couple of art creations from school. Tasha's shelves are filled with an assortment of science fiction novels, a softball, and the broken ballerina jewelry box.

The room is small, so her bed is valuable real estate, but I can't bring myself to put my bag on the pink comforter. Instead, my duffel is sitting open on the desk chair.

I wonder whether Nick Winston notices small details. I have a feeling he does, and I think maybe he understands.

It's clear where I slept last night because I didn't bother to remake my bed this morning. My childhood comforter is in Manhattan. This bed has a fuzzy blue blanket and white sheets with yellow flowers. The pillow is nearly thirty years old and lumpy, but I don't care. I don't sleep much when I'm here, anyway. Last night Alicia tried to be my snuggle buddy but eventually gave up after I accidentally turned and nearly tossed her off the bed.

The walls are the same pale warm yellow; the curtains are a groovy orange and pink, and the floor is laminate with a hot pink circular rug. Tasha loved pink. It was never my thing, but I didn't care unless I was mad at her.

It's a pretty basic teen girl bedroom. Tasha left no secrets hiding here. She was a simple, sweet girl who never had a chance to learn who she might become.

"Thanks for letting me look," Nick says and steps back into the hallway. "Who's the photographer?" He motions to the framed photos that cover almost every inch of wall space. Mama and Dad when they liked each other. Mama from her childhood in Ukraine, in black and white. Tasha and me in national parks and campgrounds and in front of presidential graves and monuments. Our old dog Lucy. A pretty grouping of flowers in the backyard. A family birthday party. Memories. There are two photos after 2002: my high school graduation in 2007 and my white coat ceremony in 2011.

"Mama, mostly, but Tasha also loved to take photos. The animal and nature scenes are hers." I pause at a photo of me hugging Lucy's neck. I used to be animal crazy. I still love the idea of them, but a pet is a responsibility. Commitment. Vulnerable.

Mama is in the kitchen, futzing. That's what she does when she's unsure of herself. In the days following Tasha's disappearance, she rearranged every cabinet in the kitchen. I couldn't find my favorite cup for a week. She meets us in the living room. "Was that helpful?"

Nick smiles at her. He seems like an okay guy. His warmth feels genuine. I don't *not* like him. I just don't understand what he's after, why he's come to us to talk about a twenty-year-old case. Does he really think Elspeth Bridges is connected to Tasha? No one else seems to.

"It was very helpful, thank you. I appreciate you talking to me. I don't want to take up more of your time. I may see you at the Bridges, Olena." He turns to me. "I understand you're headed back to New York, so I may not see you again. Let me give you my card. In case you think of something or need anything at all. I mean that." He pulls his wallet out and hands me a simple business card. The logo is trees against the sun. He has no title. Just Nick Winston, his email and phone number. I slip it into the pocket of my hoodie.

STASIA

After Nick leaves, I make my bed and repack my duffel with the few things I've taken out. Mama joins me, sitting on the chair.

"Already?" She fingers a pink ribbon tied to a knob on one of the desk drawers and I swear I smell Tasha's Herbal Essence shampoo.

"Afraid so. I've got to talk to some people." I fidget with the ballerina pendant hanging from my neck, and avoid looking Mama in the eye. Although I know what she's going to say, I've got to make the offer. I'm glad I hadn't suggested she join me this time. "I've decided I'm not going to do the road trip this year. I'll fly to Seattle the day before the conference."

"No! Anastasia, no." Mama jumps to her feet. "Why? What is the point? You can't do anything here. This isn't our case. This isn't about us."

"I worry about you being so deeply involved. I love that your heart makes you give so much, but you're putting your own well-being in danger." I can already see lines in her face that weren't there the last time I was here. Her eyes are missing their spark. She looks tired. No, not tired—depleted. Like someone let the air out of her.

"I will be involved whether you are here or not," her tone is sharp, her accent prominent. "You will go. You will call me. You will post photos on the Instagram like you always do so I can enjoy the trip with you. But you will go. This is not open for discussion."

I open my mouth to argue, but she shakes her head, cutting me off. "Don't 'Mama' me. It's important for *your* mental and physical health. I worry about you, too, you know. You have no personal life. You work, you rollerblade, you stay in your apartment, and you visit me. This trip is the only thing you do that you will look back on as an old woman and have memories. You must keep with the plan."

She does not know how accurate her words are. Am I strong enough? I have to be. I wrap my arms around her and kiss her on the cheek. "All right. I've got to get going. I'll check in with you later."

AVA

We're hosting a party. After being gone most of the last week, I wish we were on our own tonight, but entertaining is a big part of our lives. Real estate development is a complicated puzzle of government approvals, money, and union contracts, which means Jamie has to hobnob with people of influence. As President of the DJ Group, Jamie's responsible for the puzzle's progression.

Every year, David James spends less time in his birth state. He has significantly different priorities these days, which rarely relate to the real estate business. Tonight he'll be in attendance, along with Bishop Oliver, his chief of staff, so a big deal must be on the horizon to get them to come to Virginia.

David James once told Jamie, in front of me, with his own weird version of respect, that I was not 'the marrying type.' Jamie was furious and determined to haul me down to city hall then and there. He wanted to shout from the rooftops that we were together. I refused. I told Jamie flat-out I didn't want to get married, at least not now, and it had nothing at all to do with David James' declaration. I could care less about the legalities. What would be different? I have all the benefits—companionship, our rescue babies Voom and ZoZo, and a beautiful home. It's all I ever wanted. That, and peace in my soul.

Jamie put the house in my name when I agreed to live with him. Again, not my idea. After watching his mother's intrigues to keep her claws in David James' pockets, and the games David James plays in return, Jamie is determined to be forthcoming and transparent in all his relationships. He despises the way wealthy people try to hide their assets, which is one of the things I love most about him. He has a Robin Hood soul.

Jamie is the majority shareholder in the DJ Group. Not because David James loves his son; it's just part of their long-term strategy to keep assets safe should something go awry. *Something* is a bomb just waiting to go off. There's no way

David James can keep playing his dangerous games without consequences. It's only a matter of time.

When the David James empire does blow up, the University will blow up, too. I've known that for years. I've been a long-term thinker my whole life, and my finances don't rely on any Ellington, father or son. I've squirreled away most of my salary and bonuses from DJU and work closely with a financial advisor. I will not be a victim of anyone else's whims.

Besides, if I were ever to leave behind this glittering, dangerous world and start over somewhere else, the Ellington name is a freight train worth of baggage I don't want. The trouble with that is that I would never leave without Jamie, and he can't hide from who he is.

The dogs sprawl across my dressing room floor, forcing me to step over them as I debate what to wear tonight. Voom's dark eyes watch me curiously. ZoZo could care less, according to her snores. My guardians. My loves.

Option one is a vintage Oscar de la Renta cocktail dress from the 1970s, highly graphic with bright colors over a white background. Option two is an Alexander McQueen dress, hot pink, very short, with a tight bodice and poufy skirt tiered with tulle bands to show off my long legs. I finally choose the vintage simply because it will take less physical space, and I'll be able to leave my waist-length blonde hair loose. Sometimes I want to be the center of attention, and sometimes I'd rather be background noise. Tonight, I have a feeling the latter is better.

I may live a champagne and caviar life in public, but pizza and beer is my preference. I grab a local IPA from the small fridge in my dressing room and take a long drink to steady my nerves. I hear Jamie in his dressing room on the other side of our bathroom, which I joke is bigger than the house I grew up in. He always plays Motown when he gets dressed for parties, and right now, he's singing—badly—along with the Temptations. "Ain't too proud to beg…"

I put the finishing touches to my makeup, down the rest of my beer, and give myself a pep talk to improve my mood. In just under two hours, I will have a hundred and forty virtual strangers to entertain. My nerves are jangling, and I'm not sure why. I study my reflection in the silver-framed floor-to-ceiling mirror. It feels as though I'm looking at another woman, a woman who looks like me but isn't me. I shake my head. "Snap out of it, Ava. It's going to be fine."

AVA

When we have parties this size, we execute "The Plan." My assistant Angie manages the cleaners, the caterer, the bartenders, and the musicians. Hendrix oversees the valets and additional security. Jamie and I are in charge of the guest list and the guests. It's a well-choreographed effort.

The only thing about our parties that is personal is the bouquets of coral tulips that fill vases all around the house and patio. They're my favorite.

The invitation, mailed ten days ago, announced a start time of eight o'clock. People will begin arriving just after nine. Tonight's event is hors d'oeuvres and cocktails. A popular R&B singer with multiple Grammys will entertain from the gazebo by the pool. Our friends and acquaintances are not coming to eat; they want to see and be seen, rub elbows, and make deals.

Angie takes ZoZo and Voom into her office to hang out. Poor Angie is a total introvert, and parties of this size are her least favorite part of her job with us. I love her for being willing to suffer through them for me.

David James and Bishop walk through the front doors at eight fifteen, catching me completely off-guard. When they come to these events, they're usually hours late. I compose myself and greet them.

David James is tall and slim with dark, shoulder-length hair thinning at the top. With his small round-framed glasses, he reminds me a bit of both Kevin Spacey and John Lennon. He's not your average billionaire. He doesn't dress in suits. He collects arty wearables on his travels. Hand-painted tunics. One-of-a-kind boots from Madrid. Long scarves and caftans. If you didn't know better, you might think he's the head of a cult, and you wouldn't be entirely wrong.

Bishop is a few inches shorter and a foot rounder. A jovial Santa. He's addicted to expensive suits and shoes. He leans into the stereotypical Wall Street uniform. Bald and always smiling, the laugh lines around his blue eyes are deep and well-earned. When he laughs, he accentuates the Santa image. Piss him off, and Santa turns into a vengeful, spitting cobra before you have time to realize your mistake.

David James holds me by the shoulders and pecks each of my cheeks while Bishop pulls me into a firm, full-frontal embrace and cups my ass with both hands. I don't cringe or try to wiggle away. This has been my life since I was eighteen.

"Good to see you!" I say in my best hostess voice. "Jamie is finishing up and will be down in a minute or two. What can I get you?" I usher them into the main salon. Everything is white. The giant white sofa is a sectional. There are several spare pieces in storage. The ultimate subconscious message: "I'm rich. Spill your red wine wherever you'd like."

David James asks for his usual club soda with lime and Bishop his favorite tequila, and a server hustles off to fetch their drinks. The minute we're seated, Bishop's hand finds my thigh, exposed thanks to the short skirt of the vintage dress. Bishop knows he won't get anywhere with me. For men like him, that makes pushing the boundaries all the more fun. I wouldn't want to be caught alone with him.

"How are the recruiting trips going? Anything exciting?" David James asks, giving me a boys-will-be-boys wink as Bishop slips an arm over my shoulder and dangles his hand dangerously close to my left breast.

"They've been successful. Good girls," I make a show of playfully moving Bishop's hand just before he closes in. "Our friends will enjoy them. Nothing special for you this time, but I have a strong lead in Seattle next week."

David James nods then says, his patience gone, "Bish, leave the girl alone."

Bishop laughs and accepts a tequila from the server, who, fortunately, is male. We never hire female servers for these events. I don't want guests to confuse the University with the Group or David James' private interests. And I don't want Bishop assaulting anyone in a hallway or dark corner.

"I was pleasantly surprised when Jamie said you were coming tonight. It's been a while." I squeeze David James' hand, and he returns the squeeze affectionately. He's fond of me and doesn't hesitate to show it. I'm one of the few women he speaks to like a real person—most of the time, anyway. He's much nicer to me than to Jamie's mother, Madeline. Theirs is a purely financial arrangement at this point. Maddy spends her time in South America, far from her husband's varied interests and affairs. Pun intended.

"We're in Virginia for a few days on business, so of course, we wouldn't miss it," Bishop announces as if his presence is a gift.

"Well, I'm glad you made it." It's not a lie. Exactly.

Jamie appears, and I can tell he's equally surprised to see them so early in the evening. He recovers quickly and puts on his best welcoming smile. "Dad! Bish. Comfortable here, or should we go to the office?"

I watch the three men disappear behind closed doors and prepare to greet the rest of our guests.

NICK

A trick I learned from Peter is to pick up a trifold cardboard presentation display at an office supply or drugstore as soon as I hit town for a new project. That, combined with my go bag and the hotel's business center, gives me everything I could possibly need—except a solution —to work a case. My go bag is packed with a portable photo printer, rolls of blue painter's tape, a variety of Sharpie pens in different colors and thicknesses, sticky post-its of various sizes, and push pins, as well as disposable booties and gloves, plastic storage bags and containers, and a few other forensic items.

I use the painter's tape to secure the yellow cardboard trifold display to the glass doors of my small residence-style hotel room. Elspeth's smiling school photo is front and center, her parents and sister's photos beside her. Other pictures include her teammates and coaches, the expansive Madalena property and parking lot, the Bridges home, and Elspeth's Instagram profile. According to big sister Margot, Elspeth uses Snapchat for communication and will post sports photos on Instagram. She watches videos on TikTok but has never posted, at least not on the account Margot follows. Margot doubts she has a second, secret account on Instagram or TikTok. When she says this, Margot blushes, so I suspect Margot herself has a secret account. Margot doesn't think her little sister is 'super into' social media.

The files Rass gave me on both the current Bridges case and the long-closed King case are on the small table next to the kitchenette. I've mapped out a timeline, and written up mini bios on key individuals, which are tacked onto the middle third of the board.

In the far left portion of the display board I've posted pictures of Natasha, Olena, Stasia and George King, and Homer, Cindy, Willow and Xander Williams. Mini bios on sticky notes are next to each of their photos. Next to Tasha, I've written in thick black Sharpie:

14 days abduction to discovery.

I grab a large lined sticky note and make a list:

SIMILARITIES: ages, caucasian, no history of trouble, "good" kids, loving families, The Madalena

I write on another:

DIFFERENCES: 20 years, Dead perpetrator, Employee vs. Guest, Bike alone / team bus

According to Rass, since Elspeth's disappearance, there have been 114 reported sightings. None have been substantiated. An idiot kid at her school claimed he'd chained her in his treehouse and made her his love slave. Bullshit, of course.

Hockenberger mentioned there's a man named Brad that some of the tween and teen female guests call 'creepy.' He wasn't working the day Elspeth went missing, but Rass and I paid a visit to the duplex Brad shares with a friend under the supervision of Brad's mother who owns both units and lives next door. After an enthusiastic tour of Brad's Lego collection, and introduction to his geckos Leroy and Jimmy, and a long conversation about the various types of brooms and their unique purposes, Rass and I agreed Brad is not our suspect. Also, teen girls can be assholes.

We made another stop at the home of the driver of the bus that delivered and picked up Elspeth's volleyball team to The Madalena. The man dutifully informed Rass his 40-year-old son, who lives with him, is on the sex registry, but has never been involved in his father's job in any way. The son has a very solid alibi and seems to be an upstanding citizen these days. But no lead can go unfollowed.

XANDER

The Cherry Tree was an upscale bar in the nineties, popular with the professional happy hour crowd. Now it's a bit of a dive. We have a lot of daytime regulars, mostly retired, who consider this their place. Afternoons are popular with tourists needing a break from shopping, and nights and weekends are packed with college kids looking to get rowdy.

The Cherry Tree is my source of income and my home, the only adult responsibility I have managed without screwing up too much. I've worked here for fifteen years, on and off. I live in the studio apartment over the bar, which is convenient on nights I get a little too friendly with the customers. I've learned over the years one night's fun can become a pain in the ass when last night's girl won't take "no" for an answer. For that reason, there are two deadbolts on the door that separates the bar from the staircase to the second floor.

We're a block from the river, and there's a ton of foot and car traffic. If someone wanted to put some effort in, they could turn the Cherry Tree into a trendy pub. It would do well. But that would require actual work. Neither the owner nor I have the motivation to do actual work.

This is the kind of place with a long, polished bar, pinball machines and pool tables, and booths with cracked vinyl. The walls are plastered with license plates from every state. There's a train whistle between the doors to the men's and women's restrooms, and when a good-looking girl goes to the ladies, one of the regulars will pull the cord to blow the whistle. If it's her first time, it'll scare the crap out of her, and she'll be embarrassed. After that first time, she's gonna be offended if no one pulls the cord.

We serve a limited menu. Food is an afterthought, not the main event. The only thing crave-worthy is the pizza fries—thick fries covered in sauce, pepperoni, and mozzarella. They're tasty, especially if you're drunk.

Even though it's barely 7, Saturday nights are busy, and I've got a handful of regulars seated at the bar watching the game on a TV above the liquor bottles. Both pool tables are occupied. A drunk girl is yelling at the jukebox. I'm in a decent mood.

The door opens, and a lone woman slips onto the stool nearest the door. My heart pounds in my chest. I know who she is. She knows who I am. I continue to wipe down the counter and throw out a casual, "What can I get ya?"

"Shot of tequila," she says, her eyes meeting and holding mine for what feels like an eternity. It's just a few seconds. She picks up a book of matches from a bowl on the counter and flips it open for something to do. It's been years since you could smoke in the bar, but the owner accidentally ordered a dozen gross—meaning 1728—*boxes* of the branded matchbooks in the mid-90s. Smokers usually have a lighter, so the matches have become nothing more than a souvenir. As I pour a shot of Patron, I watch her twirl the matchbook between the index and middle fingers of her right hand.

I set the glass in front of her with lime and salt. She ignores both. She lays a ten dollar bill on the counter, downs the shot, says, "See ya later," and floats out the door as quietly as she came through it.

I lean against the counter behind the bar to give the adrenalin time to calm. *Stasia King. Shit.*

MAY 10, 2003

XANDER

Xander found out his father was dead from a reporter.

There were three television crews outside their house before sunrise. The sound of van doors sliding open and then slamming closed jarred Xander from a dream, a pleasant dream for a change. Once his eyes were open, he heard his mother's soft sobs coming from her bedroom across the hall. Angry, he jumped out of bed and ran to the front door, not giving a shit that he was only wearing boxers. "Go away! Leave us the fuck alone!"

"Were there any signs your father was contemplating suicide?" A pretty blonde reporter asked, without a drop of compassion.

"What?" Xander rubbed his eyes. Anger changed to something else. Confusion. Fear. Dread.

"Oh, shit, he doesn't know," another reporter said in a stage whisper.

The blonde said, "My bad," and added, "But now that you know, how do you feel about your father killing himself? Do you feel it was a cowardly act? Or did he have no hope in the appeals process? Was he afraid of being executed and decided to take his own life instead? Did he ever mention his intention to you?"

Xander heard the barrage of words and memorized her face because someday, he hoped she'd feel pain the way she was causing his pain now. But for now, for today, fuck them all. He slammed the door and went to his mother's room. He raised his hand to knock, changed his mind, and pushed the door open. She was rocking back and forth like a little kid. When she saw him, her soft cries grew in strength until she was wailing, screaming, and hammering her fists against her legs.

Willow flew into the room and jumped on the bed to wrap her arms tightly around their mother. She looked up at Xander and mouthed, "What happened?"

"Dad is dead." Xander mouthed back. "Suicide." If his world hadn't been rocked before this, it was changed forever now. He didn't believe his father committed suicide any more than he believed his father had killed Natasha King. He didn't know when or how, but he was going to learn the truth and make sure everyone recognized it, starting with that fucking blonde bitch of a reporter.

Chapter 5

DAY FOUR

STASIA

A pair of cable news anchors are gasping and oohing when I drop onto the bed post-shower. The woman announces, "Well, this is horrific. A Virginia attorney was violently assaulted overnight, and the whole thing was put on social media by the assailant!"

Her co-anchor, a man with a face so sculpted he looks like a Ken doll, nods with a mix of feigned horror and enthusiasm. "We are all left asking the same questions: who is this Sabine, and why does he/she/it need to be stopped? Is Sabine the person who did this unspeakable thing? Are they challenging the police to stop them? Or are they someone the attacker has issues with? It's all so mysterious."

They're annoying, but I want to know what's happening, so I turn off the TV and open my laptop. The story is everywhere—national news, social media, and tabloids. According to the headlines, attorney Miles Cameron was attacked in his suburban Virginia home. An unknown assailant surgically removed his eyes from their sockets. It was all recorded on video and broadcast on Facebook, YouTube, and TikTok and was quickly reshared to Instagram and Twitter. The more prestigious national news channels don't include a link to the video, but the tabloids do. I ignore the suitability warnings and click the first raw video I find.

At first, the screen is black. For a few minutes, nothing happens. Suddenly lights come on, spotlights directed at a man bound with rope to a high-backed executive-style desk chair in what appears to be a home office. The space around him is dimly lit at best. He's sitting behind a wide old-fashioned antique desk. There are three monitors on the left side of the desk, along with an old-school office phone. He was working, or at least that's what the viewer is supposed to think. A manilla folder lays open on the desk, loose papers, sticky notes, and pens scattered across it. The camera is stationary. The scene is confusing for the viewer. There is no clear indication of where the threat will come from. It's an establishing shot of sorts.

A strip of duct tape covers the man's mouth. The man is in his fifties, greying at the temples but still has a full head of hair. He's tanned, and probably handsome. His eyes are the only part of him that moves, and they're telling a story: pain, confusion, terror.

Another figure steps into view. From the angle of the camera, the person appears to be somewhere between five foot ten and six feet. Not thin, not fat. Blue surgical pants and a long-sleeved V-neck top under a surgical gown, a surgical cap covering what seems to be dark hair. Gloved hands. A mask covers the lower face, and a surgical shield blocks the top. Even without the mask and shield, the person carefully controls what the camera catches. They move intentionally to ensure the focus is on the man in the chair.

The person in scrubs does not speak. They set a surgical kit on the desk and open it, exposing various scalpels, retractors, surgical saws, scissors, tweezers, and clamps. They disappear from the screen and return with a small glass jar the size of a container of cottage cheese.

The man in the chair struggles, trying to free himself, to no avail. His hands and forearms are strapped to the chair's arms. Since he isn't rolling away, one would assume his feet are also secured.

Instruments are laid out; the person in blue moves behind the man. The man's head is strapped to the headrest at the top of the chair, holding him still. He tries to move to shake his head 'no,' but the strap holding him is too tight. Sweat beads at his forehead and catches on the strap. When the strap is in place, it forces his chin up. The man in the chair attempts to jerk away, but he is absolutely helpless.

There is no sound to the video, which adds to the eeriness.

The attacker collects items from the table and moves into position. The spotlights aimed at the man in the chair give the audience a clear view of what will happen.

The attacker uses speculums to retract the lids of both of the man's eyes. Then the attacker chooses surgical scissors from the collection of instruments on the desk.

The attacker maintains a stance that keeps the camera focused on the movement of their hands while keeping their face in shadow. As it becomes clear what's about to happen, my stomach lurches. The person in blue uses the curved medical scissors to slowly and carefully dissect the muscles that hold each eyeball in place. In the medical world, it's called an enucleation. To the average person watching, the man's eyeballs are being popped out.

It's a very clean procedure, with little to no blood in the operating area. Once the orbs are free, the attacker puts them into the container on the desktop. The attacker closes the container when both eyes are floating in clear liquid. They clean the area, replace their tools, check for a pulse at the neck, disconnect the IV drip, and disassemble the equipment. The attacker moves in and out of the camera's view. No rush. No concern about being discovered.

Finally, the attacker comes to the desk, which has been cleared of all medical equipment. As the man shows signs of consciousness, the attacker puts the container with the man's eyes front and center, then holds up a letter-sized piece of cardboard facing the camera. Two words, printed in Comic Sans font, intentionally ridiculous.

STOP SABINE.

That's it. The screen goes black.

I breathe in deeply to settle my gut.

The original video is easy to find on YouTube using the search term 'StopSabine.' There's no description, but there are hashtags: #stopsabine #thesurgeon #seethetruth #seenoevil #timetopay. It has over four million views since it was posted this morning at 2:30 am eastern standard time. It was loaded by an account called StopSabine.

I close YouTube and return to the news sites to see what they say about the victim.

Miles Cameron, attorney, age fifty. Divorced, three adult kids, lives in a single-family home in a wealthy DC suburb in Virginia. That's where the attack took place. Neighbors are shocked. This isn't 'that kind of neighborhood,' which might make a person wonder what kind of neighborhood is the kind where masked doctors remove people's eyes in the middle of the night?

Another article says Cameron's current practice is focused on corporate law. The reporter can't imagine he generates a lot of enemies establishing LLCs and arranging franchise sales. He was a public defender until 2007. The reporter theorizes that perhaps one of his clients was released from prison and is seeking revenge.

As good a theory as any, I suppose.

STASIA

My weird obsession with presidential grave sites began when I wrote a report about David Rice Atchison in the eighth grade. He was president for exactly one day, although he didn't want to be. He was kind of a jerk, to be honest, but I found the rules around the presidency fascinating and it set me off on a path. I guess that qualifies as a hobby, albeit an odd one.

If she couldn't go to Space Camp, Tasha's was content to spend our summer vacations visiting national parks. She loved the outdoors, the majesty of forests, waterfalls, rock formations, and meandering paths. Neither of us thought to ask for a week at Disney World or even a nearby water park. We didn't have that kind of money. Back when things were mostly good, we'd load up Mama's Kia with coolers of food, sleeping bags, air mattresses, and a couple of tents and head off for a week. That was the best we could ask for, and we had a blast. Even Dad was in a good mood. Those summer vacations are one of my best childhood memories, one of the rare reminiscences that feels happy.

There were no trips after Tasha was gone, and I didn't understand how much I missed them for a long time.

The summer between my freshman and sophomore years of college, I was bored and lonely and feeling restless. I loaded my backpack with shorts, jeans, T-shirts, and underwear, hopped into my third-hand station wagon, and headed west with no specific destination. I wandered through West Virginia, Kentucky, and Ohio for two weeks, visiting presidential graves and camping in some of the most beautiful parks. That was the trip that started my annual pilgrimage. Since then, I've seen nineteen presidential graves and twenty-three national parks. I keep a marked map in my glove box, and even though it's getting kind of ratty, it's one of my most valued possessions.

When I finally got home early this morning, I had to wrap up some details, and at that point sleep wouldn't come. Now I'm running slow. The double espresso I sucked down didn't help much but it's the best option I've got.

I printed out the detailed road trip map with stops at parks, camping spots, gas stations, and even some restaurants. This year's plan is to explore the upper portion of the U.S., heading west until I arrive in Seattle for the conference. I add the map to a plastic Ziplock bag with cash, a credit card, and other important information and put the bag in the glove box.

I feel guilty leaving Mama. This year will be especially difficult. Keeping her updated will be more important than ever.

My hard-sided suitcase is filled with what I'll need for the conference—a couple of professional outfits, makeup, hair products, nicer shoes. I stow it behind the driver's seat for easy access, and fold down the rear seats to open the back of the SUV. A plastic bin holds towels, shampoo, conditioner, toothpaste, deodorant, tampons, etc. A cooler and a duffel are in the passenger seat and wheel well. An inflatable mattress and sleeping bag are set up in the back, and the curtains I jimmy-rigged for privacy are in place with the curtains open to provide clear visuals while driving.

The last thing I add is my backpack, which holds jeans, T-shirts, underwear and my rollerblades. You never know when you might want to skate away.

The clock is ticking and I've got to go. I have to be at the Hackettstown rest stop in New Jersey by ten.

NICK

There's been little to no progress on the Elspeth Bridges case. She seems to have disappeared into thin air. Many times someone sees something even if they don't realize it. Or surveillance cameras capture an image. Or neighbors noticed a stranger hovering around the edges. Not this time.

When we meet for breakfast, Rass confirms that, except for the King case in 2002, no missing children were connected to The Madalena. A few times, a little kid has wandered away from their parents, but they're always quickly reunited with family.

He gives me the timeline.

At 2:25 p.m., Elspeth was with the rest of her teammates when they enjoyed an after-practice snack courtesy of The Madalena. This was the fifth and final day of the camp. She was seen on CCTV at 2:45 p.m. when the coaches instructed the girls to head toward the parking lot. Somewhere between the restaurant patio and the parking lot, Elspeth Bridges disappeared.

The coaches were irritated by their missing charge at 3:15 p.m. They became anxious at 3:30, forty-five minutes after Elspeth should have been on the bus. That's when they contacted The Madalena staff, who set out *en masse* to hunt for the girl. At 4p.m., announcements had been made, and the grounds had been searched, but Elspeth was nowhere to be found. They called the police. Elspeth's parents were contacted at 5:30 p.m. Their daughter had been missing for almost two hours.

The Bridges and King cases are more alike than they're different. Both girls went missing from The Madalena. They're about the same age. Neither has a history of running away, and neither had a boyfriend. The only real difference is twenty years. That's a pretty big gap, sure.

"Have there been any disappearances or attacks on the bike trails Natasha King used to get to and from The Madalena each day?" I ask between mouthfuls.

"Maybe a few dozen incidents over the last two decades. Mostly panhandlers, unwanted flirting, or dogs misbehaving. No abductions, successful or otherwise." Rass says.

That strengthens my conviction that there's a connection, and that connection is tied to The Madalena. For now, I won't push. I'll do some poking around, and if I learn something interesting, I'll share it. Probably.

I've got Komorebi's team checking out the employees of The Madalena to see if any ugly surprises are hiding there. But I'm going to do some firsthand investigation on my own.

Rass and I part ways, and I head to The Madalena. According to the file Rass shared, the large parking area where Elspeth should have joined her teammates to board the bus doesn't have working security cameras. Most of the active cameras are in the clubhouse and other buildings surrounding the pool decks and immediately next to the golf course. Because it's an old analog system, scope and quality are limited.

The Madalena is a beautiful facility with buildings that date back to the 1950s, situated on 250 acres of pristine grounds. There are a number of large buildings, most in a colonial architectural style that suits the physical and historical location. The Madalena is the most exclusive golf and country club in the area, with annual dues in the $15,000 range, *after* an initiation fee of $150,000. You'd think they could afford to update their cameras.

Joel Hockenberger, president of The Madalena, has made himself available to me, maybe because I name-dropped Peter Baden's name. My partner in anti-crime still has celebrity status, even though he left the media world years ago.

Hockenberger meets me in the beautiful lobby of the Main House, which he tells me is the heart of the entire facility. The large circular lobby is a mix of overstuffed seating and Persian rugs on top of marble floors. Recessed sections of the walls hold copies of famous sculptures. I recognize the David, and Venus, and a couple of others look familiar. There's a replica of the Sistine Chapel on the ceiling. "Our owner is fond of Italian art." Hockenberger explains.

He gives me a tour of the administration area, and focuses on the security center. The club's approach to security is grounded in discretion, since the club's 3,000 members are wealthy business leaders, government leaders, or scholars. A twelve-member uniformed team is responsible for all aspects of safety at The Madalena. Most are retired law enforcement or fire fighters. The team is on the grounds 24/7 and works under the supervision of the Executive Director's second-in-command.

The entire campus is fenced with one gated entry and exit point with a parking gate that can be lowered but is left raised most of the time. The gatehouse is staffed from three in the afternoon until nine in the evening, seven days a week, and from eight in the morning until midnight on the weekends. A camera records the gated area. The gatehouse staff makes a note of everyone who enters and exits the facility in a digital log. If the gatehouse is unstaffed, visitors give their name to a security box connected to the receptionist in the main clubhouse. Members also have a sticker or hanging placard on their car that is captured and can be reviewed on demand. Guests' names must be provided by their sponsoring member.

"Cameras are used to protect the staff, members and guests but are not used to invade privacy." Hockenberger explains. "Recordings are only accessed when there is a specific need to do so."

"I'm surprised that you have so few cameras considering the size of this place. And the system is older technology," I comment, keeping my tone bland to avoid insulting Hockenberger.

He doesn't seem bothered. "What we have has suited us fine. The security team is mostly called upon for health emergencies, minor traffic events in the parking areas and an occasional theft. We don't have a lot of violent crime here.

But if we do, The Madalena has a good relationship with local police and first responders."

Membership is by invitation only, and members must be sponsored by an existing member. Once in, members have access to the two 18 hole golf courses, indoor year-round golf learning center, pool complex, tennis courts, fitness center, overnight accommodations, helipad. The community boasts sprawling multi-million dollar estates around its edges, an 85,000-square-foot clubhouse, a more intimate 40,000 square foot event center, restaurants, boutiques, and an 18,000 square foot spa and wellness center. It's as big as some college campuses.

Hockenberger and I get into one of a dozen golf carts for a tour.

"I wonder how many football fields would fit onto the property," I muse as we cruise at fifteen miles per hour across paved hills.

"One hundred and eighty nine." He smiles. Apparently I'm not the first to ask.

"What's happening over there?" I point to a cluster of people and cameras near the tennis courts.

Hockenberger glances over. "The Madalena is highly sought after by photographers although we are very careful about what we allow. Today I believe one of our members is shooting some portfolio shots."

"You have a member who is a photographer?" Considering the membership and initiation fees, the photog must be very successful.

"He's one of the best in the business. Flip through the pages of any high-end fashion magazine and he's likely responsible for a good portion." Hockenberger confirms. "But today they're shooting for David James University, I believe."

"David James University?" That's an odd name for a school, I think.

"I'm sure you've heard of it. It's a charitable entity operated by David James Ellington." He gives me a glance. "You're familiar with him, I assume?"

When I nod, he continues.

"A school of sorts. They provide young women with an education in—well, socializing, I suppose you might say."

I'm relieved when we come to a stop, and Hockenberger guides me into one of the restaurants to continue our conversation. A server brings us both coffee, and a staff member in a crisp uniform glides up to hand Hockenberger a note, which he reads, and slides into his pocket without comment.

"I'm afraid I have a meeting in about fifteen minutes. But you're free to spend as much time as you'd like exploring. I'll make sure my team knows to give you access and answer any questions you may have, although I believe the police were very thorough." Hockenberger says.

"Thanks, I appreciate the time you've given me. You weren't here in 2002, were you?"

He nods. "That's the year I began my career at The Madalena. I was hired as a shift manager for The Lodge. Why do you ask?"

"A girl named Natasha King went missing after work here at the daycare center."

"Oh yes! I remember the law enforcement activity. If I recall correctly, Natasha was said to be a nice girl, quiet, well-liked, good at wrangling the kids. I couldn't tell you anything about her other than that, really. Don't even recall what she looked like." Hockenberger is trying to be helpful but it's obvious his focus has shifted to his upcoming meeting.

"Is there anything about that time that sticks out? Not necessarily related to Natasha?"

It's a basic cover-the-bases question, and I'm not expecting much, so I'm surprised when Hockenberger tilts his head and says, "There is one thing. I never thought there was a link, but it was just before the King girl went missing, so...." He frowns. "Around that same time, the wife of one of our members accused another member of molesting her niece, who was visiting from London. That caused a bit of a stink, especially since the accused was someone important to the Club. In fact he is the one who sponsored Kodak, the photographer you saw. I'm trying to recall what the outcome of that incident was...."

He stares through the large windows at his domain. "Oh, yes, now I remember. The woman recanted the accusation and said it was a misunderstanding on her niece's part. She stopped coming to the club after that. It was a topic of gossip for a bit until someone else found themselves in the spotlight."

Interesting. "Do you remember much about the niece? How old was she? What exactly did she say the member had done?"

"She was young, maybe 15, I think. Otherwise, it wouldn't have received much attention since some girls practically invite so-called 'molestation' with their behavior and what they wear."

I keep my expression neutral, although I'm not feeling particularly neutral.

"I believe she said the member forced her to, shall we say, perform a service for him." Hockenberger looks uncomfortable.

"Do you remember the member's name?"

Hockenberger pauses, debating member confidentiality. Eventually he shrugs. "It would be hard to forget his name. His personal and professional profiles have skyrocketed in the last few decades. He's one of the wealthiest men in the country, perhaps the world. And we were just speaking of him."

"What's his name?" I ask again, giving Hockenberger my best FBI agent stare.

Hockenberger considers once more, glances around to see if anyone is in earshot, then says under his breath, "I guess it doesn't matter if I tell you. The young woman recanted and no charges were filed. It was David James Ellington."

Well, hot damn.

XANDER

At 9 p.m., I pass control of the bar over to my assistant manager and head upstairs. On the other side of the old six panel door, I pause a moment and survey my space, grateful that it's mine, grateful there's something I haven't fucked up. Yet.

The apartment above Cherry Tree is a long, rectangular space with enormous glass windows overlooking the street below and allowing a distant glimpse of the river. I've lived here for ten years now and made it my own. I'm no Martha Stewart, but I'm also not a frat boy. There are framed photographs, mostly of food, on the brick walls. The leather couch was bought on a payment plan, not found on a curb or in Mom's basement. My bed sits on a frame and has a headboard. The sheets don't match, but they're good quality bamboo. There's not a lot of stuff, but what's here is intentional and of decent quality.

The kitchen is the exception. I love food, everything about it, and I tend to splurge on things that matter. My fridge is the most expensive thing I own. Even though I bought it used from a friend I could've got a good used car for less. My gas range is a dinged model from a high-end contractors store. I have a beautiful collection of plates, bowls and serving vessels from various travels, domestic and abroad.

And then there's my knife set. The oldest pieces are from my time with Paco & Patches, where I apprenticed. There are boning knives, carving knives, breaking knives, and a heavy cleaver. Two of the knives are at least thirty years old, 'inherited' from Homer's hunting collection. My butcher knife is a 10" cimeter that lets me power through tough skin and sinew. I have a hand saw, also leftover from Dad, to process game when I go hunting. I keep everything but the saw in a knife roll Paco gave me when I completed my first processing test. He had my initials burnt into the leather. I love that damn thing.

Now's not the time to think about Paco, or how I messed up a career I loved; how I hurt the adopted family that took me in and gave me possibility. I need to be careful how much anger I let out. I think of it as a teapot: I can open it a smidge, and release some steam, but if I open it all the way, someone will get burned—probably me. I'm not strong enough to slam it closed if the rage escapes.

I open my laptop and start typing the email, careful to leave the addressee line blank so I don't prematurely send it. The words have been flying around my head since I saw Gifford at the diner, which makes it easy to get a violent first draft out. Every emotion I've carried for twenty years spills onto the digital page. I spend another thirty minutes paring it down. Mark Twain was right when he said it's easier to write long than short. I repeat a mantra to myself: *Careful as she goes, my man, careful as she goes. Imperative to maintain the fine line between intimidating and illegal. If you end up in the slammer, everything goes to shit.*

I re-read the email three more times, change a word here, rephrase there, remove a line, then save it into drafts. *You're overthinking, man, you're overthinking.* I head downstairs for a smoke, navigating friends and strangers in the now-packed bar. I only make it through half my cigarette before I'm back upstairs, telling myself to shit or get off the fucking pot.

I hit send, and my missive flies through the ether toward its target.

I have one more to deploy.

Someone could make a lot of money designing and selling greeting cards with 'fuck off' sentiments. Since my local CVS carries nothing like that, I go with second best: a dog squeezing out a giant steaming pile with "Surprise!" written in shit. It'll have to do. Inside, I print, "Someday, the world will know what a self-serving piece of crap you are. Do the right thing and tell the truth before the truth is told for you."

Damien Simpson's office is in the historic district, not far from the Cherry Tree, and the daily mail delivery is shoved through a slot in the glass door. No postmark.

I don't sign it, not because I'm afraid there'll be consequences, but because I want them to work for it.

Let the games begin.

STASIA

After dinner, I open my phone and check my Instagram account. There are a couple of interactions on today's posts, mostly from Mama, but also from a couple of coworkers. There are two mercy 'likes' on photos from the Ohio tomb of Warren G. Harding, the 29th president of these United States. Mama commented on a shot of a Cracker Jack collection at the Wyandote Popcorn Museum. We're big popcorn fans. Mama and I used to experiment with popcorn recipes most weekends when I was growing up.

I text her. "How are you? Taking care of yourself?"

Mama hits the thumbs-up icon as I add, "Any news on Elspeth?"

"Not that I've heard." Mama types. The screen goes blank, and I try to think of something to say. Then more words from Mama. "Nick is trying to persuade Detective Rasmussen there's a connection between her case and Tasha's, but I don't think he's gotten very far."

Many thoughts, including that Mama calls him 'Nick' instead of 'Nick Winston' or 'the investigator.' They've spent more time together if she's that relaxed with him. I suppose if he thinks there's a connection, as she says, that makes sense.

"Don't get too involved, Mama. I don't want your heart to be broken."

"My heart broke in 2002. It's held together with spit and old gum." Mama types.

I 'heart' that since I have nothing brilliant to say. "Does he have any real theories? Or just a hunch?" I want to think positively and keep an open mind. Easier said than done.

"He strongly believes it's somehow connected to David James Ellington," Mama explains. "Those girls of his."

Hmmm. Now that's interesting.

After Mama sends a stream of XOXOXOs, I stretch out and study the ceiling. Maybe I should tell Nick Winston a bit more about back then. Maybe I should tell him about Willow.

SEPTEMBER 5, 2005

STASIA

The first day of her sophomore year started decently. Stasia got the classes she wanted. She'd made some friends last year, they'd hung out over the summer, and she was on the math team. It felt like she was finally finding a stride. She and Mama had built a little nest at home, removing all traces of George except for a few old photos from the good days. When she was especially sad, Stasia would stop at the photos of their summer vacations because those were the ones that included everyone, and they seemed happy. Her favorite was the one of Tasha and Stasia at Grant's Tomb in Manhattan. They almost didn't stop because there wasn't an immediately available parking space, and George didn't have much patience for Stasia's obsession with presidential graves. Tasha saved the day when she spotted someone leaving and begged their father to stop. It was a good day after that.

Mama's new job wasn't so new anymore, and she was comfortable with her coworkers and had even made a couple of friends. Things were okay.

Until fifth period, when Stasia headed to Spanish class.

Willow Williams was walking toward her, head down, as she and a friend looked at something in Willow's hand.

Stasia saw Willow coming and stopped in her tracks, trying to decide whether to avoid conflict, even as her skin itched and her head buzzed.

They hadn't seen each other over the summer. They hadn't seen each other since Homer Williams was found dead in his cell, an apparent suicide. Stasia was furious about that. She wanted him to rot in that jail cell until the time came for him to be executed. She wanted other people to do to him what he'd done to her sister. She wanted him to feel pain in every form. But the coward had taken the easy way out. Willow would get the brunt of her anger, especially when she put herself in the way.

Willow nearly crashed into Stasia. She glanced up, ready to apologize, but her mouth clamped shut when she saw Stasia. Her eyes narrowed, and her voice lowered. "Move."

Stasia said, "Okay!" in a singsong voice and 'moved' right into Willow with all the force her petite body could manage. Willow didn't need to be asked twice. Slaps, punches, hair and clothing pulls, with both girls on the floor, a circle of enthusiastic students cheering them on. Stasia had no memory of the physical fight itself. She just remembered a teacher dragging her away from Willow and jerking her to her feet. In the bathroom, she saw the beginnings of a black eye. There were scratches on her arms. Otherwise, her body was intact. But her mind was still furious. *Bitch. Bitch. Bitch. Bitch.*

They were given after-school detention. Not only did the new high school administrator not realize the feud between the King and Williams families was along the lines of the Hatfields and McCoys, but Ms. Vincent also thought it would be a good idea to put the embattled students together in a detention classroom with a first-year teacher who wanted to be everyone's friend. The idiot teacher told them to sit at their assigned tables and write 250 words on what they found positive about the other. Then the moron left the room to fill his water bottle.

Willow was out of her chair before the door closed behind him. Stasia rose, ready to continue their fight, but Willow held up both hands. "Truce. Truce. I want to talk for a minute. Please." She looked worse than Stasia, which gave Stasia a moment of satisfaction since Willow was taller at 5'9" and much thicker. The girl had put on some padding. Her breasts were impressive, which helped balance the rest. Her brown hair was wavy and frizzy. Pimples glowed red between the scratch marks Stasia had left on her face. Willow used to be pretty and would easily be pretty again if she tried. She wasn't trying. Stasia felt a moment's guilt. She hoped no one judged her as harshly.

"A minute. Go." Stasia remained tense, prepared to launch the second Willow said the wrong thing. She didn't trust Willow Williams for two seconds and couldn't imagine what the hell she'd want to talk about, much less that Stasia would give two hoots about anything she had to say.

Five minutes later the teacher returned and ordered Willow back to her own seat. Stasia, to her great surprise, realized she did in fact give two hoots. He didn't notice the change in the room. Both girls were feeling hurt and angry, but not at each other. Stasia had started the day believing one thing, and now her mind was swirling. The anger she'd felt toward Willow had morphed into a weird sisterhood.

That was the last day Willow Williams came to school. Rumor had it she moved to California to start a new life. Stasia hoped she would find what she was looking for.

Chapter 6

DAY FIVE

NICK

Cindy Williams has no record, not even a speeding ticket, and seems to be an upstanding citizen. As Stasia suggested, there's no information on Willow after 2005. Xander, on the other hand, was a busy boy for a while. Rass provides a copy of his sheet, which lists a number of traffic violations, two assault charges that were dropped, and one that was not. The last incident was more than ten years ago and the details are interesting.

Immediately after high school Xander went to work for Paco & Patches as an apprentice butcher. Paco & Patches is a group of family-owned butcher shops with a long history of providing exceptional quality meats and seafood to the people of DC and northern Virginia. This fact is included in Xander's legal record because, in 2007, there was an incident at the Paco & Patches Fredericksburg location and Xander was in the middle of it.

According to the report, Xander and another employee had recurring tension between them. The other employee, an older man named Wallace, would often 'jokingly' call Xander 'Homer' and imply that Xander got his interest in butchery from his father. Most of the time Xander managed to ignore the insults, with his mentor Paco doing his best to protect him. But one day the taunting got to be too much, and Xander snapped.

Wallace reported that Xander grabbed his arm and pressed it down on the table of a standing bone saw. Xander turned on the saw while Wallace screamed in terror, chasing customers out of the store. Wallace insisted on filing a complaint with the PD. Xander was charged with assault.

A small collection of outraged citizens learned of the case and made it their business to stand outside the courthouse, demanding Xander be put away for a long time because he was clearly destined to follow in his father's footsteps. Paco paid for Xander to have decent counsel, and offered up a strong statement of support to the judge, but Xander still spent three months in the Fredericksburg city jail. Paco had no choice but to let Xander go.

Xander must be in his mid to late thirties now, about the age Homer was when he attacked and killed Natasha King. Could Xander be following in his father's footsteps after all?

AVA

An investigator working on the Elspeth Bridges case contacted me to talk about DJU. I have no idea how he got my name or information, but I've agreed to meet him for coffee. Hendrix and Jamie say I shouldn't worry. Winston isn't an actual FBI agent or even a cop, just a private investigator helping the Bridges family. I'm all for anything he can do to help them. That doesn't make me any less nervous. I ignore the little voice in the back of my head that reminds me I wouldn't be nervous if I had 100% faith in my employer.

"What could he possibly want to talk to me about?" I mutter as I slide my feet into Louboutins. My favorites shoes are my Converses, but I don't wear those on the job.

As I get dressed, Jamie lifts my hair and kisses the back of my neck. "Maybe he's heard how hot you are...."

I smack him. "Seriously. Why would he want to talk about DJU when he's here investigating the Bridges case?"

Jamie rubs my shoulders, staring at our reflections in the dressing room mirror. His expression is serious. "David James is a lot less discrete than he used to be. And younger people are not as committed to privacy as the old guard was. Maybe one of the girls said something on social media that got his attention."

I really don't like the idea of DJU being associated with that part of David James. The very thought makes me want to vomit. Outside of the safety of our home, we don't even acknowledge that we know about David James' other activities. That would be dangerous for us and the girls at DJU. I don't give a shit about his friends; the assholes that enjoy those activities alongside him.

"You're right. Of course, you're right." I'm trying to convince myself. He pats my shoulder, kisses the top of my head, and leaves me to finish getting ready. He's been up since five. He and Hendrix take the dogs for a long run every morning when Jamie's in town. Today he's going to New York and won't be back until Wednesday. I'm already stressed. I don't need this. But I'm a pro at dealing with things I don't need. This, too, will pass, and it might even be a blessing in disguise.

I said I'd meet Nick Winston at a Starbucks near the airfield since my schedule is tight. Hendrix is driving me. He pulls into a spot to wait, and I go inside.

I don't need to look around. The guy greets me at the door and waves me to a table. "What can I get you?" He brings me a double espresso, and a black coffee for himself. The place is crowded.

"Thanks for agreeing to meet with me," he says after we're settled. He doesn't look like what I imagine a PI to look like. He's tall, dark, and handsome, with a warm smile. "I don't need a lot of your time, but I have a few questions I'm hoping you can help with."

"I'm not sure how much help I'll be, but I'm more than happy to try. I feel awful for the girl and her parents."

He nods. "It's a terrible situation. As I explained on the phone, I'm a private investigator, part of a group that supports the families and survivors of stranger abductions. Sometimes I can go places and ask questions law enforcement can't."

I swirl thick espresso in its paper cup. The true crime fan in me is intrigued by this and wants to ask questions. The everyday me is still nervous, although I won't show it. "I'm sure the families are grateful. So, what can I tell you?"

"I'd like to know more about David James University. What it is, what it does, who its—students—are, if that's what you call them. I looked online and there's not a lot of information. That's unusual for a school, isn't it?" His face is neutral, without judgment. I'm sure he's got thoughts behind those dark eyes.

I sip my espresso, set the cup down, look him in the eye, and give him the spiel I use whenever I speak about DJU. "I suppose the 'University' is abstract. It's a private institution, not open to the public. DJU helps young women make the most of themselves personally and socially, giving them the skills and knowledge to increase their self-esteem. We teach them to conduct themselves in any environment, in any situation, with anyone from any part of the world. They're taught how to dress, style themselves, walk, speak, and have an intelligent conversation. They learn etiquette and grace. In the end, they can walk into any room with confidence and the knowledge they belong. Schools like this are more common overseas."

He looks fascinated. "That's not what I was expecting. It sounds like a great opportunity. How do the women apply? How do they pay for this education?"

That's where DJU differs from traditional finishing schools. "They don't apply, and they don't pay." I run a fingertip around the rim of my empty cup. "I find candidates and invite them to join. Based on certain criteria we've learned will give them the best chance for success. The David James Foundation, a 501c3 organization, funds their time at DJU."

Winston tips his head and makes a 'hmmm' sound. "I guess that explains why Google did me no favors. Why would the Foundation do that? What's in it for them? What's the desired outcome?"

"David James is a philanthropist. He came from nothing. His mother was beautiful and smart but had no opportunities. He aims to help young women like his mother gain a foothold she never had, never could have dreamed of. It's a passion project for him." I tap my finger on the table and smile. "The Foundation funds other projects, as well. Medical and scientific research. Food access overseas. Tech in underserved countries. DJU is but one piece of the giving pie."

My watch buzzes, and I glance out the window. Hendrix has pulled up to the door. "I'm so sorry. I have to go. Here's my card. If you have more questions, text or email me. I'm at your disposal." I smile. "You can call, but it will go to voicemail. I'm one of those annoying people who think talking on the phone is torture."

I stand and head for the door. Before I step out, I turn back and see him staring at me. "I hope you find that kiddo."

NICK

Yesterday was a long, frustrating day, which isn't unusual but doesn't make it any easier. In most cases, there's a flow of worthless leads. Valuable ones are few and far between. That's no different now. What's frustrating is that I feel in my gut David James Ellington had something to do with Natasha King's disappearance two decades ago, and he's involved with Elspeth Bridges now. I just need to find the missing link before it's too late.

Just. Angel's obsession with words is rubbing off on me.

"You *just* need to chill out!" the husband says to his abused wife. "The trip you want to give your kids is *just* $10,000!" The salesperson says to the overworked, underpaid teacher. "You *just* need to wait a little longer." The government worker says to the houseless family waiting for an apartment. Or the one I hear most often from my darling Angel. "I *just* need a few more minutes."

The thought of Angel makes me smile, a smile I really need. Last night we ate dinner together via Zoom, me scarfing down a room service burger while she dug into a hearty bowl of Cheerios. When we first became the us we are now, she was a burgeoning foodie working hard to develop her cooking chops. Then I moved in with her on the Utah ranch, and we started cooking together. She says it's no fun cooking for herself, and she's reverted to what she calls the C Diet—chips, cheese, cookies, and cereal.

Our dogs, Nope and Asa, enjoyed the video chat as much as we did, showing off their wrestling skills under Angel's feet. Nope is a three-legged corgi/beagle mix Angel adopted from a homeless guy named JR. Nope is a klutz and a dork, and I love everything about her. Asa, her slightly older brother, is half pit-bull, half blue-heeler, 100% daddy's boy unless Angel has him working. He's brown with black and gold speckles, and his ears are black triangles that stand straight up all the time. It's amazing how, with ears that resemble small satellite dishes, he can't manage to hear "Not yours" and "Move."

I miss my weird little family. I'm going to shower and get to bed early. Tomorrow I'm meeting with the woman who runs the David James University recruiting program. Hockenberger generously provided me with her contact information after we spoke.

I'd forgotten how muggy it is on the east coast, and I'm a sticky mess. I should have showered last night but I was otherwise occupied. My phone pings as I'm about to step into the shower, and for a minute, I think about ignoring it. I change my mind, grab it off the dresser, and head back to turn off the shower. There's a long string of texts from Stasia King. There is no preamble.

> *In high school, I got into a fight with Willow Williams. I blamed her father for losing my sister, she blamed my sister for losing her father.*

> *One day, she tells me why she doesn't think her dad killed my sister. By the time she was done, I agreed with her. Or at least I had serious doubts.*

> *Homer never showed any sort of violent tendencies except for one incident when he was startled in his sleep. Have you seen the file on Tasha? What was done to her? That's not what happens when you're startled. That's intentional, brutal, sexual, and prolonged violence. Nothing about that says PTSD, and I can't imagine someone who could do that was a beginner.*

She's right. The Homer she's describing is not someone I'd peg for this sort of crime. Not at all. I reach for the King file on the second bed and flip it open to the photos. It's hard to tell this was a living, breathing person. Her legs and arms are broken, bone protruding through bruised and bloody flesh. There are diagonal knife cuts deep across her ribs. Her nipples have been sliced off. There are burn marks on the remaining patches of solid skin. Her lips are torn and swollen, her teeth shattered. She's been partially scalped. Her inner thighs are black with bruises, bloody from the carnage.

Stasia—via Willow—isn't wrong. This was done with thought and purpose. This is not the work of someone experiencing PTSD or even hallucinations. This happened over a period of time, and it would require a secluded place. From what I've read, Homer didn't have any place at all.

Why didn't the cops recognize this? His attorney? Worse, why didn't I pick up on it the first time I read the file?

I type, *You're right. Willow was right. This doesn't fit PTSD. Where's Willow now?*

> *I haven't seen Willow Williams since that day. Have you talked to her brother Xander? He might know.*

I type my thanks and see it marked delivered, but Stasia King is done.

XANDER

The Cherry Tree doesn't open until eleven, but Joe, the cook, comes in at 9:30 to accept deliveries and get ready for the day. Usually, I sleep until noon, but not today. I'm wired. I feel like I did coke, but I haven't had a line in at least a year. Eh, well, maybe nine months.

When the knock comes at the front door, I'm eating over easy eggs and toast. I'm on my third cup of coffee, reading the newspaper. We get the print edition delivered every day. It gives people something to do if they're uncomfortable sitting at the bar alone.

Elspeth Bridges is still on the front page.

"Come back at eleven!" I yell over my shoulder, not bothering to look toward the door.

The stubborn fuck knocks again. Maybe the guy is hard of hearing. I get up, crack the door, and repeat through the gap, "We're not open. Come back later."

A tall, dark-haired beast of a man is on the other side, dressed too nicely to be looking to get his morning buzz on. He presses his hand against the door to keep me from closing it. "I'm looking for Xander Williams."

Huh. Okay. "That's me. What can I do for you?"

The man smiles. "I'm hoping you can help me with a case I'm working on. I'm not a cop." He adds the last bit quickly.

Inquiring minds want to know. "What case?"

"Elspeth Bridges."

Well, fuck. I'm torn between closing the door in his face, and letting him in because I'm curious. Curiosity wins. I open the door, wave him inside, and point to the bar. "Have a seat. Coffee? Juice?" The guy shakes his head. "No, thanks. You're not open. I'm not here to hassle you. Just wanted to ask a couple of questions, if you don't mind."

129

"And you are…?" Breakfast forgotten, I wipe down the bar top even though it was cleaned after closing last night. The guy doesn't look like a cop but feels like one. Is this about the email and the card? Already? The energy I felt earlier morphs into tension.

"Nick Winston. I'm with an organization called Komorebi. We help with cases involving stranger abductions." The guy slides his card across the bar.

I ignore the card but feel myself loosen up. Not a cop. "Huh. Okay. And what might I possibly be able to do for you, Nick Winston of—whatever the hell you said?"

"Komorebi," Winston laughs. "We really need to rethink that name."

He's trying to relax me. What the hell is this about? "Maybe, yeah. So, what can I do for you?"

"I'm in Virginia for the Elspeth Bridges case. You've heard she's missing?"

"Of course," I nod at the pile of newspapers where I was eating a few minutes ago. "Everyone knows she's missing. But that's all I know. I'm not into teenage girls, and the women I *am* into come willingly." In another situation, I'd grin at that, but no grins available just now.

Winston nods. "No, no worries there. I'm here to ask about your sister, Willow."

Willow? What the fuck! "What about her?"

"Someone told me Willow didn't believe your father was responsible for Natasha King's death. She shared Willow's reasoning, and I find myself agreeing." Winston says. "I was hoping to speak with her."

I lean against the rear counter where the liquor is kept, arms across my chest. "A little late for anyone to agree since my old man was killed in prison twenty years ago."

"Killed?" Winston frowns. "I thought he died by suicide."

"Fuck, no. Ironically, he was getting decent help with his head in there. Finally. More than the VA ever did, anyway. We'd see him sometimes. He was feeling okay and even cracked a smile occasionally. There was an attorney who thought he was innocent and wanted to try to get him off. He had hope." I don't mean to spout so much, but it feels good to get it out. I haven't talked about any of this in years.

"Do you remember the attorney's name?" Winston asks, poised to make a note on his phone.

I shake my head. "Sorry, no. Like I said, it's been years. But he didn't kill himself. He was murdered because it was convenient."

"Convenient?" Winston has the playing dumb thing down. I sense he's anything but.

"He didn't kill Tasha, and anyone with a brain would know that. He was framed by whoever did." My blood pressure is rising. *Chill, Xan, chill.*

"Any idea who that might be?"

I debate whether or not to open this can of worms. Finally, I shrug. "I have a theory. But I can't prove anything."

"Care to share?"

I consider. *Will it be helpful or harmful to put this guy on the scent?* "How did you hear about me?"

Now it's Winston's turn to contemplate. After a long pause, he says, "Stasia King."

Aha. Now it makes sense. "You know David James Ellington, yeah?" Something clicks behind Winston's eyes. "There are rumors about him and his activities. Everyone knows about the women he collects. That school of his. But there are stories where he and some of his closest pals take things farther. Much farther. That they have a club of sorts where they do the darkest of deeds." I can see him digest this and turn it around in his brain. "I think Tasha King got caught up in that, somehow."

Winston is silent. After a few minutes, he asks, "Do you think Elspeth Bridges might also be caught up in that?"

"I hope to hell not. But it all feels kinda similar."

He nods. "It does. Since you've been forthcoming with me, I'll share with you. I think you're right. I think this somehow ties to David James Ellington, and he also was connected to Natasha's death years ago. So thank you." He slides off the bar stool and heads for the door. Halfway there, he pauses and turns back. "And Willow? Do you think she'd talk with me?"

"Dude, I haven't seen Willow since she was seventeen. She took off one day and has never come back."

Winston nods, half-smiles his thanks, and closes the door behind him.

I pour a splash of whiskey into my coffee cup and stare at the newspapers sitting where I left them. I feel a weird burst of hope for the first time in years.

AVA

There was another attack in Virginia overnight, and it's a popular topic even as far away as Oklahoma City.

Taking the eyes of the first guy was shocking. Removing the tongue of the second guy may be worse. The Surgeon—that's what everyone calls him because of his clothing, the method of the assaults, and the hashtag he showed during the events—is precise and exacting.

I wonder if others have connected "Sabine" with the Rape of the Sabine Women from Roman mythology.

"It's so scary," the woman across from me says, nodding up at the television screen. I decided to freshen my manicure while I have time to kill and Caty had an opening. "I mean, can you imagine just plopping someone's eyeballs out? Or chopping off their tongue?"

Like the first video, this one is shot in near darkness again. The Surgeon straps his involuntary patient onto what appears to be a dining room table, head positioned in a way that provides him access to his mouth. The lights are focused on the victim's head. The camera points toward the man on the table rather than the person in the surgical scrubs and mask.

"Did you watch the video?" Caty asks as she massages oil into my cuticles.

I make a face. "I saw parts of it, but not the whole thing."

People worldwide watch as the Surgeon attaches the IV, checks the flow, and gets to work. He severs Damien Simpson's tongue at what the reporter identifies as something called the frenulum, the place where the tongue anchors into the mouth.

When I glance at the TV, the reporter is demonstrating where the cut was made by wiggling her tongue. The reporter tells us this procedure is called a glossectomy. There's more blood this time.

Caty and I are silent as we get a biography of the victim. For several years, Damien Simpson was the district attorney in Spotsylvania County in Virginia. Now he has a private practice specializing in international real estate law. The reporter assures us Simpson has been communicating with his doctors and law enforcement via an iPad. He told them he was leaving his country club when a delivery van backed into his car. The last thing Damien Simpson remembers is the driver getting out of the van.

"In the early morning hours, Simpson's phone was used to call an Uber to a quiet industrial area. Sam Davis found Simpson slumped on a bus bench holding a cardboard sign: STOP SABINE. Simpson tells police he doesn't remember anything except waking up in great pain with police and EMTs all around." The reporter makes a show of looking upset on Simpson's behalf. "Just like with the first video, the Surgeon posted on Facebook, Instagram, TikTok, and YouTube with the hashtags: #stopsabine #thesurgeon #speakthetruth #speaknoevil #timetopay. Police are working tirelessly to determine what the hashtags might mean."

The screen pauses on a blurry shot of the Surgeon. It's hard to get much detail, because the person is covered head to toe in blue scrubs, a plastic face shield, and gloves. They appear to be relatively tall, at least five ten, perhaps taller. Straight build, no obvious curves. "Do you think that's a man, or woman?" I ask Caty.

"Man, for sure. There's no ass." She laughs.

The Surgeon is becoming a national obsession. Americans being Americans, he's developing a fan base. There's a lot of speculation: who will be next? We're all curious.

Caty shivers. "So gross." She begins applying Chanel Rouge Noir on my nails. "Glad we're not lawyers!"

THE SURGEON

The house is small and neat, at the back of a full acre of land. A dense, six-foot hedge blocks the view of neighbors on either side. It's the perfect place for someone having an affair or doing other things you wouldn't want eyes on.

While the homeowner was at the gym and nail salon earlier today, I took advantage and left a bag of tools in a safe spot on the property. I've been monitoring 1312 White Oak Road for a few years, and the routine never changes.

For example, I know every Friday night at eight o'clock, the resident slips into something black and leathery, turns on a favored playlist of theme-appropriate music, and pours a glass of Henry McKenna single barrel whiskey while she waits.

Her regular Friday night visitor arrives between 8:10 and 8:20. The same nondescript black sedan drops him off, a sedan I know is registered to the city. The visitor is picked up by the same car and driver promptly at midnight. This visitor has only missed two Fridays in the time I've been watching. Both times he was on vacation with his wife.

I appreciate that. Consistency makes my life much easier.

Homeowner Lydia Latella is a petite, attractive, deep-voiced dominatrix. Seeing her in the black corset, booty shorts, and seven-inch heels with shiny silver buckles on the front, you'd never know she was born Gary or that she was the number one high school wrestler in her Texas high school. As far as the neighbors are concerned, Lydia is a divorced work-from-home corporate recruiter who keeps to herself. Lydia is very, very good at what she does and enjoys her work.

Fortunately, Lydia is not as proficient at security as she is at her profession. I enter the garage through a side door, then continue into the kitchen without Lydia realizing she's not alone. It's quarter to eight. She's still getting ready for her 'date' and doesn't see or hear me as I quietly make my way down the hall toward her bedroom, which is next to the special room she keeps locked when she doesn't have a certain kind of company. The door to the special room is open and waiting.

It takes no effort to subdue her, because she's completely caught off guard. When she steps into the hallway, her eyes cast down as she finishes closing a leather cuff around her wrist, I simply put a hand over her mouth and lift her tiny body off the ground. She's not the target, and I have no interest in hurting her, so I bind her wrists and ankles with extra attention to detail since she's a pro when it comes to binding, and I owe her that respect. She's mad as a wet cat when I put the ball gag in her mouth and tuck her safely into the far corner of her walk-in closet. I wonder if she's ever been on the other end of her games. As I close the door to her bedroom, I see panicked understanding in her eyes. I could tell her she's going to be okay but decide it's better for me that she stay afraid. She'll be less likely to try something stupid.

A convenient mirror hanging in the entry makes it easy to watch the front door from the kitchen. Retired Chief of Police Jim Gifford doesn't knock when he enters the home. Gifford puts his hat, keys, wallet, and gun on a table inside the door. Then Gifford goes into the bedroom, following his usual routine.

While this isn't my first Friday night visit, it's the first Friday night I will make my presence known.

Once Gifford is dressed only in white boxer briefs, he crosses the hall and enters the special room. It's easy enough to step behind him and jab the big man in the neck with a preloaded syringe.

Chief Gifford is not a prime physical specimen, carrying at least eighty extra pounds. He's also caught off-guard, and he's been out of active field duty for thirty years or more. His intellectual response is sharp enough, but his physical ability to follow through is not. When he sees me, his mouth opens in surprise, fear, and finally, understanding. He takes a step backward and trips over a thick rope laid out across the floor. He makes sputtering sounds as his butt hits the rubber matting and tries to crab crawl away. It only takes a couple of minutes for the drugs to kick in. His panicked state pushes the drugs through his system more quickly.

Dragging him by the ankles to a massage-type table in the center of the room is easy, but it takes significant effort to navigate him onto the table since he's nearly three hundred pounds of dead weight. I cuff Gifford's hands with straps provided by Lydia and raise his hands over his head. Then I attach him to hooks conveniently installed on the table. It's quick and easy to repeat the process with his feet. Chief Gifford is now stretched out, six feet of unconscious lawman.

It takes a few minutes to set up the cameras and the lights.

When everything's ready, I go to the garage and open the side door. The tool bag is where I left it, as is the most important tool.

Let tonight's game begin.

Chapter 7

DAY SIX

NICK

Rass and I have breakfast each morning before going to the Bridges. I respect Rass's approach to working with the family. Whether or not he has new information, he spends time at the Bridges' home every day, sharing what he's learned, any leads, any new theories. He won't let them lose hope.

The diner's television shows the aftermath of last night's Surgeon attack. There's a rhythm: sometime overnight, the Surgeon attacks, and we all discuss it over coffee the following day. Anyone in this town involved in the legal world must be anxious about their safety right about now.

"The Chief of Police. Seriously? This guy has balls." Rass mutters. "Although I've heard stories about Gifford, and there are probably a lot of folks thinking he deserved it."

"Say more about that?" I'm sticking to toast and a bowl of fruit this morning.

"Chief Gifford was—is—kind of a dick. Definitely racist. There are stories about him being corrupt, too. He's from another town, so I have never worked with him, but word travels, and we have a couple of guys that used to be in his department." Rass orders the same each day: two over-easy eggs, four slices of bacon crisp, wheat toast, a side of peanut butter, and a glass of milk. He's a growing boy.

We go quiet as the local TV news details the latest assault. This time they've brought in a doctor to explain what happened for us lay folks.

"Chief Jim Gifford is the latest victim of the man known as the Surgeon. At approximately nine o'clock last night, Chief Gifford was attacked while visiting an acquaintance." The newscaster says.

Rass and I exchange puzzled looks, and I'm sure we're thinking similar thoughts. The Surgeon's attacks are—well, surgical. He seems to know the habits of his victims well enough to incapacitate them, perform the procedures, and then get out undetected. It's unlikely the Surgeon would just follow a victim around and take his chances. This 'acquaintance' is interesting.

The reporter is saying, "Chief Gifford's ears were brutalized. It's unlikely he'll hear again. We've brought in Dr. C.H. Minnick to explain."

The camera swings to Dr. Minnick, who looks simultaneously nervous and pleased to be on TV. "Chief Gifford's pinnas—"he traces the exterior structure of his ear and ends by tugging on his earlobe, "were surgically removed at the skull. That would affect his hearing but would not destroy it. Then, the Surgeon surgically damaged the Chief's tympanic membranes. That is key to transforming sound waves into mechanical vibrations within the inner ear."

The reporter's face reflects well-practiced shock. "Will the Chief ever hear again?"

"Unlikely."

The camera swings back to focus on the reporter. "As with the previous two attacks, the Surgeon released the video on social media channels around midnight, with similar hashtags as previous videos: #stopsabine #thesurgeon #hearthetruth #hearnoevil #timetopay."

"I wonder how the Chief was found. And what happened to the so-called acquaintance?" I ponder.

Rass studies his phone, then swings his attention back to me. "According to my sources, the 'acquaintance' is a dominatrix who specializes in servicing politically at-risk clients. Like, you know, a cop. Gifford was found when the dom's ex came by to drop off their dog—they share custody; she gets Spot every weekend—and found the dom tied up in the closet and the Chief in another room. The ex called the cops."

"That must've been awkward for everyone involved," I say, then rethink. "Or, maybe not."

"Doesn't the pace of this bother you? It suggests either a lot of victims or a timeline we don't understand." Rass says. "I mean, why else would this Surgeon guy go so fast? Don't psychopaths usually relish the rush for a minute? Take some time to enjoy the moment. And this guy seems all about the press. Hell, it almost feels like an antihero movie. Where are the Avengers when you need them?"

I'm a big fan of Shazam, personally. "You're right. It's not typical that a bad guy would spring into life fully formed and run at this speed with such a determined focus on bringing the outside in to watch. I would guess this isn't the beginning, so much as the start of putting it out to the public. It does feel like a movie. Maybe not superheroes. Maybe a war movie with an urgent mission. There's a game plan at work. It's not random. He's screaming that he's a vigilante with all these hashtags and messages, and he believes it. I don't get the impression the Surgeon is getting off on what he's doing, at least not sexually." I spin my spoon on the table and watch it bump into my cup, my napkin. "He's moving toward some big climax. But what? What he's done so far is plenty climatic. And I can't imagine him keeping up this pace for long. No matter how good he is, this has to be draining his energy and drawing on his adrenalin."

"It's personal, right? He's not a hired gun, someone with medical training brought in from overseas." Rass is shredding a napkin, making a small hill of thin white paper. We're both fidgeters when we think.

"I imagine your folks are bringing in professionals to assess the Surgeon's skill level." Something else comes to me. "What was that 'See no evil, speak no evil, hear no evil' story from a kids book...."

"It wasn't a kid's book, it was a Japanese folk tale. Three wise monkeys, I think." Rass says. "It makes a weird kind of sense, and even better, that would mean we're done with this, but it sure doesn't feel like that's the case."

Rass clambers out of the booth and drops cash onto the table. "I'm sure they'll bring in pros to check out the surgeon. I haven't heard anything yet, but when I do I'll keep you informed."

I follow him out of the booth and add my own cash to the pile. "Ready to tell Patrick and Anna that we're no closer to finding their daughter on day six than we were on day one? Sometimes I hate this job."

NICK

Olena King is at the Bridges' home when Rass and I arrive for daily check-in. It saves me a trip. After greeting the family, I ask Olena to join me in the living room, which is currently empty. "I have a question about The Madalena."

Just as we sit on the sectional sofa, an angry screeching sound comes from the family room where the Bridges family is watching TV. Even though Rass is with them, I jump to my feet, ready to do battle. I realize it's Margot, the older daughter, who is very unhappy and not shy about sharing her unhappiness. I sit down.

Olena, unsurprisingly, is understanding. "Margot is yelling about her birthday being spoiled, but really she's terrified and worried about her sister and doesn't want to admit it. Stasia behaved similarly. Life is hard enough at that age without unthinkable events like this."

Olena King's kindness and empathy are unending, despite her pain. I admire her. If I can get her to join Komorebi, she'll be a good fit. She's certainly got lived experience that could help others who are newer to the reality of losing a loved one to abduction. And there are a lot of services that might be truly useful for her, as well.

"You said you had a question about The Madalena. What can I tell you?" Olena crosses one leg over the other, hands knitted together in her lap. Her emotions are easily read. The Madalena isn't a welcome memory.

"Do you remember hearing the name David James Ellington?"

She looks surprised. Not surprised that I'm asking, but that I'd think she doesn't know the name. "Of course, I know of David James Ellington. You'd have to live under a rock not to know who he is."

I nod. "Yes, but do you remember hearing his name in 2002? Around the time Natasha was taken?"

She frowns, and her eyes narrow into puzzled slits. "No, not at all. Why would I have? What could that man have to do with Tasha?"

I wave a hand. "Nothing specific that I know of. He was a member at The Madalena that summer and had a run-in with a young woman. I was curious if you'd heard anything about it, either from Natasha or the police during the investigation."

She shakes her head. "No, nothing. I'd have remembered that. He's big news to most of the world now, but he has always been a big deal here in Virginia."

"Thanks. I knew it was a long shot, but I needed to ask." I change the subject. "How are you holding up? Have you heard from Stasia?"

Olena nods. "She's good about texting, and she shares photos of her stops along the way on Instagram to bring me along. These road trips are a ritual, something that keeps her tied to her sister. Stasia loves visiting presidential graves, and Tasha was obsessed with national parks. So Stasia maps out a journey that takes her to both. It's the only time she really seems like my little girl."

"What do you mean?" I haven't figured Stasia King out. Something about her makes my Spidey senses tingly, but I can't say what.

"When she was a kid, she was silly, funny, adventurous. After Natasha's death, that changed. She had no life outside of school and home. My husband's—ex-husband's—drinking became an issue before Tasha went missing, and it got much worse after they found her. When we divorced, George ended his relationship with his living child. The last time Stasia saw him was the day of the car accident." She throws me a questioning look. "Do you know about the accident?"

When I shake my head no, she continues. "George and I had been on the rocks before Natasha's death, and that was the final straw. He wanted nothing to do with either of us, not me, not Stasia. I deluded myself, thinking he was just in pain, that time with his surviving child would help him mend. I was wrong. So wrong. One weekend I forced him to be her father. He picked her up from school, drunk and angry. They fought. He crashed his truck and killed a young woman and her new baby. The son of a bitch died the next day. Stasia carries the guilt of that with her. George made it clear he loved Tasha and Stasia was a distant second. I've never understood why he felt that way, but he did. Stasia thinks if she'd been the one to die, he wouldn't have become a drunk and would not have been in that position to kill the woman and child. That's what inspired her to become a doctor."

This is new information to me but gives a deeper look into the woman who has, until now, been a puzzle. So much to carry; none of it was ever her fault.

Olena sighs. "Do you have kids?"

I shake my head no. My sister and I were orphaned at a young age, but a great family adopted us. It's made me nervous about having kids of my own. That's a conversation Angel and I have never had, although we've talked about pretty much everything else.

Olena continues, and I give her my full attention. "Stasia focused on college, then medical school, and then being a doctor. As far as I know, she hasn't had a personal life of any proper sort. No boyfriend or girlfriend. She doesn't hang out with friends during her off-time. No company on her summer road trips. It's all work for her. Coming to see me is the closest she gets to taking time away from her job—if you can call it that. It breaks my heart. She's a good girl. A good woman. She's smart and very talented, and so caring. But her life changed forever that summer."

STASIA

Usually, Mama waits to hear from me when I'm on a trip, so when she texts mid-day, I find a quiet spot and call. "Everything okay?"

"Sure, of course," she says, but I can tell from her voice something's going on. "I was talking with Nick Winston this morning, and he asked if I remembered David James Ellington's name coming up back in 2002, somehow associated with The Madalena, or Tasha's disappearance. I didn't, but I wanted to ask you."

I chew my lip. "Well, not then, no. But I heard rumors about him a couple of years later."

"Rumors? What kind of rumors?" Mama's tone is sharp. She's surprised.

"That he likes young girls. I mean, it's common knowledge he spends a lot of time with young women, but the gossip was that he's involved with much younger girls."

"*Svolota!*" Mama utters a Ukrainian word I know means 'bastard.' Until now, I had only ever heard it attached to my father when Mama didn't think I was within earshot. I repeat the word silently in my head.

"Will you speak to Nick Winston about this?" Mama phrases it as a question, but we both know it's a command.

"Yes, Mama, I'll contact him." When this started, I had no desire to insert myself into the story. But maybe some of what I know can be useful. If he's going to poke around, might as well send him in the right direction. "Everything else okay? Any news?"

"No, no news." Mama's tone levels. Her blood pressure is returning to normal, I think, with a wan smile. "Another thing Nick said is that his company, or whatever it is, has resources for people like us. The families of people who have been taken. He thinks it might be helpful for us, you and me. I told him we would be open to learning more. No commitments, of course."

149

It's too late for his program to help me. I've got to help myself. I don't say that. "Sure, Mama. I'll look at it. Let me know what I need to do."

"When you talk to him about Ellington, you let him know, okay? Okay. I need to go. I have neglected work in the last few days. Much to catch up on. I love you. Be safe. Check in." Mama makes a kissing sound before disconnecting.

Nick Winston wants to know about David James Ellington? I will tell him about David James Ellington.

STASIA

Even though it's after eight, Nick Winston answers on the second ring. He sounds alert. Apparently, he doesn't keep office hours. "Hey, there, Stasia. Thanks for calling. How's the trip so far?"

"So far, so good." This man makes me uncomfortable. He's too late, much too late, to do anything for my family and me. He should focus on Elspeth Bridges. But if he insists on digging around in the past, I'll help. I just don't want to make more small talk. "Mama says you want to know about David James Ellington."

"Yes, if you have anything you can share, that would be great." I appreciate that he doesn't seem put off by my abruptness.

"A few years after Tasha's death, I heard a rumor about him. I'm sure you've learned he keeps a harem of girls. He has this thing called David James University. A friend of mine's sister joined, which is how I know the little I know. Other women, older women, act as recruiters. They go around the country and find attractive young girls—I can't call them women because they're barely out of high school. They're invited to the 'university.' It's a big, fancy house in New York City. One of those Golden Age mansions with a zillion bedrooms and servants' quarters, the whole decadent show. They're taught etiquette and conversation, given wardrobes and hair styling, all the stuff that will make them desirable to people of a certain type. My friend said it's like finishing school, but for companions. Not escorts—apparently sex isn't *officially* part of the deal." I make a noise that tells him how I feel about that. "She said she heard that sometimes there are girls that are too young for the University, too. Really young. Illegally so."

Nick is silent. Maybe he's already heard about the University. It's not a secret, or at least the girls aren't. David James Ellington and his friends appear in photos at glamorous events worldwide, nearly always with young women on their arms.

"Anyway, that's what I know." I'm ready to get off the phone now.

"Do you still talk with the friend? Could I have her name?" He pushes.

"The friend and I lost touch. It was twenty years ago."

He's silent for a moment, hoping I'll give up the name. I'm quiet, too. Finally he says, "I'd heard stories, of course, but it was always anecdotal. I've never met anyone who could vouch for its existence."

"Well, you still haven't, legally. A judge would say this is nothing but hearsay," I laugh humorlessly. "I heard it from a friend who heard it from her sister, who could've made the whole thing up."

"Good point. Still, I appreciate you telling me about it." He pauses, then continues onto the second topic, which she'd hoped they could skip. "When your mother and I spoke earlier, I told her about Komorebi. Did she mention it?"

I'm glad he can't see me rolling my eyes. "She did."

"It may sound 'too little too late.' I get that. But I believe there might be help, even now. There are excellent professional resources, but the program's greatest part is that there are others like you. These are probably the only people in the world who understand what you've been through because they've been through it, too. It's not a support group; it's more of an extended family. It's a safe space to get angry, be sad, or share something you found helpful."

"Hate to tell ya, but that sounds exactly like a support group," I snap before I can stop myself.

"Fair enough. But it's not any kind of support group you've experienced, I promise. Before I joined Komo, I was with the FBI and sent several people to them for help. Not one has regretted it." His voice changes, and I think he's not telling the whole truth about that last part. Interesting, but not interesting enough to stretch out the conversation.

"When I get back, after the conference, I'll check it out. No promises. But I'll check it out. Now, I need to go. I've got an early start tomorrow."

"Sounds good. And thanks. If you think of anything else..."

"I'll call," I hang up. Tomorrow will be here in just a few hours. It's going to be one of the longer days, and I need to get some sleep.

XANDER

My mother lives in the same house her mother grew up in. She and Dad bought it from her grandmother after they married. Mom says they barely waited until she had her high school diploma in hand before they ran off and did the deed. They were that sure.

Even though she's approaching sixty, she's still a beautiful woman. Her dark curly hair is cut short, and her big blue eyes are still clear and sharp. Her job as an OR nurse keeps her on her feet for long hours at a time, and her knees are starting to bother her, but she's still in great shape. She's had a boyfriend, Danny, for nearly fifteen years, but she won't let him move in, and she won't sell the house and move in with him. Dad is her one true love. Anyone else is runner-up. Danny seems okay with that.

Once a month, I stop by for dinner and a chat. We love each other and need the connection, but it's hard to put the past away. It's always simmering, just under the surface. Dad. Willow. It's complicated. For the first hour, I feel like my best self, the kid overflowing with possibility and hope. Around the second hour, memories of birthdays and Christmas past, of Dad's return from the military, of the trial raise their ugly heads, and we both get edgy, dread and resentment seeping in.

Tonight, Mom is in a weird mood. She sets out the fixings for tacos and hands me a beer. She heads back to the kitchen but tips her head toward the small secretary inside the front door. "Got a postcard from Will."

I find it and study the photo. The text reads, *Greetings from Hollywood, California. City of the Stars.* The letters are filled with a graphic collage of famous spots in Los Angeles. On the back, Willow wrote, "Who knew pollution caused such beautiful sunsets? Miss you! Tell Xan hey."

Hey, Will.

"Dinner!" Mom chirps, sliding into her chair. I take my usual seat, and she pushes taco meat towards me. The smile drops a bit as she builds herself a pair of tacos. Something's on her mind. I think I know what it is.

There's the usual small talk. "Are you dating?" *No.* "How's the bar?" *Fine.* "Have you done anything fun lately?" *Depends on your idea of fun.*

Once we've run through the chitchat, she downs the balance of her beer and fetches two more. She takes a deep breath and looks me straight in the eye. I try not to squirm, even though I'm thirty-four years old. "Xander, these names, they were involved in your father's trial..."

Yep, that's what I was expecting. "Yeah."

"Doesn't that seem strange to you?"

"Maybe." I nod and tip back my beer. "I'm sure those clowns worked on lots of cases together, Mom.

She takes in another breath, her expression dark with concern. "Xander, you're not hurting these men, are you?"

I laugh uncomfortably. Because she thinks I could do something like that? Because I think I could do something like that? It's a reasonable suspicion after the incident that got me fired from Paco & Patches. "I'm envious of whoever has had that pleasure."

Relief washes over her face. "I can't say I'm terribly sorry for them, although I feel guilty for thinking that way." She plays with a bit of shredded cheese that fell from the bowl and builds a small mountain. "I try to be a good Christian, but those men, what they did to your Dad, I'm sorry for their families, but maybe the Lord is sending a message through this Surgeon person."

"If I believed in God, I'd like that theory," I agree. "I'm sure they worked on a lot of cases together. And Gifford oversaw any cases in his jurisdiction. Dad's can't be the only one that brought them into contact, though, can it?"

"Do you remember what an arrogant ass that prosecutor was? And the judge. He had his mind made up before Homer even sat at the table." She mutters.

I cover her hand with mine. Hers is so tiny, so soft. It's more wrinkled than I remember. "Mom, don't let yourself go there. Please. There's no good there."

We're both silent for a few minutes. Finally, she nods and changes the subject. "Danny says to tell you hi."

Danny, the boyfriend, who is a very patient guy and loves her. "Tell him hey back."

"He wants to know if you'll come to the beach with us later this summer."

I shrug. "Sure, if I can work it into my schedule. Let me know the dates when you have them. And thanks for the invite."

"I'm glad she's doing well," Mom says as I stand at the front door, keys in hand. "Sometimes... I wonder... if it's really her sending the postcards."

That stops me short. I turn back. "What do you mean?"

"Why does she always send postcards? She could call. It's been years. I'd love to hear her voice." Mom's voice catches.

"Who else would it be?" I ask.

"I don't know," she looks defeated. I hate it.

"I'm sure she's fine," is all I manage because there's nothing else to say. If I told her the truth it'd break her heart all over again. "Gotta go. I'll see you soon."

SEPTEMBER 6, 2005

XANDER

"No! No!"

The last few years had given Xander the super power of extra sensitive hearing. Despite the shampoo mohawk in his hair, he stepped out of the shower and grabbed a towel. By the time he wrapped it around his waist and found his mother in the living room, she was curled into a ball on the couch, sobbing. "What is it? What happened?" He looked at the windows to see if someone had thrown another brick. The glass was intact. There was nothing he could see—until he spotted a folded paper clutched in her hand. "Did one of those assholes send another note?"

Without waiting for a reply, he tugged a sheet of notebook paper from her clenched fingers.

Mom, Xan, I need to go. I'm fine, I promise. I'm not running off with a guy or anything dumb like that. I hate the person I've become. I miss the old me, but I can't be her here. I'm going to head out into the world, put the pieces back together, and find myself again. If I stay, I will be over. I don't want that, and I know you don't either.

Don't worry. I sold some of my Beanie Babies (who knew those dorky things would be worth actual money), so I have a little nest egg to keep me safe while I figure stuff out. I promise I'm okay, don't worry, I know you will, but I'll stay in touch, let you know I'm all right.

Mom, don't be hard on Xan. He's trying.

Xan, don't drive Mom crazy. She's got enough to deal with.

Both of you, I love you so much. You'll always be with me wherever I go. Someday, we'll see each other again when the world has righted itself.

Take care of each other.

Willow

He dropped onto the couch next to his mom, who was still crying, her heart breaking yet again. He understood what Willow was saying. He felt the same way. The Xander that was before was long gone, and he wasn't sure he liked the new one. But he couldn't leave Mom, too. He'd have to stay and take care of her. Otherwise, she'd be left with nothing, no one, and he couldn't stand the thought.

Xander made himself a promise: If he had to stay, he would find out the truth. Because he knew Homer Williams did not hurt Natasha King, and he also knew Homer did not commit suicide. If it killed him, someone was going to pay.

THE SURGEON

This is the last of them that will survive—well, he'll probably survive. I don't think of them as 'victims' because that implies they're innocent. These men are not innocent, not by any means. Their greed and vanity have led them to kill at least one person unjustly. It's doubtful that was the only time. They're lucky to leave with their lives. It's more than they deserve, really, but it's all a matter of degrees. Those who come next have earned the attention of Satan himself.

Tonight's player, Judge Wesley Miller III, is coming up on retirement. He could have—should have, for his own sake—retired this spring, but he's holding out one more year until his wife is ready to quit her job as a high school principal. Then they're moving to a million-dollar home on a pristine beach on the Atlantic Ocean, where they'll live their best lives. Judge Miller can't wait to perfect his golf swing.

Sadly, he'll be able to enjoy his view, but he won't be playing much golf.

It's easy enough to get into the courthouse's so-called secure parking. A fake sign on the van, a standard issue uniform, and an order form created in Microsoft Word make it all too simple to get past the tired security guard who probably has at least one other job and could care less what happens here as long as it doesn't come back on him. The guard doesn't care where the van goes once it has passed his shack and the security arm.

Once inside, I pull the van onto a patch of concrete near the elevators and a cluster of mechanical equipment. It's not designated for parking, but no one questions what worker bees are doing as long as the bees stay out of their way.

There's a chance there's additional security on the Judge after the Surgeon's activities, but I doubt it. It's only the fourth day. The cops might have figured there's a connection somewhere, but it's unlikely those idiots have connected the actual dots yet. They probably won't understand everything until the end when they're handed a gift-wrapped box full of evidence.

Judge Miller does not notice the repair man standing near a collection of pipes when he steps off the elevator alone. The Judge's jacket is folded over his arm. He carries a briefcase in his right hand. His attention is on his phone, which is in his left hand. It doesn't appear he's retrieved the fob to unlock his car. It wouldn't matter if he had; it's just nice knowing as much as possible about the people I'm going to introduce myself to.

The Judge is clueless. He doesn't realize he's got company until he feels the sharp stick of the needle in his neck. When he turns, shocked, he's still not in a defensive posture. He believes himself to be so important puffing up his chest will control the situation and remove the threat. But it doesn't take long for his eyes to widen and his brow to furrow.

We've met a few times. Does he recognize me? Then I remember I have a mask covering my nose and mouth. I doubt the Judge is observant enough to identify anyone from their eyes alone.

It is easy to navigate the Judge to the van, despite him being limp. He's much lighter than the fat-ass Chief. The van door is open a crack. I slide it wider to get the Judge in and join him in the van. I lock the door, strap the Judge down to the rings on the floor, clamber into the driver's seat, and we're off. The van, the Judge, and I leave the courthouse parking with a wave at the guard and an instruction to him to have a good night.

Our destination is an old auto shop a mile away in a seedy part of town. A click of the remote on the visor and the automatic door opens. I pull the van in and close the door.

The auto shop is dusty, but that doesn't matter. A twelve-foot square area has been cleaned, sterilized, and tented with plastic sheets. A metal table is positioned in the center. The toolbox sits on a rolling mechanic's bench with drawers for various implements. Conditions aren't perfect, but they're good enough.

If he dies, he dies. Not my concern, although I will do my best—my minimum best, that is—to not kill him.

The IV feeds his veins with happy juice.

My partner prepared all the necessary components. The surgical tray is organized with the needed tools: knives, Metz scissors, clamps, vascular clips, absorbable and non-absorbable stitches. And, of course, the bone saw. Tonight's event will take roughly ninety minutes: three-quarters of an hour to amputate each hand.

I doublecheck the lights and the tripod holding the camera. The red light is flashing: recording.

This is the last video that will be edited before they're uploaded. The rest will be live, and the 'patients' will die.

How many people who watched the first StopSabine event will be around for the last?

When the Surgeon is done, two masculine hands lie side by side on a surgical tray, cleanly cut at the wrist. Both are slightly curved as if they are beseeching. Without the visible bone and red flesh, you might not know they're no longer part of their owner's anatomy. I hope the sight makes people around the world quiver in fear.

The Surgeon speaks for the first time. I'm glad I tested the voice distorter beforehand. The robotic sound is off-putting. "If you've enjoyed this free preview and want to watch future episodes, find us on the onion website at StopSabine. The next show will air live in 48 hours, and you *really* don't want to miss it." The Surgeon holds up a piece of cardboard with the printed hashtags in large letters: #stopsabine #thesurgeon #seethetruth #timetopay."

The lights go out, but it's not done. The next part involves a bit of finesse and good timing. It won't be long until the Judge starts to rouse.

Every social media video, every hashtag, and every word spoken or written has been planned to the nth degree. It's time the public starts to understand why this is happening. It will all come together as the roller coaster approaches the crest and prepares to race toward the ground below.

This piece is like a cut scene in a superhero film, a bonus for those who stick around to the end. Those who didn't stay will discover this small addition when they wake tomorrow.

Using the remote that controls the spotlights, I click one strategic light. Before, the spotlights pointed at the so-called victim. The Surgeon is in a pool of darkness, a silhouette.

Robotic voice or no, anger and disgust are clear. "You've watched as I performed surgeries on four men. You probably wonder why I chose these men. Why I performed these specific procedures. Happy to tell you."

"Each of them put his self-interests above the job he was trusted to do. Each of them chose money and personal reward over doing the right thing. They set the duties of their jobs aside and traded their souls for material gain. They made a bargain with the Devil, and I'm here to collect."

The Surgeon holds up a photo. "Jim Gifford, the Chief of Police, hid evidence and misdirected facts."

A second photo. "Public Defender Miles Cameron intentionally disregarded the truth."

A third photo. "Damien Simpson, prosecutor for the state of Virginia, knowingly told lies."

And the last. "The Judge, Wesley Miller III, set aside his oath when he did not demand honest and accurate information from those who appeared before him."

"Each of them prioritized money and position over doing the right thing. As a result, innocent people died cruel and unnecessary deaths. Their lives were cut short."

"The next victim will pay for taking what was not his, for doing intentional harm, and for directly ending a life. You might think he's the worst of them all, and while I wish that were the case, he is not. As a society, we are a rotting mess. We're more likely to turn on our cameras than offer a hand when we see someone in trouble. Some of your friends and neighbors will even pay for the opportunity to watch another human suffer in ways that are so cruel, so unimaginable, they seem fantastical. They're all too real. Think about that for a minute. Look in the mirror, and let the truth sink in."

"It is my deepest hope that you will not watch what comes next. I won't tell you how. You'll need to find StopSabine. But I have faith many of you'll find the way on your own. I'll see you there."

The lights go dark, the camera's red light turns off, and I growl in anger and frustration, because I know too many people can't wait to log in and see what atrocity comes next.

Chapter 8

DAY SEVEN

NICK

There's been a small break in the Surgeon case, and even though the Surgeon isn't the reason I'm in Virginia, it's fascinating. The FBI agent in me will never go away.

Over the past week Rass and I have developed a good rapport and that's important. My relationship with local law enforcement agencies is what makes me effective at my job. It's important for Rass, or any officer I work with, to trust me and to see me as a tool at their disposal. As I told Olena and Stasia King, I can poke around in places and ways others can't because of rules and protocol. I can pursue threads Rass isn't allowed to chase. He shares anything of interest, and I've done the same. My presence also acts as a subtle spur and keeps the locals engaged, so they don't settle into a mindset of inevitability. I'm not worried about Rass. He's a good guy, and I don't think he'd let this case fade. But his superiors have a lot of masters and might be tempted to move resources, without the added pressure of me.

Neither of us wants to watch the news as they obsess about Judge Wesley Miller III. The poor guy was left on his courthouse steps in the early morning, minus his hands. He was just starting to gain consciousness when he was found. A cardboard sign with the hashtags we've all come to recognize was at his feet.

As we finish our meal, Rass tells me what he's learned about the Surgeon.

It took a bit of digging, but now they know the first two victims, both attorneys, worked opposite each other in several cases in the late nineties and early two-thousands. Simpson was a prosecutor, and Cameron was a public defender in the same jurisdiction. They shared more than a dozen cases before both moved on to separate lucrative private practices. Something about the timing of their career changes tickles my brain, but it isn't clear yet. Rass says the Judge presided over some of those cases, and the Chief of Police was likely involved, too, at least at a superficial level.

"There's a rush by the Surgeon tactical team to locate the relevant parties in each of the cases, to determine whether they're alive, in prison, recently released, or might have a family member who has been showing signs of emotional distress," Rass says.

Polly, the sweet woman who serves us each morning, stops by to refill our cups.

I smile at her and say to Rass, "That's gotta be an extensive list."

"It is. There are eight prosecutors. The average prosecutor's load is between 80 and 100 cases. There were almost thirty public defenders during that time. I'm no mathlete, so I don't know how many combinations that makes, but it's a lot." Rass mops up the last bit of egg from his plate. "Throw in the Judge and the Chief, and it's a hot mess of possibility."

"Any luck figuring out what Sabine means?" I've done my own poking around, using Dr. Google, of course. The most common reference is the Rape of the Sabine women. I spent twenty minutes reading about the historical event, and checking out the various pieces of art representing the attack. That's another thing that tickles the back of my brain but delivers nothing solid.

"Not yet. And the hashtags had no traction until the Surgeon appeared. Now they're trending on everything. There's even a freaking TikTok dance." Rass rolls his eyes. "People are idiots."

No argument there. "I wonder how many everyday people understood the Onion reference. I bet a lot of them thought it was the satirical news site." We're confident the Onion is The Onion Routing Project, aka TOR, aka the Dark Web.

"That'd be okay. Fewer people watching this asshole do his deeds." Rass grunts.

Again, I can't disagree. "The Surgeon wants people watching; he has a message to deliver. He understands marketing. There's definitely a plan. Very few killers come out the gate publicly and randomly attack multiple days in a row. Granted, our guy hasn't killed anyone, but I feel as though there's a great big 'yet' hanging over that statement. I'm pretty sure there'll be another today or tonight. But who? And how many targets are there total?" Rass understands I'm thinking out loud, not asking, and I can see from his nods he's had the same thoughts.

"The 'Stop Sabine' messages tell us this is vigilantism. The Surgeon feels wronged." Rass chews on a toothpick and adds, "Maybe it's not something from the past. If he's saying 'Stop Sabine,' it sounds like whatever Sabine is doing is happening now."

"And there's been no connection between the attorneys in recent years? I'm sure your folks have spoken with each of them," I grimace, thinking about the man without a tongue. There'll be no more speaking for him. Jesus. "And they claim no relationship between them?"

"They say they haven't seen each other since the mid-2000s." Rass shrugs. "If it's revenge, and it's for something happening now, they're lying."

OCTOBER 28, 2005

STASIA

Mama didn't ask for child support, and George didn't ask for shared custody. He didn't even ask for visitation rights. Stasia saw her father only when Mama had to go out of town for business. Stasia had spent exactly nine days with George King since her sister's death three years ago.

This weekend, Mama was in Atlanta at an accounting conference of some sort. Stasia thought there might not be two more boring words than "accounting conference," but she'd rather go than spend three days with her father. But Mama absolutely refused to let Stasia stay home alone.

Since Stasia rarely stayed at George's, Mama wouldn't let her find her way to his house alone. George would pick her up, damn it, Mama hissed last night when she called her ex-husband to remind him. Stasia couldn't hear his response but could guess.

Of course, George was nearly an hour late, and she could smell the Jack Daniels through the open window before getting in the passenger seat of his rusty old pickup. Back in the day, when he still had his construction job, he drove a new truck. That truck went away along with the job when his drinking got him fired.

George didn't acknowledge Stasia, just slowed enough for Stasia to jump inside before he hits the gas again.

Five minutes into the ride, Stasia made herself try to engage him. "Thanks for picking me up." As if he was an acquaintance. She supposed he was.

Unsurprisingly, he didn't answer.

Stasia took in the rumpled T-shirt and the jeans that were stiff with grime. He was barefoot. A mostly empty pack of off-brand cigarettes stuck out of the small compartment above the ashtray, which was overflowing with butts. A naked girl air freshener that had lost its scent long ago dangled from the rear-view mirror, its string yellow. George's dark hair was thinning badly, and what remained was overly long and haphazard. His nose was red, a telltale sign of his addiction.

He caught her studying him and turned to glare at her. "What the hell you looking at?" There were no whites in his eyes; they were bloodshot and yellow.

"Nothing," Stasia replied, facing forward.

"I can see what you think of me in your snotty little expression. Don't you judge me, girl. My life is hard!"

Stasia tried to stay quiet but couldn't. "My life is hard, too! I lost my sister. And apparently, I lost my father, though I guess I never really had one."

His hand fisted and swung backward, connecting with her nose and cheek. There wasn't a lot of power behind it, but the angle was effective. Her teeth knocked together. "You little bitch, just like your mama. What a thing to say. What a thing to say! You should have been the one, not Tasha."

Stasia knew he felt that way, but he'd never come out and said it. She couldn't speak, couldn't come up with some snappy comeback to tell him she didn't care, he hadn't hurt her. Because she did care, and he had hurt her. She rubbed her jaw and whispered, "I'm sorry you feel that way."

George grunted, reached between his legs, and pulled out a small bottle of whiskey. He gripped it between his thighs while he unscrewed the top. "I should just leave you right here, see what happens." He tipped the bottle up and took a healthy shot.

"You should. Leave me here. It's okay. I won't tell Mama." She'd rather take her chances in an unknown part of town than deal with him drunk, in this angry mood.

"Like I give a shit if you tell that bitch!" He slammed the steering wheel, forgetting the bottle was still in his hand. Whiskey sloshed onto his skin, and he jerked, moved the bottle away from the wheel, looked down to see whiskey on his jeans. He didn't notice he'd missed a curve in the road, and the truck was crossing grass, headed toward a house, at forty miles an hour.

"Dad! Look out!" Stasia screamed, bracing. Her eyes widened. A woman was sitting on a porch swing, nursing her child. As if in slow motion, Stasia's brain took inventory. Toys, a small table, a stroller. Stasia screamed again. "Dad!"

"What the fuck are you—" George demanded, looking up. Too late, he saw what was happening. Too late, he tried to steer away. Too late.

The sound of the truck smashing through wood would never leave Stasia's memory. Glass rained through the shattered window when the truck continued across the porch and into the home's living room.

Stasia's head hurt from smacking against the windshield. She felt a goose egg growing on her forehead. She rubbed at it and shoved the door until she could get it cracked enough to climb out. Brick, glass, and unidentifiable bits of someone's life littered the floor under her feet. She moved carefully. She had to clamber over a chunk of the living room wall to get around the truck. Her foot caught and twisted on something—the bent frame of the stroller.

She couldn't see the mother's body or the baby. She dug around in a panic. Finally, she spotted a hand raised as if hailing a cab. "Ma'am? Can you hear me? Ma'am?" There was no sound. No screaming. No crying. Nothing.

Stasia crawled around the wreckage, moving pieces of the broken swing until she found the young woman's upper body. Her eyes were closed. She looked asleep until you saw her lower body, nothing but blood and things Stasia wouldn't think about.

"The baby. The baby. Where's the baby...." Stasia muttered. Her head hurt, and her vision was fuzzy, but she had to find the child.

Finally, she found her, still wrapped in a pink blanket, pinned under the porch swing bench. She might still be alive. Stasia wasn't sure, but all the 10th graders watched a CPR video in health class a while back, and she had to try. She lifted the porch swing carefully, picked up the baby, and laid her across her lap. She covered the child's mouth and nose with her mouth and pushed air into her. *Breathe, breathe, breathe.* She positioned two fingers on the child's chest. *Push, push, push.*

That's how the neighbors found her. A woman tried to coax her away, but Stasia wouldn't stop until the police and fire department arrived and confirmed the little girl was gone.

Only then did Stasia think to look for her father. The bastard was alive. Barely, but alive.

STASIA

Tasha was our father's favorite. That was never a secret. It was okay with me. Mama more than made up for it, and Tasha never used it to her advantage. Well, not too often. After Tasha died, my father went from not good to terrible. He'd started drinking too much when I was eight, so that couldn't be blamed on Tasha's murder. But back then, he was a quiet drunk, parked in his recliner day after day, watching daytime TV or passing out. After the murder, he was out of control. He crawled into himself and his bottles and stayed there, only coming out to spray anger at anyone foolish enough to get near him.

Mama was left to deal with the aftermath all on her own. She not only had her emotions, but mine, to manage. She had nothing left to try to pull Dad out of the hell he'd crawled into.

When Tasha was still alive, Dad was a silent, sorrowful drunk. After her murder, he became a belligerent, mean man. He'd scream at Mama that it was her fault. If she hadn't let Tasha have her summer job, none of this would have happened. She'd tell him they'd have a consistent income if he had been able to keep his own job rather than wallowing in self-pity after losing his small construction company. Mama wouldn't be away for such long hours, and Tasha might have been willing to take a lesser-paying job closer to home. They fought and fought and fought. Even after the divorce, the battle raged on.

Dad died the day after he killed the mother and her baby. No one missed him. For the second time, I was the one who survived.

He might have been paying attention if he hadn't been focused on screaming at me. He might not be so angry if I had been butchered instead of Tasha. The drinking might not have gotten so bad.

I am the sister of the dead girl and the daughter of the murdering alcoholic. I couldn't wait to get away from Virginia. The nightmares. The waking horrors.

I wanted a fresh start, where no one knew me. And more than that, I wanted someone to pay.

AVA

Lazing around the pool after a delicious late lunch is one of my joys. It's early still, a warm and sunny day. Voom is hogging half of my chaise. ZoZo is in the pool, one of her favorite places to be. In a few minutes, she'll clamber out and find one of us to receive a dousing as she shakes herself dry.

I stare at nothing in particular and listen to the boys talk animatedly about security. They get giddy over the newest this or that. All of it is gibberish to me, although I love being included in their excitement.

Jamie is so very different from his father. Where David James holds his emotions close to the vest, Jamie never holds back from sharing how he feels with those he loves. Where David James is driven by ego and vanity, Jamie is sweet and thoughtful and generous. Where David James gets off controlling others, Jamie is driven by service. How can he help others? How can he make the world better? When we first met, I thought it had to be an act; how could you be born to a man like David James and really be that kind? But he is. We've been through thick and thin and if it was a veneer, I'd have seen cracks by now.

Jamie would never admit it outside of our little group, but he's ashamed of his father and his 'extracurricular' behaviors. Hendrix and I are the closest thing Jamie has to family. The boy's relationship, though, is what guided them to manhood, and the world is a better place for it.

When Jamie invited Hendrix to move in with us, one of the first things the two of them did together was 'upgrade' our in-home gym from basic to professional. The two of them were kids in a candy store as truck after truck pulled into the drive and brawny men pushed heavy-duty delivery dollies into the garage bay the guys decided would replace the original gym in the house. I was happy with my elliptical, treadmill and basic weight set, but they were not. Power racks, bench presses, rowers, bikes, balls, barbells and dumbbells and kettlebells. Machines that do things I can't envision, much less understand. Benches and platforms. Even a boxing ring.

I told the boys this was now their domain, and I would continue to work out in the house.

Jamie mostly trains to stay in shape, but Hendrix is obsessed with staying strong and lean. Whatever. As long as they're happy, I'm good.

There are definite advantages to this setup. The roll-up door opens onto the pool patio, so I can hang out without risk of getting their sweat on me. With Hendrix's apartment and the security office upstairs, it has become a self-contained command center.

Right now they're in the weight center with the door up, talking about updating the computers, the cameras, the phones, and some new tracker doohickeys Hendrix is excited about. He's telling Jamie about gizmos and gadgets he learned about from buddies on the Dark Web. When I hear those words and give him a look, Hendrix informs me, "The Dark Web isn't just for bad guys, ya know."

"Really? Good guys use it too?" That doesn't fit what I thought I knew but my only real knowledge is from TV and books.

As always, Hendrix is happy to share knowledge. "Most of the users on the Dark Web are legal, even law enforcement. But the bad-doers are the worst of the worst. They like it because the Dark Web browser issues a false IP address, using a series of relays, that hide the user's identity. It's a safe space to do terrible things."

After thirty minutes of listening to their conversation has lulled me into a relaxed half-sleep, Hendrix drops into the chaise beside me and hands me a phone. "This one is for family use only." I examine it. It's small and thin compared to my others. I have two iPhones—a personal device and a phone for DJU. It's important to keep space between most of the girls and me. "What's so special about it?"

"It runs on Linux, has very few features, and is hard as hell to track. There's also some anti-spoofing tech built in. There are just five in the world, all designed and commissioned by moi." Hendrix grins. He loves his toys. "You can make a call, send a text, take a photo, or record a conversation. That's it."

"No gossip? No shopping? No games?" I gasp in fake outrage.

He shakes his head, beaming with pride. "You have lots of other tech for that shit."

"I do have lots of other tech for that shit," I grin back. "Thanks. I'll keep it with me always."

"Until this business is done, use this phone for important calls to Jamie or me." He's serious now, and I nod my understanding. Teasing aside, this man keeps Jamie and me safe.

He adds, "Please keep your dirty talk on the regular phone," to keep the mood light. "I don't want to hear that accidentally." He makes a face that makes me roll my eyes.

This new interest in DJU and all things David James Ellington by one ex-FBI agent, Nick Winston, has got us all nervous. Nick has asked for a tour of the DJU house in Manhattan, and I agreed. Best to be open about things. It's a perfectly legal enterprise. That's not what's making us jittery.

Now that Hendrix and Jamie are done talking tech, they've started a volleyball game in the pool. Even though they're both approaching forty, they're 18-year-olds at heart. They are two of the people I love most in the world, and I need to be sure they're safe. If that means carrying one extra phone, I'll use larger handbags for a while.

APRIL 16, 2017

AVA

Hendrix in real life wasn't at all what Ava was expecting, based on Jamie's stories about his best friend.

One early morning she woke to find Jamie and a man she'd never seen before huddled in the kitchen of their suite. No one entered that private space, not even the cleaning staff, so finding a stranger there was a shock. Ava stood in the bedroom doorway, quietly observing, unsure whether to be worried.

They sat side by side on bar stools in the kitchen. Jamie was dressed in navy sweatpants and a tank, his 'hanging at home' preference. The stranger wore jeans, an old leather bomber jacket, and a baseball cap. Ava couldn't see his face, but dark reddish-brown curls brushed the jacket's collar, and she caught a glimpse of a beard and mustache that needed the attention of a good barber. He took a swig of beer. Jamie had a beer, too, before 8 a.m. *What the hell.*

The man said something. Jamie responded. Ava couldn't hear what they were saying, but their body language told her it was a serious conversation, maybe an emotional one. Jamie put a hand on the man's shoulder and left it there. The intimacy of the gesture gave her the hint she'd been searching for: *Oh. This is Hendrix.*

Ava heard about Hendrix on her first proper date with Jamie. They were talking about Jamie's childhood. Hendrix and Jamie met in the fifth grade when Major General Daniel Hendrix moved his family to Virginia for his new job at the Pentagon. Before that, the family was in a horrible-sounding place called Fort Irwin, California. To hear Hendrix tell it, Fort Irwin was Satan's waiting room. For a long time, Ava thought Hen was being overly dramatic. Then he dragged them there one weekend. He was not.

Jamie and young Hendrix met on their first day of fifth grade at the prestigious Wallace Academy. The two became instantly inseparable. They took vacations with each other's families, charmed girls as a team, and got into trouble together. Jamie confessed he felt closer to Hendrix and his family than he ever felt to David James and Madeline. Jamie went on to Harvard to pursue his business degrees. Hendrix was accepted into Westpoint and became part of the Army's Green Berets.

When Hendrix came to their home that morning, he'd been in the military for fifteen years. He told Jamie he was not going back. Something bad happened. He pulled strings and retired early.

Ava wavered between staying where she was or joining them. She decided she was being a creep. As she moved closer, she heard Hendrix say, "It was too close to what we saw on your dad's computer. Brought back the nightmares. I will not be part of that shit."

She felt a change in the room. Ava made a point of circling wide enough to avoid startling them and smiled. "You must be Hendrix. Welcome home."

NICK

During tonight's virtual dinner, Angel brings up the Surgeon. "Have you heard anything? Does Rass talk about it? What about the other LEOs?" LEOs are what she calls law enforcement officers, a term she picked up during her years riding with CB, a five-foot-nothing, sassy-mouthed Latina long-haul truck driver. For CB, it's not always a term of endearment. Fortunately, Angel still loves the men and women with badges... with one notable exception.

I'm trying not to inhale a Cobb salad with chicken, and Angel is feasting on a cheese and cracker buffet. We're both drinking pinot noir. Angel tells me she 'had a day' training her newest charge, a pit mix pup who will soon be a psychotherapy service dog. I tell her I 'had a day' going in circles trying to connect the dots, which feels very loosey-goosey. Yeah, that's an official investigative term. Wine is necessary.

"The scariest thing about this Surgeon guy is that he's so calm and measured, you know? Nothing seems to faze him. He has a goal; he accomplishes the goal, he's done, and he moves on. But not without reminding the viewers at home he has a message." Angel breaks off a chunk of cheese and offers it to Nope, the three-legged wonder dog. I miss my crew, but I'm not sad that I'll miss the dog farts tonight.

"The LEOs are trying to find the right link between the victims. All four victims worked on several cases together years ago, but there's no apparent recent connection. The task force is working hard, but as far as I'm aware, they haven't found anything yet." I pick chunks of red onion from my salad and set them on the tray.

"I would think the national press on both the Surgeon and Elspeth would put pressure on them to get it together," Angel is sitting on the patio, wearing my Celtics basketball jersey and her own bright blue boxer briefs, bronzed legs stretched out in front of her. I can hear the dogs tussling nearby. The sun is just going down over the Utah hills behind the house. It's beautiful, and I'm homesick. Before Angel, I was never homesick. But then, I never had a place I called home.

"I don't think it's from lack of trying. They're separate police departments, but neither is used to cases like these. The Surgeon, especially, is extraordinary." I may be making excuses for them. I haven't met the Surgeon team. I've just heard second-hand from Rass.

"Anything at all on Elspeth? Her family joined Komo. Dr. Lisa asked me to meet them, and we spoke today," Angel says. Dr. Lisa is the lead psychotherapist on the Komorebi team. She's brilliant, kind, and dedicated, and one of the first folks Peter Baden hired when he built Komo, using the extensive funds he'd inherited when his father died. "I'm worried about her sister. So rough to be going through something like this at that age. I'm going to ask Hannah to reach out."

Angel understands the complexity. She was a victim herself, more than once. The woman finds trouble. Less so now that I'm around, thank God. I'm not sure whether I'm protecting her, if I'm a positive role model, or if she just has other, safer trouble to get into nowadays. "I'm glad they're in. Nothing definitive." I tell her about my conversation with Stasia King and about Xander Williams.

"Their mom must have been a big Buffy fan," Angel says, stretching to paint her toes with a bright blue polish.

"Buffy?"

"The Vampire Slayer. Xander and Willow are two of the main characters. Angel, too, but she had nothing to do with naming me." She laughs. "Xander thinks David James Ellington—what a pompous name—could be connected?"

I nod. "There's a rumor, although Rass says he's not heard it, that David James Ellington has interests in things that are not generally considered acceptable by the public. Xander and the missing Willow believe there may be a connection between Natasha King and those interests, and possibly Elspeth. I need some way to tie it all together. I'm trying to dig deeper, get better access."

"Ava is part of that, isn't she?"

"She's part of the University," I explain DJU as Ava and tell her about my upcoming tour. "I suppose she could be involved in Elspeth's disappearance. Maybe DJU has one method of recruitment for legal girls, and another for under-aged kids. People are good at hiding their true selves, but my gut tells me she's not involved."

Angel nods. People hiding their true selves is another thing she has too much experience in. First she was abducted by a madman who presented as normal to the world, then she was hunted by a sheriff, and not long ago she was stalked and nearly killed. "So what now?"

"I'm going to keep digging into this David James thing. At the very least, I'll check out the University in New York. Someone, somewhere, knows something. I just have to find out who."

Chapter 9

DAY EIGHT

AVA

Criminal Minds lied to us. The FBI doesn't fly its agents around in private jets. So when ex-FBI agent Nick Winston is completely unfazed by the experience, and I'm curious. I smile. "Most people are a bit gob-smacked the first time they're in a private jet. I'm guessing this isn't your first time."

He smiles back. "The organization I work with was started by Peter Baden. You may know him from his news days."

"I do. I also remember when his daughter Olivia was kidnapped. And what happened later? That was absolutely heartbreaking." I remember hearing about her death and how shocking it was. "I'm so sorry." I tilt my head and confess, "I'm a true crime addict." To prove it, I open my Dolce & Gabbana bag and pull out my current read, *If You Tell* by Gregg Olsen.

Nick makes a pained face. "That's a brutal story. I don't think I'll ever stop being shocked by how truly terrible humans can be to one another."

'Terrible' is an understatement. I tuck the book into my bag and get comfortable in my seat. "I'm sorry. I sent us on a tangent. What were you saying about Komorebi?"

"Peter was successful in his career, and inherited a lot of money from his father. He's invested most of it back into Komo. That's why I'm here, working with the Bridges family. We're fortunate to have access to resources like private planes for situations when time is of the essence," he laughs. "But most of the time, I'm parked in business class with everyone else."

"It's hard to deal with the congestion and stress of public air travel after you've flown like this." The attendant zips by to announce we'll be landing momentarily. The flight from Virginia to Teterboro is less than an hour, barely time to get settled and have a drink before landing.

Hendrix was already in the cockpit with the captain when Nick and I boarded, so I doubt Nick is aware of his presence. One of the regular DJU drivers will have delivered a black SUV to the airfield, but Hendrix will drive us. I won't draw attention to him unless Nick notices and asks. He hasn't met Hendrix, so I can't imagine he would.

Hendrix and I agreed it would be good to have Hendrix's eyes and ears available, too, just in case. 'In case' what neither of us can say, but it's making me feel better knowing he's here. I just have to remember to use the fancy new limited edition phone he gave me.

The switch between drivers goes without a hitch. As soon as we're comfortable in the back of the car, Hendrix slips behind the wheel, his black trousers and polo the same as the other man's. All our drivers wear baseball caps with the DJ Group logo; frankly, they all look the same, even to me. I'd never thought of that before. I wonder if Hendrix hires them based on their looks. I'll ask later.

Teterboro is only fifteen miles from Manhattan, but the drive will take 45 minutes to an hour at this time of day, almost as long as we were in the air. Once the car is over the George Washington Bridge, we turn onto the Henry Hudson Parkway. "Have you been to New York before?"

Nick nods. "Several times. It's fun to visit, but I wouldn't want to live here. Too many people."

"There are a lot of humans packed into this small space. Where are you from?" I rarely mind silence, but I'm so nervous. I hate that he has me off-center like this. The worst part is that he hasn't done anything to cause it. I'm doing it to myself.

"Now I live on a small ranch in Utah. But I was raised in Philly and based in Virginia when I was with the Bureau." Nick is a foot bouncer. The constant movement adds to my stress, and I want to ask him to stop. Of course, I won't.

"Utah. Wow! That would be a big change from Philly or anywhere on the east coast. I'd like to live somewhere quiet like that." Hendrix catches my eye in the rearview, and his mouth tips up in a grin. He doesn't think I could stand living somewhere quiet. I'm going to prove him wrong! Someday.

"It's definitely different. I think it depends on the company." He grins, a wistful look in his eye. Someone important is waiting for him in Utah.

Hendrix glides the SUV into a spot in front of The Fifth. This is the primary residence of DJU. The Fifth is seven floors of luxury, built at the turn of the 20th century for one of the wealthiest men of the period. I'm sure that's why David James wanted it. Its seven floors feature sixteen bedrooms and twenty-one bathrooms. The interior is marble and gilt and velvet and brocade. There are millions of dollars' worth of paintings and sculptures. The Fifth is for the star students. Stellar performance earns a room here. There's a second residence near Gramercy Park that we call the undergrad house.

We climb the steps to the front doors, where we're greeted by Adam, the uniformed doorman-cum-security chief for The Fifth. He welcomes us into the impressive foyer, where Mercedes, the housemother, takes control.

"Hello, Ava! Welcome to The Fifth, Mr. Winston," she beams. She leads us past the impressive circular staircase that rises from ground level to the top floor. The steps are eight feet wide, beautiful Italian marble, the railing black wrought iron. The smaller staircases to the basement and the attic are slightly more subtle, but not by much.

Mercedes motions for us to take a seat in the Great Room and offers beverages. We both decline. "What can I tell you? Show you?"

The sound of giggles and high heels clicking on the marble floor gets Nick's attention, and he swivels his head toward the stairs and the Grand Foyer. He smiles as three young women pass, but the smile doesn't reach his eyes. He returns his attention to Mercedes. "Let's start with you telling me about the students. How many girls live here?"

"We have fifteen women here, Mr. Winston." Mercedes answers. She's perched herself on the edge of one of the five sofas in the room. Mercedes has been with DJU since the beginning. In the early 1980s, Mercedes went to a traditional finishing school in France. Now she's nearing sixty years old, and she makes sixty look fantastic. I've never seen her look anything less than stunning.

Her thick hair is steel gray and short-cropped, highlighting the sharpness of her cheekbones and the graceful tower of her neck. She's wearing a simple black dress that shows off her curves and long legs. If I'm still in this business when I'm her age, and I sincerely and passionately pray I am not. I only hope to look half as good.

"And the girls are recruited? How?" I already went over this with him, so is he testing me? I don't buy for a minute that he's forgetful. But Mercedes is a pro; if I were lying, which I was not, he still would not trip us up.

Mercedes tips her head in my direction and says, "Ava has a wonderful instinct for young women who will succeed in this environment. There's a certain magic in finding just the right blend of beauty, brains, and personality. Someone might be attractive but lack the intelligence to do well. Or she might be both beautiful and intelligent and have no personality, or worse, an unattractive one. We don't want to waste anyone's time." She smiles. "The women who are fortunate to be here understand that they're exceptional."

Again, Nick's smile doesn't reach his eyes. "How long do the women stay at the university?" The way he says 'university' has just a tinge of sarcasm, and I don't appreciate it, but I keep my expression even.

Mercedes shrugs. "Most of them are here for a year before they move on to their new lives. They're still part of DJU but rarely live on the premises. If you're asking what percent of women are unsuccessful, very few cannot complete the program. Ava is an excellent judge of potential." She smiles at me. "I believe fewer than two drop out each year."

"What sorts of things might get a girl kicked out?" His wording is intentional, another test.

Neither of us is ruffled. I respond. "Women are never kicked out. They may be encouraged to leave, but they're never abandoned."

"Okay. What sorts of things might cause a girl to be encouraged to leave?"

"Please, Mr. Winston, we prefer to give them the respect they're entitled to and call them women or students, not girls," Mercedes instructs. "I might encourage a student to leave if she's not absorbing the knowledge shared with her. Some young women simply find conversations about politics, world issues, or the economy boring. That young woman would not enjoy her time here, even with a beautiful wardrobe. Still, others prefer their own fashion sense and comportment to the sophistication we expect."

"What about addiction issues? Do the—women—drink too much or get involved in drugs?"

Mercedes laughs. "Many people drink too much occasionally, but it's not a practice we encourage. We advise moderation in all things." She shakes her head. "As to drugs, none of the students use illicit drugs on DJU premises. I cannot speak about what they do in their personal time. But we have no students who are abusers. I can assure you of that."

Nick looks from Mercedes to me, and his expression is apologetic. "And there's no sexual component of this? I'll be blunt; David James Ellington is well-known for his sexual tastes. It's hard to believe that having a stable full of women at the ready wouldn't be tempting to him. A little quid pro quo."

Mercedes' eyes flash angrily. "Mr. Winston, this is not a brothel. There is no tit for tat. Of course, the women sometimes enjoy friendships with guests, but that is entirely up to them. There is no pressure. And certainly no reward."

Nick makes a conciliatory gesture. "Got it." He pauses, and I can tell he's about to ask something else we'll find offensive. "Are any of the women under eighteen? Now or historically?"

Mercedes's face turns pink with anger. "The students are all of legal age. Mr. Winston, I understand you're doing a job, but we are not what you're implying we are."

"I'm not implying anything," Nick says, and he seems to mean it. "I'm just trying to figure out how a thirteen-year-old girl disappeared."

"And while I appreciate that greatly, I still find your questions insulting." Mercedes snaps. "What information have you that DJU might be in any way connected to the girl's disappearance?"

I'm trying hard to keep from smiling. Mercedes riled up is a thing of beauty and something I've never witnessed before. I'm eager to hear Nick Winston's response to the question. Does he have something specific that's brought him here?

But no, he shakes his head. "Just my gut telling me something isn't right. Are you aware another young lady disappeared under similar circumstances from the same location in 2002?"

Mercedes clearly did not know this.

"Or that David James Ellington was accused of sexually assaulting a young woman at The Madalena around the same time?" Nick adds.

This is news to both of us. And surprising to neither of us.

"My job is to find tiny threads that may have gone unnoticed and pull on them to see if they lead anywhere. Another girl went missing at the same location, and there were whispers—*are* whispers—that David James is attracted to little girls he has no business being around." He's kept his tone calm and non-confrontational, but his eyes tell a different story. He's angry and frustrated and convinced that something is happening here. He just has to find it.

Mercedes takes a deep breath before she says, "Mr. Winston, I can assure you there has been no one at DJU during my tenure who was underage or here against her will. Ever. I would not only resign, but I would contact the authorities myself."

I chime in. "I have to agree with Mercedes, Nick. I have never been involved with, or suspected, anything like that happening within the University. If I did, I would not be silent."

Nick studies us both, then nods. "Fair enough."

There's a moment of uncomfortable quiet as each of us finds our composure, then Mercedes offers a tour of some of the more notable parts of the building, and Nick agrees.

I finger the small phone in my jacket pocket. I hope Hendrix heard all that.

STASIA

My schedule for today is low key: savor a cup of coffee snuggled up in pajamas while enjoying the hotel's free cable, and wait for a decadent breakfast via room service. Food, TV, and a nap, even though I've only been awake a couple of hours. Sleep has been rough the last few days, either filled with nightmares or eluding me entirely.

The phone rings and the sound makes me jump. I lick spilled coffee from my hand, set the cup on the nightstand, and reach for the phone resting on its charger. Nick Winston's name appears on the screen, and my gut clenches. He better not kill my appetite.

I could let it go to voicemail, but then I'll obsess, my do-nothing plans ruined. "Hi, Nick."

"Hello! How's the trip?" His voice is warm and friendly, as usual. He can't possibly be this happy all the time. It sounds like he's in the car. We just spoke yesterday. Is he checking up on me?

"So far, so good. Visits to four dead presidents and one national park. What's up?" I force myself to sound calm, although I feel anything but.

"Sorry to intrude. I just had a quick question and thought you'd be a good person to ask." Nick explains. "Have you seen the news about the person who calls themselves the Surgeon?

What the hell? "Of course. Mama is freaking out about it."

"I'm sorry to hear that." He says. "I was wondering, as someone familiar with surgery, what do you think? Is he an actual doctor? Someone with medical training? Maybe a medic or a veterinarian?"

Interesting. "I work in the ER so don't do surgeries, but you're welcome to my two cents. In the videos I saw, he seems competent. He achieves his apparent goal and looks confident while doing it. Although they're attention-getting for sure, none of the surgeries so far are especially complex. You could probably find educational videos on the Internet showing you how to do each of these procedures. If he's self-educating online, I will say he's an excellent student and has practiced. I suppose he could watch a video off-camera and follow along, although that would be risky, especially with all the ads YouTube plants in videos nowadays. But I don't get that impression. So maybe the Surgeon is a doctor, or used to be—"

"Used to be?" Nick's confusion is evident.

"Doctors sometimes lose their licenses for various reasons. Maybe the victims are somehow connected to that. Malpractice lawsuit, maybe."

Nick is silent. It's a good theory.

I concede the obvious. "It's also possible the Surgeon is a doctor with a reason to seek vengeance against these folks in a very public and dramatic way."

"If you had to bet money, which way would you go?" Nick finally asks.

"I'd start with the lost license." My gut is returning to normal levels of stress. "Can I ask why you're even thinking about this? Aren't you there to focus on Elspeth Bridges?"

"I am, yes. But it's hard to turn the law enforcement brain off sometimes." He sounds a little embarrassed. "Thanks, Stasia." He offers a few words about having fun and taking lots of photos, then disconnects.

After we hang up, I realize there's one more thing I should tell him. I'm not up for another chat, so he'll have to settle for a text.

Remember Xander Williams? Homer Williams' son. He was a nice kid before everything went to shit. After Homer's death, he changed. He was an apprentice in a butcher shop for a while, but they fired him. The rumor mill said it was because he had a flash temper and couldn't be trusted with knives, saws, and such. Butchery and surgery are different, but if you're comfortable handling a knife, that might be a gateway. Just a thought.

I return the phone to the charger and lean back against the headboard. I wish there was a human charger. Since there isn't, I'm going to eat my pancakes, then try for a dream-free nap without Elspeth and Tasha and Nick and Mama running through my brain.

XANDER

Dear Editor,

In the year 2002, a fourteen-year-old girl was abducted, tortured, and killed. Chief Jim Gifford and his team immediately accused Homer Williams, a homeless veteran battling PTSD. They did not investigate other possibilities. They did not look deeply or logically at whether it even made sense that Williams could have committed such a crime.

The skills of Sherlock Holmes and his man Watson are not needed to recognize that Williams could not possibly have done what was done to Natasha King. He lived in a small tent near a freeway underpass. The vile and unimaginable things that were inflicted upon that young girl could not be done in the open. They could not be done without tools. Homer had no location and no tools.

Nevertheless, Homer was arrested and convicted of the crime. Less than a year later, while in prison waiting for his appeal, Williams supposedly died by suicide.

Homer Williams did not commit this crime, and he did not commit suicide.

While I could not say who is actually responsible for the death of Natasha King, I know who is responsible for the death of Homer Williams:

> ***Miles Cameron**, Williams' public defender. This man did absolutely nothing to represent his client and did not attempt to prove him innocent. He did not encourage the pursuit of other leads or present evidence that could have helped exonerate his client. He never once questioned the reality of whether his client had the opportunity and means.*

Damien Simpson, the state's attorney who prosecuted the case. At no time did he look for or consider another possible perpetrator. He accepted the blatant lies presented to him by the police and enthusiastically pursued a false victory.

Chief Jim Gifford chose to oversee this case personally. It was his job to explore all options, to be sure he identified and held accountable the true monster. As such, he has significant culpability. He decided early on—with no actual evidence—that Homer Williams was guilty.

And finally, there's **Judge Wesley Miller III**, who may bear the most responsibility of all. His job is to listen to the evidence, weigh its veracity, and guide the jury to find an appropriate conclusion. He did none of these things. He ignored the blatant lies and misdirection presented in his courtroom, and he allowed an innocent man to be represented by someone who clearly had no interest in providing his client with any sort of defense.

As a result, the person or persons who actually committed this horrendous crime continue to move around in society, free to attack other young girls.

You'll realize the men named here have recently been victims themselves. No doubt they worked on many cases together. How many other families have had their lives destroyed through their intentional incompetence and voluntary blindness?

The attorneys left their courthouse careers for cushy, high-paying practices that significantly grew their wealth. Chief Gifford recently retired and *purchased a beachfront home valued at substantially more than a public servant's salary could afford.*

Is it possible that their self-serving deception hurt another family and someone has sought retribution? I do believe there's a reason this is happening to these specific people. While they are victims, they are not innocents. I hope the police do a better job finding the actual attacker in this case than they have in the past.

Signed,

Xander Williams, loving son of Homer Williams

THE SURGEON

This fuck. The son-of-a-bitch is watching a preteen girl being violated by a very large man, a tennis ball in her mouth preventing her screams. There will be no regret killing this one. If there was any doubt Bernard McNeill needed to be held accountable, it's gone now.

This is the man who bought Natasha King's life twenty years ago.

The son of a bitch is sitting on the sofa in his living room, wearing nothing but a ratty Grateful Dead t-shirt. His belly is so big it's amazing he can find his dick under it. McNeill's eyes are at half-mast as he watches the girl being raped and terrorized on a giant flat screen hung over the fireplace.

As I move closer, I see a blonde head between the bastard's thighs, and rage races through me—does the son of a bitch have an actual kid here? Oh, shit, it's just a doll. Well, the head of a doll. The motherfucker is getting a blow job from a decapitated sex toy.

I pause a minute to let my adrenalin slow. Intense emotion causes accidents.

The very bland beigeness of this uninteresting tract home seems to amplify the monster that lives inside. I can only imagine what a UV light would show on that ugly brown corduroy sofa. The only non-disgusting thing I see is a large framed photo of a preteen girl with long reddish brown hair. She's wearing a navy school blazer over a white blouse. Her hand is supporting her chin, a pink watch on her left wrist. The watch ignites another flame of rage in me, and I force myself to tamp it down.

When McNeill's thirteen-year-old daughter told Mommy that Fat Fuck Daddy was raping her, Mom didn't report him. No, she used the information to access Fat Fuck's trust fund money. Fat Fuck was banished to a tract house in the suburbs. Mom and daughter kept the fancy house in Arlington. Daddy hates them with a terrifying intensity. Since he couldn't punish his daughter, he chose Natasha King as a stand-in. *I wonder if others ever made the connection to Natasha King.*

Fat Fuck is so engrossed in the scene on the screen and the plastic head between his jiggling thighs he doesn't notice the needle slide into his neck. He half-heartedly slaps at his flesh as if chasing away a pesky fly. McNeill manages to orgasm just before the medicine takes hold. The last orgasm he'll ever have.

Getting the Fat Fuck where I want him is no small task. The kitchen island may not be wide enough to hold this man whale. At least McNeill is short. Magazines and paper plates caked with grease and old food fall off the counter as I push and pull him onto the cheap laminate. It takes longer than I'd like, but this mass of dead weight would be hard for anyone to move.

I've had a small flicker of doubt a few times in the last few days. Am I playing God? Who am I to take a life? But now, there's no doubt at all. This man needs to die.

NICK

My days are structured around food and conversation. Breakfast with Rass. Dinner with Angel. Both are important.

"Have you found the StopSabine site?" Angel asks as she makes a sandwich out of crackers and cheese slices. If I don't get back soon, she's going to starve to death. Nope, the three-legged hound slips in and steals a bit of cheese. This particular certified therapy dog only has manners when she's on the clock and wearing her vest. Asa, my handsome best boy, sits patiently waiting for a tidbit. Nope is very much like Angel; energetic and imperfect and precisely who and what you want and need in a time of crisis. Asa is like me: calm, steady, and lethal when necessary. We're the perfect family.

"As we expected, it's a Dark Web site." I'm enjoying a burger and fries and an ice-cold beer. Old school.

"Do you think it really is a red room site?" Angel frowns. "I mean, that's just an urban legend, right? No one has ever actually found one. It's always a friend of a friend."

"Here's the thing. I don't think there are actual red rooms where people can log in and watch the torture and eventual killing of someone. For one, the streaming quality isn't there. The functionality that makes the Dark Web desirable is the same thing that slows it down. The traffic that passes through Tor, AKA the Dark Web, is encrypted and bounced between at least three relay points to obscure the origin of the data. That makes it hard to track IP addresses. If a lot of people are going to watch simultaneously that just makes it worse. That said, we both know there are tons of all-too-real child abuse and torture videos and streaming sites worldwide. I don't for a minute believe the bad guys have a line they won't cross. So I have no doubt there are legitimate snuff videos, and even that people can pay to direct what happens in them. If I were into buying and selling that kind of stuff, I would not be putting it out on the web, dark or otherwise, to watch. I would use the Dark Web to transfer files and collect funds."

Angel makes a vomit face. "People are horrible. I'm staying here on the ranch and may never come back out. Hurry up and find Elspeth so you can come back to us. Please."

"I'm not sure how much longer I'll stay here. I'm going to talk with Rass about what Ava told me, and I have some ideas left to check into. But I can probably do as much from home as I can do here, depressing as that is. I might be home next week." I say, and she beams, which makes some of the crud of the last few days fade a bit.

"Yay! I'll even go shopping. I think the only thing in the fridge right now, besides cheese, is beer."

"I feel catfished. When we started being us, you were so into food. Where'd that woman go?"

"She's still here. She just needs company to motivate her." Angel shrugs. Her tone darkens. "I'm not watching the StopSabine thing." Then she frowns. "Could I even watch it if I wanted to? How do you access stuff like that?"

"I'm glad you're not watching. Whatever happens, it's not going to be pleasant. If you wanted to, you'd have to install a VPN and then download the Tor browser. Even then, everything on your computer would be at risk. I bought a cheap laptop to watch it—I'm not about to risk exposing Komorebi to the villains of the Dark Web."

NICK

We're in my hotel room with the new laptop on the table between us. Neither of us thought it would be a good idea to watch the proceedings at Rass's place, with his wife and kids in the next room. We're both expecting this new phase of StopSabine to take it up another level. Why else would they move to the Dark Web, a place with very little monitoring? The Dark Web appeals to these folks because of the way it uses relays and masks IPs, giving everyone—good and bad—anonymity.

A small box in the bottom left corner of the StopSabine site shows how many viewers are tuned in. Nearly four million. Jesus. And that's just the people who know how to find a site on the Dark Web. There'll be copies on YouTube and other mainstream platforms before those entities take them down.

In addition to the view counter, there's a countdown clock. When we first found the site, the clock was the only thing on the black screen except the words **'Stop Sabine'**. According to the clock, whatever happens, will begin in three minutes. It's 10:16 p.m. east coast time.

"What do you think it's going to be?" Rass asks nervously. Neither of us wanted food, although I haven't eaten since breakfast, and I don't think Rass has, either. We may be badass law enforcement dudes, but there are just some things that screw with your system, like watching someone pluck out eyeballs and chop off hands.

We've both asked this question a few different ways over the last few hours and have yet to come up with an answer. This entire event is so far out of bounds it's hard to wrap my head around it. I'm glad Angel told me she wouldn't be watching. "I've seen and been a part of enough fucked up shit. No thanks."

The countdown clock disappears, and the screen goes entirely black.

The number from the view counter is nearly five million. It'd be nice to think they're all law enforcement folks trying to figure out how to stop this, but that's not reality. The Surgeon's little speech after the Judge's assault was accurate: We've become a rubber-necking society, and too many people get a thrill from violence against their friends and neighbors. On a good day, I tell myself maybe we're all just numb to it. Today's not a good day.

The screen stays dark for a minute, then two past the timer hitting 0:00. Maybe it was a false alarm—but no, the Surgeon suddenly appears on the screen in what looks like an anywhere USA kitchen. Initially, the only light is over a center island. A naked man with a bulbous belly is flat on the counter, straps holding him down. Three spotlights come on, all pointing at him the same way they've been positioned in the past. The man's skin is pale but blotched with pink, a thick fur of gray hair coating the center of his chest, down toward his groin. His arms and legs are equally furry.

The Surgeon is, as always, in partial shadow. When he speaks, the cadence of the altered voice reminds me of the opening of a *Twilight Zone* episode. "This is a very bad man who is about to have a very bad day. Twenty years ago, he paid other bad men to kidnap a young girl. Why? Because the girl looked like his daughter, and he was very angry with his daughter for telling their 'secret.'"

"I debated long and hard about revealing his name. By doing so, I would be outing his daughter, who didn't deserve this then, and doesn't deserve this now. Knowing what her father did to another child... horrible. There's one more player in this tragedy, and that's the bastard's wife. She knew what he'd done to her daughter. She knew how dangerous he was, and that he wasn't going to stop being a pedophile just because he got caught. She let him continue, for money. In the end, protecting the daughter outweighs the wife."

The Surgeon smacks the belly again, and I get the impression he wishes it was the man's wife.

"Not only did he lose access to his favorite toy, but he also lost most of his money. The missus kicked him out but kept control of the family finances. He couldn't punish his child—not because he's a pillar of morality or even because he loved the child of his loins. He just didn't have the balls to risk getting caught.

Instead, he took an innocent girl away from her family and made her a stand-in for everything he wanted to do to his daughter. Today, he is going to pay for that decision." The Surgeon is pacing, but it's focused.

I'm sure several cops and media folks are trying to identify the man on the counter with the faint hope of finding him in time to save him. My brain is doing that itchy thing. The Surgeon is smart.

The Surgeon stops pacing and steps closer to the man, one hand resting on the mound of flesh that rises from the counter like a mountain. The Surgeon's gloved hand slaps the belly twice like you might greet a friend. Then the Surgeon goes to work.

It doesn't take long before Rass groans and drops his head between his knees. My skin crawls in horror as the Surgeon performs what he tells us is a "penectomy"—the total removal of the man's penis and testicles.

The Surgeon lifts the amputated penis to present it to its owner, and the camera zooms in so we, the audience, can see that the man is, in fact, conscious. Can he feel this? Jesus! Whatever drug runs through the IV into his arm keeps him still, but his eyes tell the story. They are huge and dark with pain and fear, and tears roll into the crevices of his nose and jowls. I have mixed emotions. *Should I feel sorry for a man who's done what this man is said to have done?*

"Interesting fact. If I had used a serrated blade on this man, he could have a chance to survive since his veins would constrict because of the rough edges of the wound. However, I used a scalpel so if I were to leave him right now, he would bleed out. But that won't be the cause of his death."

The Surgeon holds up the penis for the camera, pries open the man's mouth, and slowly with great care, fits the penis inside, balls first. Once it's in, the Surgeon begins to push it deeper, a centimeter at a time, intent on causing the man to suffocate on his own genitals.

That's my limit. My belly sends up an alert and I look away taking deep breaths until the feeling passes. I assume the man died. The Surgeon seems satisfied by the outcome. He turns toward the camera and holds up a cardboard sign, similar to those used in the earlier videos.

#stopsabine #whoisnext

Chapter 10

DAY NINE

AVA

We all have secrets. Big secrets, little secrets. Things that embarrass us, things that shame us. Jamie, Hendrix, and I have shared many secrets over the years. For instance, Jamie wishes he'd been born to a guy who does oil changes for a living, or delivers the mail, or drives a garbage truck. Jamie is ashamed of his father but proud of the work he is able to do for the DJ Group. I know about things Hendrix did that tore out pieces of his heart and made him hate himself. I've told them my secrets, too.

One snowy day, the three of us were huddled around the fireplace, comfortably tipsy from day drinking out of sheer snowbound boredom. Not that we minded. Our lives are usually so ramped up it was nice to have a forced lazy day. That day we shared those kind of secrets.

Some secrets are so ingrained they're part of our very being, determining who we are and how we respond to life.

I want to tell Nick Winston a secret. It's not my secret, but my gut tells me he's the right person and now is the right time.

NICK

When Ava called and asked me to meet her at the welcome center at Maymont, I wasn't exactly shocked, but I was surprised. I hover near a rack of brochures by the front doors. When she arrives in what I presume is her personal vehicle instead of a company SUV, I realize something is about to change. I buy a bottle of water and take a seat just as she enters. Except for a young man working at the snack counter, the place is empty.

The car isn't the only change in Ava. Gone are the designer clothes, although I bet the slim-fit jeans and black tank top she's wearing aren't from Target. She's wearing oversized black sunglasses, her blonde hair is pulled back into a sleek ponytail, and she isn't carrying a handbag. She has her keys in her hand, and as she approaches, I see the tip of her phone in her back pocket. She smiles nervously, buys her own bottle of water, and then joins me at the table.

"Everything okay?" I ask in what I hope is a reassuring voice.

She nods once, not meeting my eyes, and peels the paper from the generic bottle of water. "Yeah. It's okay. I just." She stops, twists the lid off the water bottle, takes a long drink, then starts again. "I want to tell you a story. It's not my story. But I think maybe someone should know what's going on."

"Okay." The spot in my belly that jumps when something big is about to happen is going nuts.

"But first, I need to ask—will you please—can you promise me you'll use this as information, but you won't approach the person or people involved?" She raises her eyes to mine, and they are dark with worry, the blue nearly as navy as her Porsche.

That's a hard promise to make, but I'm no longer law enforcement, so I nod my agreement after a small internal tussle. "Can I use the information to obtain additional information?"

She thinks, then nods. "Yes. You can do that."

"Okay." We both offer small smiles to seal the deal.

She takes another long sip, nearly draining the bottle. "I'm going to tell you the way it was told to me." She smiles, for real then, and says, "Well, without the occasional slurred words. We were pretty drunk when they told me."

I nod in encouragement, and she begins.

They slipped through the door of David James' home office. Hendrix said the room felt cavernous, with a fireplace big enough for a man to stand inside, dark wood bookcases and paneling, and the centerpiece: a giant partner's desk near the wall of windows. When David James and Bishop Oliver were here, Jamie's father sat on one side and Bishop on the other. David James was neat and organized, nothing out of place. Bishop was a stacker. Piles of magazines and papers threatened to topple if someone sneezed.

Jamie slid into his father's big leather chair and pressed the button to start the Pentium PC that sat on the desk. He clicked away at the keyboard and told Hendrix to grab one of the expensive bottles of booze so they could get their party started.

Hendrix chose a crystal decanter filled with brown liquid and carried it to the desk. It wasn't full, so he figured no one would notice if they took a few sips.

Hendrix went to the bookcases to distract himself and looked at the titles. Leather-bound novels, business books, magazines, encyclopedias, and dictionaries filled multiple shelves. He remembered asking Jamie if David James had read them all.

Jamie said, "A lot of them, yeah. He says reading is how he learned to be David James Ellington."

The two were trying to find the address to a party they'd been sent—email, private message, group chat. Finally Hendrix pointed to the AOL icon and Jamie click and logged in. Address in hand, he exited the app and was going to shut the computer down.

Hendrix was gray when he described what happened next. Jamie closed the AIM window. A message notification popped up, and Jamie accidentally clicked the mouse, which caused it to expand. There were three words: "Tonight's Little Dove. Approve?" Under the words, a photo of a young girl, maybe ten or twelve, huddled on a cement floor. She was naked except for a hot pink watch on her left wrist. She looked terrified.

They thought it was a porn pop up, and Jamie tried desperately to close it. In his panic, he kept clicking wrong things. "Little dove is going to bring a good return. I'll report back tomorrow, but here's a preview." A small video filled the message box. The same girl, now strapped spread eagle to four steel bars sunk in the concrete floor to make a suspension rack, nothing but air between her and the cold, stained floor. The tight straps held her at least two feet above the ground.

Neither boy could move. They watched, frozen in horror, as a large man wearing nothing but a hood approached the girl. She screamed, first in fear, then in pain.

Her screams broke their paralysis.

"What the fuck, dude," Hendrix whispered. "What if your father realizes we saw it?"

You don't get videos like that unless you want to see videos like that. And if you want to see videos like that...

Neither of them was naive to think he'd simply yell.

Jamie grabbed the bottle of whiskey and upended it on top of the PC, making sure the liquid dripped into the slots to hit the fans and motherboard. "I just dumped three hundred thousand dollars on his desk. He'll be too mad to notice."

AVA

Part of me can't believe I told him this. I've never told anyone, but really, who would I tell? My only close friends are the people it happened to.

Nick is digesting. Finally, he asks, "I'm guessing they got away with it?"

I nod. "According to the guys, David James screamed at them about the PC and the Macallan scotch but never mentioned any videos or messages."

"How old were they?"

"I think they were in high school. They're two years older than I am. Maybe the first year of college. Honestly, I don't remember, and we've never talked about it again. They may not even remember our conversation, as drunk as they were when they told me."

"They didn't say anything to anyone else about it? The cops?" Nick asks.

I give him a look. "It's Jamie's father. He was young; a kid. He couldn't turn in his own dad. Could you?"

Nick doesn't answer that. "Did they recognize the girl?"

My heart is pumping so hard I think both he and the guy at the snack counter must hear it. "Not exactly. But they described her. It kind of sounded like Natasha King. Pale, with reddish hair. I've seen photos and she wasn't a mature fourteen-year-old if you know what I mean. Stupid boys might have guessed her age wrong."

Nick's eyes flash. I can't tell exactly what he's thinking, but I have a pretty good idea. "Say more about this other guy, Hendrix?"

"He's been Jamie's best friend since fifth grade. His father worked at the Pentagon, which is how Hendrix ended up at West Point and then the Army. He was a Green Beret, which I guess is a big deal. On the A-Team. I thought that was just an old TV show, but apparently, it's a real thing." I'm babbling nervously.

"Hendrix is still in the military?"

"No. He had a bad experience a couple of years ago and went civilian. He's our head of security now." I roll the empty water bottle in my hands. "Anyway. You can be angry that we haven't told anyone before, but what would be the point? Let's say they did go to the police, now. That computer is long gone. A man was found guilty of killing Natasha King, and he's dead. Case closed. What judge would give you a warrant based on the word of two boys about something they saw twenty years ago? Something that might have actually been old-school computer porn?"

Nick nods. "Okay, yeah." He's thinking, his own water untouched. "You're about as deep at David James University as possible. The other day you told me if you thought anything bad was going on there you'd speak up. But you knew about this, and you haven't said anything."

That hits hard. I feel anger and shame mingling in my heart. "If there was anything at all that was sketchy at David James University I absolutely would report it. This is not connected to DJU. This is something else, something outside. Something between David James Ellington and Bishop Oliver. I've never seen anything remotely like it." I pause. "It's a horrible story, and probably true, but there's nothing that can be done about that now. And I'm telling you."

"Yeah, you are. Why are you telling me?" His frustration is palpable.

"Because maybe there's something that can be done to save Elspeth, if they're connected." I snap. I have no reason to be angry with him but I am. "Maybe you can use this to look for her now."

He's staring at me, all signs of the warm Nick Winston gone. "Have you personally seen anything that would make you connect David James and Bishop to what Jamie and Hendrix saw on the video?"

I don't know why he thinks asking the same question with different words will get him a different answer. "I promise you, I *would* speak up. If I saw something, and I thought going to the cops would stop it, save someone, I'd be there in a heartbeat. But I haven't." I sigh. "What I will say, though, is that I wouldn't put it past either David James or Bishop Oliver to be into this stuff.

They're jaded. When you can have anyone you want by wiggling your finger, what you can't have becomes much more enticing. I've seen it with some of the DJU guests. Tell them a certain girl isn't available, and that's the only one they have eyes for. Men are pathetic." I don't apologize or add a lame, "except you, of course."

"They absolutely are. I'm assuming you know what the Dark Web is?" he asks, watching me closely.

"A bit," I say, remembering my recent conversation with Hendrix. My anger has retreated, but I'm still defensive. I squeeze the bottle, and it makes a squeaking sound.

"What they described to you sounds like a child abuse site." Nick leans back in the stiff plastic seat and stares at nothing. His anger is retreating. After a long silence, he asks, "Have you ever heard them say anything that might be connected to something like that outside of DJU? Any talk about younger girls, filming, or... I don't know... anything?"

"If I had, I would have told you. Or someone. The thought that I might be connected to this, even accidentally or at the very edges, makes me nauseous."

Nick stares me down, hard. "Would Hendrix or Jamie talk to me?"

"You agreed not to approach them. I broke trust telling you. Please keep to our agreement." There's steel in my voice.

"Got it, just checking. Okay. This is useful, and frustrating as hell, but I appreciate it. I promise to keep our discussion between us, although I'm going to share enough with the lead detective so he knows he should look deeper at David James Ellington and Bishop Oliver." He pauses. "I believe I told you when I visited The Madalena Club where Natasha King and Elspeth Bridges went missing, I spoke to the manager. He worked there in 2002 in a different role. He said a young female visitor accused David James of molesting her, but the charges were dropped."

"I remember you telling us." I mutter, "He's usually very cautious about his reputation. I'm a little surprised he would take that kind of risk." A thought comes to me. "Maybe that's why. Maybe that incident is what triggered his hyper-vigilance."

"Maybe. Do you feel safe with him? With them," Nick asks.

"'Them' being David James and Bishop Oliver, or Jamie and Hendrix?"

"Both, I guess."

"I trust Jamie and Hendrix with my life. Literally." I squeeze the bottle again, and it crumples in my hand. "David James and Bishop? I wouldn't want to be alone with them for any length of time. In fact, I'd go to great lengths to avoid that. Bishop doesn't understand the word 'no,' and David James has a God complex."

Nick's look softens. "You take care of yourself, then. Be smart, be safe. If we dig into their activities, who knows what they'll do."

NICK

Back in my room, I walk up to the sliding glass door and study the board. It hasn't changed substantially since I arrived. There have been one hundred and fourteen potential leads called in, including three dozen 'spotted' calls. None of them proved actionable. That leaves a good chunk of empty space on my presentation board, and that space is demanding to be filled by all the thoughts that have been running laps around my brain for the past few days.

I grab two pads of sticky notes, one green, one blue, and start writing.

Surgeon: (blue)

STASIA K—dead sister, medical skill, doesn't believe Homer's guilty. BUT she's driving cross country

XANDER W—Cindy's son, doesn't believe Homer's guilt, threats to legals, history of violence, butcher experience

WILLOW W—Cindy's daughter, MISSING, know nothing about her. could be surgeon?

Olena K—did she really forget the legal team? She's not the surgeon, but may know who?

Cindy W—unlikely she's connected, but she's a nurse. Boyfriend?

Elspeth: (green)

DJE—prior accusation, known for attraction to young women, power / influence / affluence cover up

Bishop—could he be Sabine without DJE's knowledge?

Jamie / Hendrix—saw video but took no action. Involved in Dark Web project?

Ava—deep in DJU. Strong connection to Jamie & Hendrix. Would she tell their story if involved or thought they were?

I post the notes side by side on the board, and draw an arrow from the blue to the green because everyone on my blue list who might be involved in the Surgeon case is also connected to the historic disappearance of a girl twenty years ago. The Surgeon case isn't why I'm here, but there are too many coincidences. I don't like it, I don't buy it. Maybe what Ava shared today will help move the needle.

I call Rass to tell him about my conversation with Ava. He finally agrees that Natasha King and Elspeth Bridges are connected, and the key is The Madalena and David James Ellington. Tomorrow he will take it to his chief to discuss the next steps while I continue with my own methods. He also agrees that the Surgeon's victims so far also have a link, but he's not fully bought in that connection extends to the missing girls. Yet.

Chapter 11

DAY TEN

THE SURGEON

The ideal location would be outside the city, in an area where everyday folks have no reason to go on nights and weekends. This does not meet that criteria, but it's the last option on my list, and so far the best one I can access on short notice. This isn't how I anticipated the final act of the StopSabine project playing out, but the plan came together so fast I've got to do the best I can with what I've got.

It's still early in the day and the world is relatively quiet, which I appreciate.

This last candidate is at the outer edge of a gentrifying area of the city that is becoming trendy with shops and restaurants. The only operational commercial enterprise is a block away and seems to work on three shifts. It will be important to time any in-and-out activity away from shift changes and deliveries. I have only hours to figure out what that schedule is. Fortunately it's a Saturday and if the Universe is on the side of the angels, the working factory isn't fully staffed on the weekend.

The building I'm looking at was a canned vegetables processor for nearly one hundred years, until it was acquired in the late 1990s and the location was closed when operations moved to a larger facility in South Carolina. The building is one piece of a real estate portfolio held in part to offset losses against revenues, but also with an eye toward future expansion as the area redevelops into mixed use residential and commercial.

From the building's exterior, I see some pros: the windows are high up on the sides of the three connected structures that form a U, and most are painted black. Light, especially deep in the guts of the interior, won't attract attention from the outside. The entire property is fenced, although there are a few spots where the fencing has been cut, presumably by squatters and drug users. That's something I'll need to investigate.

The con, and it's a big one, is that the property literally bumps up against an area that's transitioning from old industrial to retail and upscale commercial. Five years ago there would have been no one around outside of shift changes. Now, just two blocks away, cars circle the block looking for a parking spot.

After driving around the perimeter a few times, I park in the shopping district and walk back. One of the multiple vehicle-accessible gates is unlocked, which is interesting. I slip through and head to the door I've identified as the best choice for entry. A quick glance assures me there's no video security. It takes no effort to pick the lock. I have a couple of flashlights in the pockets of my cargo pants. I flip the largest one on to begin my exploration. Later, I'll switch to a headlamp, but for now, I want immediate control of the light.

Nearly 100,000 square feet of space laid out in a maze of large and small rooms amongst the three structures. The rooms closest to building entrances are marked with graffiti and trash from urban miners, partiers, and the homeless. I don't hear anything that would indicate there are current occupants.

The space is huge, and it takes twenty minutes to identify the ideal spot for my needs. Many of the rooms are completely empty, while others are graveyards for ancient machinery and equipment. I'm satisfied that the space will do, and am about to make my way back out, when I hear footsteps and voices coming toward me. I slip behind an old steel tank that smells vaguely of corn.

Two men are passing through this room on their way to another. They're walking with a confidence that says they've been here many times. They're relaxed, and excited about something. As they pass by, I recognize one of them. My gut clenches. What is he doing here?

Once the click of their footsteps is at a safe distance, I follow quietly behind to try to get a handle on what's happening. The click of shoes comes to a stop, but the chatter continues, in the next large room. A light source turns the blackness to light. As I near, I hear the men laughing about "the little dove." Before I have a chance to consider what little dove they're talking about, the terrified scream of a girl shatters the silence.

What the fuck.

I press against the wall and slowly, carefully, risk a peek around, and see the last thing I expected: Elspeth Bridges.

AVA

Someone is in the house. I hear them but can't see anyone. There's danger. I don't want them to find me. I wrap a bed sheet around my naked body and stumble from door to door, looking for a way to safety. Fear turns to panic. Each door I open leads to a grave, freshly dug dirt mounded at the edges. There's a single coral tulip in each hole.

I dash for the stairs, nearly tripping as my feet tangle in the bedsheet. Just as I start to step down, the stairs disappear, replaced by a literal mountain of coral tulips. I consider throwing myself into the soft floral bed, but at the last second, dozens of sword-like spikes rise out of the flowers. I grab the rail to stop myself from tumbling over.

I scream Jamie's name, and when there's no answer, I shout for Hendrix. Silence. Dark, ominous silence. Where are they? Why aren't they answering?

I turn the handle of a new door that appears near the bed. Another grave... this time, not empty. Jamie lies in the dark soil, handsome in his favorite suit. He clutches a single coral tulip in his folded hands. Then I realize his head looks like a bloody cauliflower.

I scream, anger and fear and heartbreak washing over me.

A long shadow falls across the grave, and I look up. The Surgeon looms over Jamie's body, and our eyes meet.

A hand touches my bare back, and I scream again. The Surgeon is gone.

My eyes fly open. I'm coiled tightly on my side. It was a nightmare. Just a nightmare. Relieved, I straighten my legs, loosen my arms, and roll onto my back to blink away sleep and let my heart find its normal rhythm. I open one eye. The sun is barely cresting the sky. Jamie's side of the bed is empty. Jamie and Hen have taken the dogs off on their crack-of-dawn run. He's fine. Everything's fine.

I yawn, stretch, and scream once more.

Bishop Oliver is sitting on the edge of my bed. "Bad dream?"

235

My brain is still clouded with remnants of the nightmare, and I briefly wonder if I'm still dreaming. How would Bishop get into the house? Why is he in my bedroom?

He pulls the sheet down, exposing my breast, and lowers his hand onto it. He squeezes it hard. "Nice. Exactly what I thought it would be like. Not bad for an old girl."

I roll away from him and wiggle across towards Jamie's side of the bed. Bishop crawls after me faster than I would expect, considering his size. Before I can slide out the other side, he's on top of me, pressed against my back. I can feel his hardness against my ass, and panic rises in my belly. *No, no, no. This bastard will not rape me!*

His breath, hot and moist, is against my ear. He jerks the sheet down to my ankles, so I'm fully exposed, then straddles me again. "No tramp stamp. Good. I've always hated those."

"Get *off* me." I hiss against the mattress. I try to move out from under him, but he grasps each of my wrists and presses me harder against the bed under his weight. He rotates his hips to be sure I feel his erection. He raises up and moves my hands to my sides, then shoves one of his knees between my thighs, forcing them apart. "Are you insane? Why are you doing this? Bishop, stop it!"

Bishop's tone goes from mocking to serious. "Let's talk about why you met Winston at Maymont yesterday?"

What the fuck. "Are you following me?"

"Let's just say we keep track of what's happening in the kingdom," Bishop responds, his voice cold.

"You know he's been asking a bunch of questions about DJU. He had a few more." *Jesus, how did I not plan an answer to this? Am I really that stupid?*

"Bullshit. You would have had Hendrix drive you. But you took your own car. You wanted alone time." Before I understand what's happening, he grasps both my wrists in his left hand and ropes them together with something that feels like his tie. Once I'm bound, his right hand moves between my thighs. I buck in shock as he pushes his fingers into me. "Ahh, you like that."

"Get the fuck off, Bishop! Jamie is going to kill you!" I shriek and try to throw him off, but he's at least twice my size. I debate screaming for help. Hendrix is with Jamie and the dogs. If Angie heard my scream, what would she do? More importantly, what would Bishop do? *Fuck!*

"Tell me the truth, now," he says in a low voice like he's trying to seduce me into something. His fingers are rough inside me, and then I feel his thumb come up and slide between my ass cheeks. He rubs himself against my backside, so I know how large and hard he is. He's intent on causing pain and humiliation, and if he can get his rocks off in the process, all the better. "Don't for a second think you belong to anyone but DJU, you little bitch. You're bought and paid for."

The hell I am.

How far is he going to take this? I'm in serious fucking trouble here. I grasp for the only thing my feeble brain can come up with. "I wanted to talk to him about Elspeth Bridges. The girl that's missing. Jamie and Hendrix make fun of my true crime addiction, so I didn't want to tell them. Winston was out in that area, and it was the only place I could think of for us to meet."

Bishop stops moving his fingers, and his voice is incredulous. "Seriously? You expect me to believe that load of shit?"

"Look in my bag on the coffee table. There's a notebook with a lot of flags and notes. It's my hobby. Amateur crime solving gives me something to do when I'm recruiting. Now, will you get the fuck off of me before I scream?" Somehow I manage to keep my voice calm.

Bishop slides away, and I roll to my side to watch him. With my hands tied behind my back, there's a sharp burst of pain in my shoulder. He grabs the oversized Fendi and pulls out my crime notebook. There are sticky flags and highlights throughout the thick spiral-bound notebook where I record my theories, and the most recent notes are about Elspeth Bridges. The only thing I wrote after meeting with Nick was "The Madalena."

Is he actually buying this lame excuse? Somehow? He flips through the pages, scanning a sentence here, a paragraph there. He gives me a mocking look. "This is pathetic."

"I didn't ask your opinion." I snap. "Now, will you fucking untie me and get the hell out of my bedroom? How do you expect us to move on from this, Bishop?" I make myself sound calm and in control, although I'm anything but.

"I expect you to say not a goddamn thing about this is how," he responds coldly. He's still reading snippets, occasionally grinning at something he sees. I wonder if he's laughing because he knows exactly what happened to some of the girls in those pages. "If you mention this to Jamie, or Hendrix, or anyone, you'll become a missing girl yourself. You got me?"

He tosses the book on the floor, dismissing it, apparently buying the story. My relief is temporary as he comes back to the bed. "I was really looking forward to continuing the interrogation." He grabs my bared nipple between his thumb and forefinger and twists hard until I cry out. He smiles. "Ah, can't resist having just a little bite before I go." He dips his head down, takes the same nipple into his mouth, and closes his teeth hard enough to cause pain but just shy of breaking the skin. "So sweet." He presses me flat and unties my hands. "Not a word, my dear. Not a word."

NICK

Rass has a meeting this morning, so I'm on my own for breakfast. I need some cheering, so I order strawberry pancakes with extra whipped cream. Polly laughs and shakes her head but puts in the order. While I wait, I open my laptop and the spreadsheet of all the cases the four 'legal victims,' as the press has dubbed them, worked on over the last twenty years.

Using my finger as a mark, I scan the rows of cases. The judge and the two attorneys worked in the same courthouse for twelve years. Both the district attorney, Damien Simpson, and the public defender, Miles Cameron, moved to private practice around 2005. Chief Gifford just retired. There are a lot of opportunities to connect these folks. We just have to find the right connection.

I ignore the fact that this is not my case.

A date gets my attention. Summer of 2002. *State of Virginia vs. H. Williams.* I know that name. Why do I know that name? The actual case files aren't included in the spreadsheet, but Virginia conveniently has some of its records available online. I click into a browser window, search for the site, and enter the case number.

It only takes a couple of clicks to find what I'm after. H. Williams is Homer Williams. Homer Williams, the convicted killer of Natasha King. Natasha King, the other girl to go missing at The Madalena. What the actual hell?

I pull out my phone and text Rass. *"This is either a mighty big coincidence, or I may have found a connection, not just to the girls, but maybe even the Surgeon. We need to talk."*

Rass calls back before my phone is out of my hand and what he says confirms my findings. "Apparently Xander Williams sent a letter to the editor about his father's case, that also ties the first four Surgeon victims together. For some reason the paper sat on it for a day, deciding what to do with it, before they contacted us."

Before I can say anything, Rass continues. "We identified the 'bad man' who died in the last video. One Bernard McNeill. In a photo at the scene, his daughter was wearing a pink watch. So was Tasha King when she was found, although her family claimed she didn't own a pink watch. It's looking more and more like the Surgeon is going after those connected to Homer William's case. We're going to find Xander Williams and have a conversation." He says he'll call me back shortly.

Holy shit.

My breakfast arrives with a refill of coffee, and I pick at it, too distracted to enjoy the treat. I've spoken with three people who should recognize at least the names of the Surgeon's victims: Xander Williams, Olena King, and Stasia King. Yet no one brought it up or has in any way indicated they knew the men. Really? Not one of them would have said, during one of our chats, "Hey, that's the prosecutor or the judge or the public defender"?

Maybe they made the connection but didn't think it was about the King case. Doubtful, but possible. I have to believe one of them would comment on it.

"What's the matter, doll? Pancakes don't taste good?" Polly asks, noticing the nearly untouched stack in front of me.

"Oh, no, they're great. Just got a lot on my mind. Can I ask you something?" She nods. "Have you ever had to go to court for anything? Not traffic court, but a trial of some sort. As a juror, a friend of one of the parties, or a party yourself. I don't mean to pry."

She laughs. "Oh, honey, you're not prying. I've been to court twice, both related to my stupid son-of-a-bitch ex-husband. What do you want to know?"

"Do you remember the name of the judge or your ex's attorney? Your own attorney?"

"I don't remember the judge's name, but I remember the asshole representing my ex. That rat bastard made it so the other rat bastard didn't have to pay hardly a thing in child support. I hated that man. I don't think I could ever forget his name, or his smirk, or his laughing eyes when the judge gave him what he wanted." She looks angry at the memory, then waves a it away. "But it turned out all right. My girl went to college. Now she's a nurse. Without his help. And I found a much better partner. One who understands me." She winks and wiggles her rainbow-painted nails in my direction.

I smile. "Thanks. And now, my appetite is back." I build a forkful of pancakes, berries, and cream and tuck in, making happy sounds.

"Good, good. Can't have you going hungry, a growing boy. Let me know if there's anything else I can do for you."

I nod, but she's done enough. Hate is a powerful glue. I find it hard to believe Olena could forget the man who tried to defend her child's killer, or that Xander Williams wouldn't remember the name of the man who orchestrated his father's death sentence.

NICK

Olena King still comes to the Bridges' each evening after work, although she's sleeping in her own bed. It's an hour's trip each way. She's a good friend.

I time my visit to coincide with her arrival. I have questions.

Patrick and Anna move like zombies, in a limbo between life going on around them and wondering where their child is. It's been more than a week, and it doesn't feel like we're any closer than when we started. It's not uncommon—I think about Olivia Baden's abduction, which set her father Peter on his mission to help the families and survivors. She was gone for more than a year, with not a single solid lead. It's a good news, bad news situation: if a victim is found quickly, they're usually deceased. If they're not found shortly after their abduction, they might be dead, but not necessarily. Jaycee Dugard was found alive eighteen years after she went missing.

Olena arrives just after I do, arms loaded with containers of fried chicken from a local chain. I help her unpack everything onto the kitchen counter. We work in companionable silence. I like to believe we've developed a level of trust between us. It will hurt if she's been holding out.

Patrick and Anna sit silently on the couch in the adjoining family room, each in their own corner of the large sectional. Their daughter, Margot, is staying with a friend for a few days. She told Olena, "I feel like I'm living in a nightmare."

"Come on, you two, have some food," Olena prompts. "I can make you a plate."

Patrick joins us, moving slowly toward the kitchen. He looks ten years older than the day I met him. His blond hair is turning an ashy gray. There are lines where there were none before. His eyes seem permanently red and hooded, swollen from tears. "Thanks, Lena, for everything you've done for us." He says this regularly, automatically. He allows her to spoon coleslaw and potatoes onto

243

his plate and watches with disinterest when she adds two pieces of chicken. He takes the food to the couch and sits with the plate balanced on his lap. He doesn't eat.

"Anna? What can I bring you?" Olena calls softly. The woman turns to look at us, shakes her head no; she doesn't want anything. "Promise you'll eat something before you sleep. Please."

Anna nods vaguely and returns her attention to the television. They're talking about the Surgeon, again. The story is big news to people all across the country, perhaps even around the world, but I am confident that, for Anna, it's a distant second to her missing child.

Olena and I make plates for ourselves, and I tip my head toward the formal dining room with a questioning look. She nods, and we sit at the large table. "God, I remember these days. The waiting for absolutely nothing to change. Being terrified that the police will finally come, but only to deliver bad news. It's the pain of having hundreds of small nails driven into your skin, hour-by-hour. You become numb to it after a while. You know it's there, and it hurts, but it starts to feel... normal."

"I can't imagine what you went through or that she's going through. I've been with families through these events many times, both as an FBI agent and in my current role, but I won't ever be able to put myself in your shoes, having no children of my own." I soak up coleslaw juice with a biscuit. It reminds me of summertime as a kid.

"Strangely, parts of that period are seared into my flesh. Other things are hazy. It all sort of blends together." Olena sighs.

She's given me the perfect opening for my question. "Do you remember the legal team who took Homer Williams to trial? Did you participate much?"

Olena picks at the crust on a chicken thigh while she thinks. "We didn't have anything to do with the case until the sentencing. We sat in the courtroom during the trial, though. I remember the judge's name, I think. Miller or something like that."

"You don't remember the prosecutor?"

She thinks, then shakes her head. "No."

"What about the attorney who was representing Williams?"

She thinks again, again shakes her head no. "Why?"

"The four men assaulted by the Surgeon were each involved in the case. The judge, the chief of police, the prosecutor, and the public defender."

Her mouth drops open, and she stares at me. I can see her brain working behind those intense dark eyes, rewinding twenty years. "I don't remember any of them except the judge. Oh my god. What does this mean? Why would someone attack these people? I don't understand." She takes a breath and repeats, with more force, "I don't understand!"

I put my hand over hers, hoping to reassure her. "They worked on other cases together, not just the Homer Williams trial. But it's an odd coincidence."

"Odd doesn't feel like the right word. Bizarre. Frightening, even. If this is related to Natasha's case, would they come after us? Me? Stasia?" She asks, her voice suddenly very quiet, nearly a whisper. "I've got to tell her!"

"What do you mean?" I'm not following.

"Well, why would the Surgeon pick those four people and do what he's doing? It sounds like revenge to me. The outcome of that event was that Homer Williams was sentenced to death. Stasia says that Homer's children don't believe he's guilty. Could they be involved?" She is absolutely pale. "If the Surgeon is angry about Homer Williams' conviction, he might also come after Stasia and me."

At no point did I consider that the King family might be in danger. Is she right? Should they be worried? I don't think so, but the idea that Xander or the mysterious Willow might be involved isn't farfetched. Hell, Cindy Williams is an operating room nurse. She'd have access to the tools and knowledge needed although she's not big enough to move men the size of McNeill. My gut says that while there may be a tie to the Natasha King case, Olena and Stasia are safe. "I can't imagine anyone would have animosity toward you, but I'll talk to

Detective Rasmussen about keeping an eye out. I'm sorry. I didn't mean to upset you."

She gives me a nervous smile. I change the subject. "Have you spoken with Stasia? How's the trip going?"

"Not today, but it looks like she's having a good time from the photos she's loading into the Instagram." Olena is clearly as relieved as I am to talk about something else, although I can tell she's still worried. She unlocks her phone and opens Instagram. She must have very few connections because the feed is almost exclusively photos related to Stasia's trip. "She's been a busy girl."

She swipes through the images. Each has a short caption and a couple of comments. The most recent post says, "David Rice Atchison's grave in Independence, Missouri."

Olena makes a face. "That's strange."

"What is?" To me, the very idea that someone cares enough to visit presidential grave sites is strange.

"Truman's grave is in Independence, not Atchison's."

"I've never heard of David Rice Atchison."

"That's because he was a reluctant president, just for one day, which happened to be Stasia's birthday, with one hundred fifty years in between. Stasia wrote a report about him in school. That's the only reason I know him. His story is what started her obsession with presidents, and eventually their graves. You can understand why I'm surprised she misidentified the location of Atchison's gravesite as Independence." Olena shrugs and stands, taking both our plates back to the kitchen.

I tackle the dishes while Olena sits with Anna. The woman leans into Olena and rests her head on her shoulder. It makes me feel better that Olena doesn't remember her team. It's good to know she hasn't been haunted by them for the last twenty years.

AVA

"Bishop texted. He and David James want to have dinner tonight. I told them yes," Jamie is moving around, collecting all the bits and pieces he needs for his day. He's swapped jeans and a polo for a navy suit. It's the same suit I saw him buried in, in my nightmare.

Jamie and Bishop have never had a warm relationship. They each recognize the other as vital to the success of David James Ellington, and therefore David James Group. On Jamie's part, at least, there's a wariness there. I think it's easier for him to place the blame for his father's greatest failings at Bishop's feet.

Bishop. That motherfucker is trying to play me. He knows the last thing I want to do is sit next to him for two hours, but there isn't a way in hell I'll let him see he upset me. I didn't tell Jamie or Hendrix about what happened. It's humiliating. I'm also a little bit worried about what would happen if I told them. I am going to keep the dogs in the bedroom when Jamie is gone. Although I'm pretty sure if Bishop wants to come at me again, it won't be here, and I won't get away a second time.

After Bishop left, I ran for the shower to wash his stink off my skin, wash away the memory of his hands on me, his fingers in me. I tried to go back to sleep, but sleep wouldn't come. I can only imagine what the next nightmare will be like.

As far as Jamie knows, I was in bed while he was off getting his endorphins. How I love this beautiful man. I tell myself the sheets smell like him and me. Not fucking Bishop Oliver. They'll be going in the washing machine as soon as Jamie's gone. Or the trash. "Sounds good. Will you pick me up for a proper date?"

Jamie dips down and kisses me, all smiles. "I absolutely will pick you up for a proper date. Hendrix has something to do tonight, so he won't be available to drive. We'll need to stay out of trouble."

"We can take my car. Nice night to go topless," I tease.

247

He smacks me on the butt through the sheet and kisses the top of my head. "Now I'll have the thought of you topless in my head all day as I talk to bankers and permit guys." He slips his wallet into his inside coat pocket, wraps his watch around his wrist, and is gone.

I yell after him, "Let the dogs up!" Two warm bodies are just what I need.

THE SURGEON

A stylized piece of matte metal with 'K Studios' carved into it sits above a large red warehouse-style door with a 12" square reinforced glass window. This is the studio of one of the most famous photographers in the country, maybe even the world. Models and actors consider a session with Kodak a sign they've made it.

My friend Sophie is nearly six feet tall with waist-length naturally red hair that would make any Scotswoman proud. She reaches for the old-school black doorbell next to the door and presses. She smiles and hands me her red leather portfolio, then bends to adjust the strap on her sandal. The arch of her back, the curve of her ass, the length of her legs, are connected so perfectly she doesn't seem real.

There's a buzz, and an audible click as the door unlocks. Sophie takes her portfolio back and enters. I follow.

"Well, hello!" Kodak bellows from the top of the metal staircase leading to his studio. His smile drops when he realizes she's not alone. His tone is chiding. "I was only expecting you, Sophie. Who's the dude?"

Sophie floats breezily up the stairs. "My manager. Don't worry. He's easy going."

Kodak makes it clear he isn't thrilled, but he's committed to the session. Sophie and I know the request was made by an important friend, the kind of friend you don't refuse. "Well, come on then. You need portfolio shots, yes? Anything specific in mind?"

Sophie coos at him. "Just adding to my book. You're the best, and I want the best."

"How old are you, Soph? You don't mind if I call you Soph, do you?" Kodak wraps an arm around her waist and leads her toward the set in the middle of the large space.

This is going to be easy.

Kodak and Sophie talk about the sorts of photos she's after. A few headshots, a full-length body shot, and a couple of editorial and commercial options. She's brought outfit changes in a large duffel bag. Kodak takes the bag and sets it near a door that presumably leads to a dressing room.

"Shall we start with the headshots? You've got a good sense of what looks good on you. That dress is perfect." He motions her toward a wall of white and drags over a tall stool. Sophie perches on the stool and beams at him. "Very nice. You're a natural. But you already know that."

Sophie follows Kodak's instruction as he directs her in various expressions: happy, sad, thoughtful, petulant, intrigued, flirty. She moves easily, and Kodak is obviously pleased with the results. He ignores me.

"You'll have plenty to work with in the headshot category. What did you bring for outfits?" Kodak swaps cameras while Sophie goes to her bag and pulls out various pieces of clothing.

"Bikini, of course. Jeans and a tank, a couple of fashion-forward bits," she pauses as she digs through. "I brought a few different necklaces to get your opinion." She holds up a navy blue suit that is absolutely stunning with her coloring. "How about this for a corporate look? I need help deciding which piece." She unties the string of the green halter dress she's wearing, and it falls to the floor, leaving her nude except for a tiny beige thong. Sophie looks around for somewhere to hang the suit and eventually slips the hanger over a nail in the drywall.

Kodak doesn't hesitate to join her, his hands on her bare body as she shows him the first necklace she brought to coordinate with the designer suit. She holds a pearl choker against the blue. "Too old school?" She drops the necklace into the jacket pocket and brings up a silver choker in her other hand, "Or this?"

Kodak doesn't notice her trade the pearls for a syringe when her hand dips into the jacket's pocket. When she jabs the needle into his neck, he yells in shock and fury and hits her hard, sending her flying into a stack of tripods. Sophie slides to the ground, but she's grinning. "Get it out of your system while you can, big boy, because you're about to lose your shit. Motherfucker."

The photographer tries to come at her, but the drugs are taking effect. Realization dawns. He looks my way and realizes his error. It's too late to do anything. His knees buckle under him, and he falls to the ground.

Sophie gets to her feet, kicking off the sandals. She pads barefoot to her bag, pulls out jeans and the tank top, and gets dressed. She slides her feet into hot pink flip-flops and packs up the rest of her belongings. "That was fun. You need anything else?"

"That's it," I grin.

"Cool. I'll see you later! Oh! Almost forgot," Sophie opens her purse, finds her checkbook, scribbles out a check, and lays it on the table next to Kodak's cellphone. "For services rendered." She wiggles her fingers at me and disappears down the stairs.

When we entered the studio, I checked for video cameras and found none, much to my surprise. Does Kodak not want a permanent record of the things he does here? Or are the cameras hidden very well? I'll have to take my chances.

I remove the equipment from one of Kodak's rolling camera cases and maneuver the skinny guy inside. He's tall, so I have to bend him, but eventually, I fold him in and latch the hard-sided case. I suppose I should move quickly so he doesn't suffocate, but it's hard to care too much.

I take a few seconds to retrace our steps over the last hour. Sophie rang the bell and touched the stool, which is fine. There is evidence of a regular shoot on Kodak's camera, and her check is confirmation she's come and gone. The only thing I touched is the case, and that's coming with me. I didn't even need to use the gloves in my jacket pocket. Clean. Nice.

I roll the case toward the freight elevator and hit the call button with my elbow. Minutes later, the case is loaded into my vehicle and we're en route to our final destination. There'll be another photo studio, but this one is deep within the bowels of the empty factory.

There are no other cars on the property. I think I'm alone, but I take five minutes to do a quick check inside. All clear. When I get back to the vehicle, the case is still.

When I was here earlier I left one of the dock doors unlocked. I drive in and lock the door behind me. I strap on a hunting headlamp to help guide me into the guts of the building. When I drag the case out of the back of the SUV, I don't worry about giving the photographer a soft landing. But there's no sound from inside. I'm a little bit disappointed.

The interior is a maze, but I've been here a couple of times since this morning so I'm confident. The part of the building we'll be using is nothing but concrete floors, with puddles of water where a pipe is leaking and patches of oil from some long-removed machine. It's a three-minute hike from the dock door to this spot. This area is cleaner than the rest. And it has a new generator. I flip switches, and a dozen industrial halogens come on. It's been a busy day.

The room is forty-feet square, with fifteen-foot ceilings, two steel doors, and no windows. There's a drain in one corner, and water has pooled nearby. There are three six-foot by six-foot steel cages on another wall with an eight-foot gap between each. The cages are the kind used to transport apes and gorillas safely. They're indestructible. Each of the cages has a raised steel floor to allow urine and feces to drop through, an attached water bowl, and an attached food dish. They're locked with heavy-duty discus non-pickable padlocks.

I wheel the camera case to the middle cage. I'm pretty sure Kodak hasn't revived yet, but to be safe, I have another syringe at the ready and a gun, although I won't use that unless I have absolutely no choice. The bastard isn't getting off that easy. I carefully unlatch the case, and Kodak is still out.

I navigate him into the cage. I remove his clothes—denim coveralls with many pockets over a gaudy Hawaiian print shirt. Kodak is wearing a florescent orange G-string. Jesus.

Once the guy is naked, I lock the door with the padlock and put Kodak's clothes into the camera case. That'll be destroyed later.

Three cameras and three spotlights are focused on a surgical table in the middle of the room. A surgeon's scrubs and safety equipment are hanging from a temporary screen. On a folding table nearby but out of camera shot, a neat stack of cardboard sits with computer-generated words applied to each individual piece of paper.

Everything is ready. Only a little while longer until we can end this, and rescue Elspeth.

I hear a sound from the hallways leading into the room and smile.

Stasia forces a smile in return. "I guess we're getting to the main event."

"It's almost over. I'll be back." I check the safety of the pistol and lay it on the table with the cardboard. "He's out cold, so I don't think you'll need this, but just in case."

She nods. "I'll be fine. See you in a bit."

I hurry back toward the SUV. I've got more work to do.

XANDER

It's a typical Friday evening, with a good crowd even though it's still early. Everyone's in a good mood, with high energy and lots of laughter. I love these sorts of nights. They're also the nights I'm most likely to make bad choices of the very best kind. Not this weekend, though. Need to keep my shit together. Once my assistant manager gets here, I'm going back upstairs.

A crew of day-drinking college kids pulled in an hour ago and took over the pool tables and surrounding booths. One cute little blonde cheerleader keeps coming to the bar to get drinks for her friends. She's the soberest of the bunch, which isn't saying much. Every time she gets to the bar, she uses it as a breast rest for her ample bosom. Used to be, I had no problem succumbing to the flirtations of barely-legal college girls. Now that I see forty coming in a few years, it feels creepy. A little too much like David James Ellington and his buddies. I send the honey back to her friends with a cold, "Move along now." If you show any warmth to girls like this, they consider it an invitation.

The door opens and two uniformed cops saunter in. They're not here for a snack. They scan the room intently, and their eyes come to rest on me.

Of course they're here. I knew they'd come. I've thought about what I'd do when this happened. How I'd play it cool. How I'd answer their questions honestly and to the best of my ability.

What do I actually do?

I run. I slip out the end of the bar into the kitchen, then dash out the back door. Apparently, I wasn't subtle because the cops aren't for a minute fooled into thinking I'm checking on an order of pizza fries. I hear shouts and assume my kitchen guys are doing their best to slow down the law. Even though they're likely confused as hell, they're team Xander.

On the street, I head north toward the busiest part of the district. Worst case, I'll blend into the crowd; best case, I'll find a friend and disappear. Either way,

I don't have long to decide because Fredericksburg's finest are not far behind. There's a concert in the park tonight. College kids and tourists mingle on the crowded sidewalk, and usually, I'd be annoyed by the congestion. Tonight I'm grateful.

I make a sharp left into the tattoo shop in a particularly thick crowd of folks. I've got lots of ink and have worked with the owner several times. Lucky for me, he's working on a memorial tattoo. "Dude, can I hang in back for a bit?"

Trey shrugs, and I slip into his office. I drop onto the old leather couch with its rips and stains and fold myself in half, wrapping my arms around my knees.

Fuck, fuck, fuck. Think, Xan. Think. Of course, I knew they'd be coming to talk after the letter to the editor. I was kind of surprised they didn't contact me after the email to Gifford. *Fuck, fuck, fuck.* Running was not the right choice. I should've just stuck with the plan and stayed put. But true to form, instinct overrode common sense, and now I've taken something uncomfortable and made it a pain in the ass. *Fuck, fuck, fuck.*

Oddly, I fall asleep. Trey wakes me with a kick to my foot. I'm dizzy from having my head on my knees. "Who you running from? Law or pussy?"

That makes me laugh. "Law, sadly. I didn't do anything. Well, I didn't do anything criminal."

"Do I want to know?" Trey falls into the desk chair and lights up his vape pen. He offers it to me, and I take a hit.

"Nah. But thanks for that," I motion to the pen, "and for letting me hang out. What time is it?"

"Just shy of midnight."

I've been here more than an hour. Good. It's a busy night. Hopefully something else has got their attention. I'll make my way to my car, which is parked on a side street, then head to Mom's and spend the night there. Tomorrow I'll go to the station and present myself for a conversation. It's not like they have anything to hold me on. Obviously, they just want to talk.

Yeah, that's a good plan.

My plan is not their plan, however, and as soon as I turn the corner to get to my car, I hear the "whoop whoop" of a police siren and an amplified voice instructs me to put my hands against the side of the building. My stupid inner child orders me to *Run!* again but this time, I manage to resist.

AVA

If Bishop thought he would turn me into a cowering mess, he's wrong. We arrive at the restaurant simultaneously, and I glide up to them, kissing Bishop's cheek first, then allowing David James to pull me in for a hug. When Bish pulls his usual touchy-feely routine, I laugh and manage him as I always do, until David James tells him to knock it off, as he always does. When Jamie and I first became a couple, Jamie would get angry when Bish pulled his usual stunts. It took a while for me to convince him I can handle myself, and if it gets to be too much, I'll do something about it. I also reminded him that my ability to roll with the punches is why his father trusts me in my position. I'm not easily offended. Jamie doesn't like it, but he understands.

We're seated at a table in a quiet corner of the restaurant, the one David James always chooses when he's in town. I'm seated with Bishop to my left and Jamie to my right. Bishop's hand brushes my thigh repeatedly, and I remove it repeatedly. If he doesn't stop, I'll cut one of his fingers off with my steak knife. I don't think David James would be upset. He has a weird sense of humor.

The men talk about business, including developments in the Pacific Northwest and Singapore. They're in discussion with 'friends' who are helping to pave the way for a new project in Saudi Arabia. David James lets me know there will be a gathering of DJU friends next month at his estate in Wainscott in the East Hamptons. Fifty guests are invited for an evening of fun, with eight spending the night. Eight and companions, of course.

Jamie and I don't attend those parties. That part of David James' world has nothing to do with us. But some of my girls will go. Mercedes will decide.

After dinner, we say goodnight as we wait for our cars to be retrieved by the valets. Bishop continues his smiling assault on my body, which I avoid by snuggling up to Jamie, who doesn't object in the least. We're driving my Porsche 911 Carrera. The top is already down since it's a beautiful night. David James and Bishop are in one of the DJ Group suburbans. Their car arrives before ours, and I watch with relief as Bishop slides across the rear seat and is finally out of my thoughts, at least for tonight.

As I'm thinking this, I realize something's wrong. The driver wears the right DJ Group uniform of black trousers, shirt, and jacket. He's wearing a baseball cap pulled down low over his eyes. At night.

"Look," I say to Jamie and nod toward the SUV. The driver's hand is on David James' back. He moves him into the SUV. He's *touching* David James. No DJ Group driver would dare touch David James.

Jamie starts to step out of the Porsche, but the SUV pulls away, moving quickly. Jamie slams the door closed. "Hold on."

I clip my seatbelt into place and grip the door handle as Jamie gives chase. The restaurant is at the edge of an industrial area with lots of quiet streets at this time of night. The SUV driver clearly knows where he's going. He turns left, then right, doing 60 in a 30 MPH zone. There are few, if any, police here this late.

"Should I call 911?" I ask as we screech around a corner.

Jamie says, "Not yet. But get ready." He turns hard to keep up with the SUV.

Four minutes into the chase, the SUV driver decides he's had enough company. He slows just enough to let Jamie catch up. When we're immediately behind him, he brake checks us. Jamie is on high alert, but he doesn't have time to stop, and my Porsche rams into the back of the heavily reinforced SUV. We have no chance. The front of the Porsche crumbles. The SUV takes off.

Jamie is swearing behind a wall of deployed airbags. The giant airbag in front of me has battered my chest and ribs, and I think my right wrist is sprained or broken, but we're both alive. I hit the final digit on my phone to connect to 911.

"911, what's your emergency?" The operator says in a monotone voice.

"I need to report a kidnapping." My voice is hoarse. I cough to clear it. "David James Ellington was just carjacked. Or, I think, kidnapped. He's in the vehicle that was taken." Then, as an afterthought, I add, "We were trying to follow, but the driver slammed on his brakes, and we hit him hard, so we need EMT as well."

I give her the location from the GPS display and hang up. "You okay?"

"I think I have a broken nose and possibly a broken leg." Jamie runs careful fingers over his face and makes pained sounds at his cheekbone and brow, where his head banged against the steering wheel. "Did you see which way they went?"

"All I saw was airbags." I try to open my door but the frame is bent and the door is stuck. I unlatch my seatbelt with my good hand, kick off my shoes and step up onto my seat. It takes a moment for the dizziness to stop. "Is the car on fire? I smell smoke."

Jamie shakes his head and groans. "No, that's the air bags. Little mini bomb type things make them deploy."

I carefully step over the passenger side window, which was down, thank God. I don't care that my short dress rides up. When I get to him, I try to pull open the door, but it's stuck, too. "Shit. Shit shit. Let me see." He turns toward me. His face is covered in blood. "You're going to have a shiner, for sure. I think you're right; your nose is broken."

"You've always admired the rugged look," Jamie tries to joke, then moans again. Sirens are approaching, thank God. He looks at me. "I love you."

"I love you too, idiot."

"Damn..." he mutters. I know he's referring to the SUV.

"Damn." I agree.

Two police cars, a fire truck, and an ambulance approach with sirens blaring. I want to cover my ears against the sound but my bum wrist complains when I try. My head has begun to pound. Stress, smoke, shock. I almost wish I was a fainter so I could sleep through this next bit and wake up in the safe comfort of a hospital.

Jamie is extricated from the car and loaded into the ambulance, and I'm directed to sit on a bench next to him. Two police officers are dealing with the trashed vehicle, and the other two are asking questions and taking notes about the carjacking slash kidnapping. When we explain for the third time who is in the carjacked vehicle, they finally get it and seem to find motivation. Suddenly there is all sorts of activity on their phones and radios.

They release us to the hospital, telling us they'll have detectives meet us there. Jamie closes his eyes on the gurney, and I grip his hand.

"Damn." He says again.

NICK

I'm on a mission. Something isn't adding up. My ever-persistent Spidey senses are whispering, "Stasia. Look at Stasia." But why? Just because she's a doctor? She's got skills, but as she said, she's an ER doc, not a surgeon. Does she have a motive? The legal team was involved with her sister's case. Even if she doesn't believe Homer Williams killed her sister, why would she want to hurt these men? And there's no concrete evidence that the victims we've seen so far had anything to do with Tasha's death. How the Surgeon described McNeill and his daughter—could Natasha King have been the girl McNeill chose as a replacement?

And none of it matters, because Stasia King has been driving west since the attacks started. Hasn't she?

The first attack happened the night before Stasia left New York.

I open Instagram and search for Stasia's account. Probably should have paid closer attention when Olena showed me the most recent photos. The account name is something about dead presidents. I play around with several possible accounts and finally get lucky with "DeadPresRambler."

On Sunday, there's a photo of a rest stop in Hackettstown, New Jersey. The next photo is the Wyandott Popcorn Museum in Marion, Ohio. There's also a Harding Memorial photo with no caption other than "#29, Marion, Ohio." A second photo is of the Huber Machinery Museum. Dinner was a hot dog and root beer float at an old-school drive-in, complete with carhop service. This is the day the attorney lost his tongue.

On day two, we see a photo of William Henry Harrison, 9th president, laid to rest in North Bend, Ohio. President Benjamin Harrison, the grandson of William and president #23, is buried in Indianapolis. That day's fun food is a giant Dutch baby pancake. It looks amazing. Angel and I will have to try making that when I'm home. The photo makes my stomach growl. Then I remember

263

that's the day the attorney lost his ears and my stomach rumbles for a different reason.

Stasia posted photos of Truman and Atchison's graves on her third travel day. That's the one Stasia messed up that got Olena's attention. I query Dr. Google and learn that Independence, where President Truman is buried, and Plattsburgh, where the one-day president Atchison resides, are less than an hour apart. The error could have been carelessness. There was a tornado in Missouri that day. Stasia posted photos of the darkened sky. This is the day the Judge lost his hands.

Wednesday, she traveled from Missouri to a park in Colorado. Dr. Google tells me it's easily a 10-hour drive. There are a handful of nature photos and a video tour of a charming Schitt's Creek-style motel. There were no attacks that day, but that was the day the video directing us to the Dark Web was released.

Yesterday was the first Dark Web video, certainly the most brutal to date, with the first death. According to Stasia's Instagram, she traveled from Colorado to Jackson Hole, Wyoming, where she bought a beautiful turquoise cuff bracelet.

There are a number of photos to document the trip.

But are there? The pictures are scenery shots. With a reverse image search, Google assures me they're originals, not borrowed. Yet not a single photo shows her face, and only a few show any part of her body.

I open my phone and find the call log. I added her number the day we met. We've spoken and texted multiple times in the days since. I'm going to have Rass trace the location of her phone. It's not technically his case, but I think I can persuade him.

I may be a victim of my own overactive imagination because there's no possible way Stasia King can be in two places simultaneously. Still, something is off. My Spidey senses are screaming at me that Stasia King is involved. Somehow.

XANDER

Officers Tweedle Dee and Tweedle Dum were generous enough to give me a lift in the back of their standard-issue SUV, then promptly handed me off to a Detective Carl Rasmussen. It's been a while since I've seen the inside of the Fredericksburg police station but from what I remember, nothing much has changed except maybe some of the faces. Detective Carl "call me Rass" Rasmussen seems okay. In a good cop/bad cop routine, my sense is, he'd be the good cop. He's got short-cropped brown hair that's starting to gray, and grey-blue eyes. I bet he was on the track team in high school.

"Can I get you a soda? Water? Coffee? Running from the police can parch a person." His tone isn't mean or mocking. He's not laughing at me, he's laughing with me. This will be an interesting conversation.

When I shake my head no, he slips into the only other chair in the small interrogation room. I don't think they've updated the decor since last time I was here. The beige table and black plastic chairs look exactly like what I remember. I even smell the same unpleasant blend of burnt coffee, dirty ashtray and sweat.

"Why'd you run when you saw the officers?" Rass asks as if we're two pals having a beer, and he's just curious. He's relaxed in his hard plastic chair, a notebook open on the table in front of him. He makes no move to pick up the pen.

That's a good question, and one I can answer honestly. "I have no freaking idea. It was stupid. Fight or flight, I guess."

"Usually people who haven't done anything wrong don't have that kind of reaction to our boys in blue." Rass says. He flips open what I presume to be my file. "Looks like you've visited us before, although it's been quite some time. Good for you for staying out of trouble." He makes a show of reading the notes. I'm sure he read them before he sets foot in this room. That's okay. *You play your games, I'll play mine.* "Wow. You nearly sawed a guy's hand off?"

"Nah. Just held his arm on the plate and thought about it a while." I grin. As he pointed out, it's been a long time. I've dealt with my anger—mostly—and talking about this particular incident doesn't bother me at all. Court-ordered therapy can be effective, apparently.

"I can read what happened, but want to give me your version?"

I shrug. "Sure. Wallace, another employee at Paco & Patches, really liked to jerk my chain. He seemed to get off on trying to rile me up. That particular day, he was successful. He made one too many comments implying butchering people ran in my family. I grabbed hold of him and held his arm on the bone saw plate. Told him if he didn't shut up with that shit... and let him guess the rest."

"Was the saw running?" Rass asks, ever curious.

"Yep. But I knew what I was doing, even being that angry. I'm not a monster. I would never cut a man's hand off," I say this clearly, while looking Detective Rasmussen directly in the eye. The door is open, he is now invited to walk through.

"Interesting you chose that wording. You haven't asked why you're here, have you?" Rass notes.

"Hmm, what could it be?" I scratch my chin in mock puzzlement. "I may not be a fancy-ass detective, but I'm also not an idiot. I've sent communications to a couple of guys who have recently turned up injured. You'd be the criminals if you didn't at least bring me in to chat."

"Did you run because you knew we'd have something to talk about?" Rass asks. He's still relaxed, nothing-to-worry-about-here.

"Nah. I think that was just knee-jerk from the olden days." I smile. "So, let's chat. What would you like to know?"

"Cool, cool. Right to it. I like it." Rass closes my file and draws the notebook toward him. "In the last week you've sent an email to Chief Gifford, hand-delivered a greeting card at the office of Damien Simpson, and just yesterday you emailed a letter to the editor of the *Fredericksburg Free-Lance Star* making some very serious accusations about four of the five victims of the person calling himself the Surgeon. And, coincidentally, you're pretty skilled with cutting instruments. Odd timing, wouldn't you say?"

I shrug. "Considering what slimeballs they are, I find it highly unlikely that I'm the only one who has less than loving feelings toward them."

"If there was any evidence that supported your assertions, that might be true. What makes you think these men are as nefarious as you claim?"

It's a reasonable question, but I can't answer just yet, at least not with proof. "My gut. Logic. Common sense." I start ticking things off on my fingers, and with each new fact my voice raises, even as I try to stay calm. "My father was homeless. He had no place to do the things that were done to Natasha King. My father had no motive. He had no history of sexual abuse. Your pals could not find a single person who would say Homer had bothered them in any way, not even to ask for change. His therapist at the VA said he was a kind, loving man who was suffering from PTSD. That is not psychopathy. There was nothing at the site where her body was found that pointed to my dad. In fact there was absolutely zero evidence that Homer Williams was responsible for the abduction of Natasha King." I pause for a breath, to calm myself down. I continue. "She was found near his tent, and that was apparently enough to stop the police from looking for another suspect. His own public defender never tried to find an alternative theory. The prosecutor could have slept through the trial the defense put on and still won—oh, wait, he did. The judge treated my father as if he had been convicted before he even set foot in the courtroom. And Chief Gifford inserted himself in the case for absolutely no reason. He had no business being there, and yet he was. It's clear to me, and anyone who wants to open their fucking eyes, that either these four men were too lazy to do their jobs properly, or they had some kind of motivation to convict an innocent man. Whatever the reason, two people died—Natasha King, and my father. And the real perpetrator or perpetrators are still out in the world, walking around, maybe even hurting other girls, because no one lifted a finger to stop them."

Detective Rasmussen has been silent throughout my rant. When I finish, he stays quiet for a full minute, I suppose waiting to see if the silence will push me to say more. It doesn't. Finally he says, "I'm not going to pretend you don't have valid points. And, if I thought four men had set my father up for a crime he didn't commit, and if my father died as a result, I'd be pretty freaking pissed. Rightfully so. How angry are you, Xander?"

I sigh deeply. "My mother has been through enough. No way I'd risk making her suffer through another trial. Especially if I was guilty."

"I want to believe you. But you see how it looks, right? The emails and letters and notes. And I hear you confronted Chief Gifford not long ago. None of it looks good, Xander. Not good at all." Rass pauses and looks at a different file. "Have you ever met a Bernard McNeil?"

"Nope. But from what we all saw last night the guy didn't generally come out of his rat hole into the real world." I realize as I say it I've made a mistake.

"The Surgeon didn't name the guy, but you know. How?" Rass asks.

"Are you kidding? Have you seen how fast the people of the internet can find someone these days? It's no secret." That's true enough, and I hope to God I'm right. *Xan, you're a freaking idiot sometimes.*

Detective Rasmussen leans back in his chair and gives me a look that hints at apology. "Well, my friend, here's where I'm at. I can't just turn you loose. Not yet. I have more questions, and I'm pretty sure you have more answers. But it's getting late. So, here's what's going to happen. You're going to spend the night at the lovely Fredericksburg PD Inn, and we will talk again tomorrow."

I start to object. I have no interest in sleeping in a fucking jail cell. Then I realize it might not be a bad idea to be under the watchful eye of the Fredericksburg PD for the next few hours. I muster up a look of disdain. "You know I want my lawyer, right?"

"Of course. I would be disappointed in you if you didn't. We'll let you make that call before we tuck you in for the night." Rass stands. "I'll call someone to get you processed quickly so you can get some shuteye. We'll talk tomorrow."

I'm sure we will, Rass. I'm sure we will.

STASIA

Each of the three cages is wrapped in a blue plastic tarp, only the front open to face the room. All three men are bound and gagged with a thin strip of fabric covering their eyes, offering them shadows and light and a sense of movement around them. Are any of them aware they're not the only prisoner? Perhaps Bishop and David James Ellington have some understanding since they were taken together. But they may believe they were separated while they were knocked out.

There are four white bankers' boxes of evidence. I squat, still dressed in my own clothes, and remove the lid of one of the boxes. There are dozens of external hard drives fitted inside, with a thick pile of stapled paper on top. The drives look the same: blue plastic frame surrounding a sturdy metal body. "Buy one, get one sale at the office supply?" I throw out to the room, not expecting an answer. They don't see what I'm doing, don't know what I'm talking about.

The stack of paper lists the contents of each hard drive. They're all videos, identified by a number. Each drive has a piece of masking tape with a date written on it. I flip through them with a gloved hand, and my gut churns the farther the dates go back in time. Naively, I'd expected 2002 to be early days for Sabine. How wrong I am. The oldest label reads "1987." I suppose it makes sense. The men in the cages didn't suddenly become villains when they were in their forties.

The next box contains photocopied images of ledger entries from an old-school paper accounts book. Amounts, dates, times, and instead of names, numbers. That might give the law enforcement folks some challenges. Oh, wait, nope. My partner has broken the code and included a key to make things easier. I test the key, and find it simple to decipher a handful of names, and my nervous gut rolls like waves on a choppy sea. Judges. Actors. Writers. Politicians. Business people. *So many.* So many eager to participate in the suffering of others. "You really are bastards," I say over my shoulder. At this point, I feel no rancor, only numb acceptance. Any qualms I may have had about this last stage of the plan are now gone.

The third box holds a large collection of both Polaroids and digital photos, printed for posterity? Each photo has the word 'Dove' followed by a series of numbers, the longest is four digits. The photos show unsuspecting women, boys and girls living their lives, presumably before Sabine swept them up and destroyed them. A disconcerting number include very young children. Toddlers. Even babies. These are scouting shots. Fan-freaking-tastic. I wonder if Tasha is in there somewhere, wearing her Madalena uniform, or riding her bike. I scrub away tears. I refuse to let these fuckers make me cry.

The last box is the most surprising, and most heartbreaking. It's a trophy box, a collection of jewelry, hair ties, small shoes, stuffed animals and dolls. Why? Why oh why would the bastards save these? This can't represent all of their victims, not by a long shot having seen the hard drives, so there must be something 'special' about the curated items. *Leave it alone, Stas.*

So we've got video evidence, we've got financial evidence, we've got photographic evidence, and we've got trophies that I am confident can be connected to victims of Sabine. There are photos showing where the contents of the boxes were found, to prove the connection to these men. *Is it enough to indict the three motherfuckers in cages not far from me?*

Yes. Absolutely yes. But I want a confession. I want one or all of them to admit what they did, to leave no doubt. They won't be slipping out of this, but I want the public to understand why we've done what we've done, and equally important, I want the names in the ledgers to be held accountable, too.

The men in the cages are still silent, although one of them—Kodak, I think—is crying. *Good. I hope you piss yourself. I hope you feel some of the terror those innocents experienced.*

I stand, and begin to construct the Surgeon's body over my leggings and fitted Lycra top. Hip and thigh pads make me larger and more square. Another pad straightens my waist. A wrap flattens my chest, and more pads give me pecs and broaden my shoulders. Under the blue surgeon's scrubs none of these details show. A special effects makeup artist or drag queen might guess, but I don't think everyday folks would be able to tell.

The bulk reduces my grace but I'm not performing any particularly sensitive surgeries so it doesn't matter. Everything I've done is basic, and I'm not invested in lifesaving outcomes. If my hand slips, I don't care. These patients are not intended to live.

The final piece of what I think of as the Surgeon's uniform is specially designed sneakers with a 5″ platform. It took a bit of practice to feel secure moving in them, but it's all good now. With the shoes, I'm just shy of five foot ten. That, combined with the physique created by the padding, effectively implies—consciously, or subconsciously—that the Surgeon is a man.

I clip the mic for the voice changer to my face shield, tuck the control into my pocket, and turn to face the cages. "Well, boys, are we ready?"

NICK

Rass isn't in my hotel room tonight. He's decided to stay home with his wife and kids. Tomorrow everyone will know what happens on the StopSabine site. No need to watch it unfold live.

I told myself I wouldn't watch, either, but here I am. As I wait for the show to begin, a thought pops into my head and I text Rass,

> *Do you know who owns The Madalena? Hockenberger referred to 'the owner' in a way that suggests it's an individual, not a holding company.*

Rass texts back almost instantly. I don't think I could sleep either, knowing what's happening.

> *Don't have that information but I can get it. Hold, please.*

On the screen, there's another countdown clock and another visitor counter. The number is even higher than last night.

Rass is back within a few minutes.

> *It's a holding company, but it took a bit of digging and guess who owns the place: David James Ellington's right hand man, Bishop Oliver. And guess who was in a carjacking tonight... David James Ellington and Bishop Oliver.*

> *Two more bits of interesting news: Xander Williams is spending the night in holding. And David James Ellington*

and Bishop Oliver were carjacked and/or abducted tonight.
Waiting to hear more.

What the hell. Before I can process this, the screen changes, pulling my attention. *Thanks. Talk in a bit.* Even though it's the middle of the night, I'm sure we will.

The lights come up all at once like a play would open on a stage. Beneath the bright lights, a naked man is strapped to a metal surgical table. There is a gag in his mouth, and sweat dots his forehead and cheeks. He is entirely on display. He is both thin and flabby at the same time. Under the lights, the glow of his skin is sickly. His penis is so small it's hard to see in the curly nest of gray hair between his pale, fleshy thighs. The man is fully conscious, and unlike the others before him, he is not paralyzed. His panicked jerking is evident as he tries to loosen the thick straps that hold him in place.

The deep, robotic voice that has come to be associated with the Surgeon booms out, and this time, it's chatty.

"Story time, as the kids say. This is Harold Weiner, but he prefers to be called Kodak. Who can blame him? The jokes as a child must've been brutal, especially considering the size of his actual wiener. Is that justification for what he's done? Lots of kids have a shitty time in school and somehow manage not to turn into monsters. Our pal Harry has spent the last thirty years making his living as a photographer. He's well known in the modeling community and has done a lot of editorial and commercial work. Good for him!"

"But that's not all Harry has done. One of Harry Weiner's hobbies is to procure innocent children and women for special photo and video shoots. I say 'procure' because they are not given the option to participate. They have no free will. He buys them, or he steals them. Then Harry sets the stage for them to be raped, tortured, and eventually killed. As if it's not enough to be a monster, he's a greedy monster. He sells photos and videos for lots of money."

"Because I don't want there to be any question about his guilt, I'll leave a box of evidence with his body. In that box, the police will find photos and videos of ninety-seven different women and children taken by Harry Weiner. There are likely more, but that's the number we're going to work with today."

The Surgeon wheels over a metal cart of tools and medical implements. "This will be relatively simple for me. It's going to hurt like a motherfucker for poor little Harry." The Surgeon holds up a scalpel and displays it to the viewers. "This is a 15-blade scalpel. I don't really need to finesse what I'm going to do, so I'm going for comfort. My comfort that is. Whatever tool I use won't be particularly comfortable for good ol' Harry here."

Harold Weiner is in a full-fledged panic, struggling mightily to free himself. It's clear to everyone but him that he has no chance.

I know I should be horrified and worried on his behalf, but with the descriptions of the crimes of the previous victims, curiosity has the better of me. I'm sure he's done something heinous. That doesn't mean I agree that he should be tortured and killed. But I at least understand the motivation.

"Did you have something you wanted to say, Harry?" The Surgeon asks. He removes the gag.

Harold 'Kodak' Weiner screams. "Help! Help! Please help! Help me!"

The Surgeon isn't fazed in the least. "Harry, my friend, you can yell all you'd like. No one will hear you. Do you know why? No? Guess where we are. Take a guess."

At first, Harry looks completely confused. Then understanding comes, and his eyes grow larger. "No! No!"

"That's right, Harry. We're in the same secret place where you brought all those women and children. You chose it because no one would ever hear their screams, and their screams are your favorite part, aren't they, Harry?"

"I'm sorry! I'm so sorry! Please, I'm sorry!" Kodak sobs, verging on hysterical.

"Are you sorry, Harry? Really? Are you sorry enough to tell the audience who you work for?" The Surgeon drops that bomb and waits.

Harry's eyes are so big now they bulge from his wrinkled orange-tanned face. From his expression, I think whoever he works for is at least as terrifying, if not more so, than his current predicament. He stops making noises. He closes his eyes. Tears leak and roll down his face.

"No? That's too bad, Harry. You're not protecting them by staying silent. Because guess what: they're here, too." The Surgeon chuckles.

Weiner's eyes flash open in shock. "What?"

There's a muffled growl from nearby.

Harry goes silent, then sobs, "Just kill me."

"Don't worry. I will." The Surgeon pats him on the knee. "Let's get started, shall we?" With that warning, the Surgeon presses down and draws the scalpel across the top of Harry's left foot. A line of red blossoms. Harry howls in pain. "That's one."

The Surgeon repeats the process, moving up Harry's left side, counting out the slices, which range from one to two inches. All of them look deep. At Harry's lower ribs, the Surgeon says, "There'll be a total of 48 cuts on each side of Harry's body. One for each of the lives he destroyed."

The process takes thirty minutes, although the Surgeon isn't moving particularly quickly. Harry stops his shrieks before the Surgeon starts on the right side of his body. Has he passed out? Or are there so many cuts he's stopped feeling them? After the Surgeon makes the last cut on the top of Harry's right foot, the photographer's body is striped with blood.

"Whew, that was a lot of work. Forty-eight cuts on each side. Ninety-six all together. But wait..." the Surgeon pauses as if thinking. "I said ninety-seven victims, didn't I? That means I need to make one more cut."

Harry wails again, but his throat is hoarse from crying and yelling. He understands it's over. "Please. Please. No more. Just kill me."

The Surgeon nods. "I bet that's something your victims begged for. I bet the little ones cried for their mommies and daddies. Maybe even some of the older ones."

Harold Weiner doesn't say anything because it's obvious there's nothing he can say.

"The youngest child I saw in your photo collection couldn't have been more than four. Four fucking years old, and you decided your greed and your disgusting desire was worth more than that child's life. You are a monster, Harold Weiner. A monster and a coward." The Surgeon raises the scalpel, and draws a deep, straight line from just between Harry's ribs down to his pelvis. The man screams then goes silent. "You're a coward, and cowards don't need guts."

The Surgeon reaches a gloved hand into the man's body and lifts out a wad of internal organs. He sets them down on Harry's upper thighs. Blood is everywhere.

"We're done here. Join us in a little while when we meet the next member of Sabine." The Surgeon says, and the camera goes off.

And I finally remember what's been bugging me about Sabine. There's a replica of the famous statue in the lobby of The Madalena.

Chapter 12

DAY ELEVEN

STASIA

Once the camera light is no longer red, I tear off the face guard and the mask and suck in huge breaths. Strangely, I don't feel like I'm going to vomit. How can that be? Every single bit of stress my whole adult life has made me nauseous, yet I've now killed two men, and my gut is fine. I'm afraid I'm a psychopath, too.

Kodak will live a while longer. He'll be in extreme pain if I don't intervene. I debate. I can quicken the end of his life and still feel justice was served. That's the crucial bit. But equally important, this whole exercise is meant to be a warning. Not to the two men in the cages across the room; it's too late for them. It's a warning to the larger world outside this chamber of horrors deep within an abandoned manufacturing plant.

I walk to the cages and study them. Both men have ball gags in their mouths, so they can't speak. Both are bound at the wrists and ankles. Both had front-row views of the show, although their eye coverings dimmed the specifics. I run a finger along the bars of their cages, and it makes a humming noise. "What do you think? Should I end his suffering? Honestly, if I do, it will be for me, not for him. I need to clean up before the next act, and dying of blood loss takes a while. Oh, wait, you already know that, don't you?"

The bigger one, Bishop Oliver, is glaring at me so hard I almost feel it as a physical sensation even through the fabric over his eyes. David James is doing an impressive job concealing his emotions. That doesn't surprise me. You don't get where he is in life without managing yourself.

I slip the shield back on, return to the table, and draw the scalpel across Kodak's throat, deep enough to sever the carotid artery. It won't be long now.

It's the right choice. Elspeth is in this building, and she's alive. She's miserable, but she's safe. I don't want to drag out her torment, or continue her parents pain, but since the men who would hurt her are contained here with me, I am not going to abandon the plan. If I were to stop here, and contact the police to come for her, these three would get away with their crimes like so many before them. I can't let that happen. I will, however, speed up the timetable. Knowing she is safe from them allows me to deal with these motherfuckers before everything is turned over to the police.

The part of me that's still human is desperate to get out of here, to go far away and claw back to the person who isn't a killer.

THE SURGEON

My partner has positioned a new body on the table. Bishop Oliver is plump but not nearly as fat as McNeill. The ball gag is still in his mouth, and more straps are holding him than were needed to restrain Kodak. Kodak was a wimp.

My friend turns on the camera, and I step into the camera's view. "Hello. I'd say I'm glad you joined us again, but really, I'm not. That you're watching makes you part of the problem. Maybe humans are just hungry for the suffering of others. That would explain beheadings and hangings and burnings. That's a depressing thought because, in that case, this whole exercise is fruitless. It won't change a thing. No, I refuse to accept that. I refuse to believe that my actions in the last week won't have a positive impact. Somehow."

I pat the new 'patient' on the belly. "This man. You're wondering what he did to get himself into this predicament. Well, I'll tell you. Way back in the way back, around nineteen eighty something, two guys were hired at The Madalena country club."

I grab Bishop's jaw and squeeze tightly. The hate radiating from him is intense. In any other situation I'd be afraid. "We'll call this guy Asshole and the other guy the Genius because he's, well, a genius. He had big ideas about how to get rich. This one," I smack Bishop again, and I know it hurts, but he doesn't give me the satisfaction of a reaction, "this guy is smart, too, but a different kind of smart. He's smart, like a weasel. He knows all the people who will do gray things for the right price."

I trace a gloved finger along his exposed skin. He's a hairy one with fur all over his chest. He probably gets waxed to keep himself from looking like an actual gorilla. "So, these two guys get to know each other while working together. The Genius has this idea of how to buy and sell real estate and make everyone rich. The Asshole moves obstacles out of the way. They get the rich guys they caddy for to invest. Within a few years, their partnership is one of the most successful in the world. Those first few years, it all goes great. Everyone's happy, and everyone's making money. And then..."

I grab the man's nipple between my fingers and twist hard. "And then, the two realize they have a shared interest they haven't dared speak of. They like it when things get rough. They like violence. It turns them on. And even better, some of their friends are turned on by the same stuff. Not pretend rough. Way beyond the BDSM stuff you can find in magazines or online. This isn't the kind of thing you can find just anywhere. No. This is the real deal, the sort of event you have to arrange, and it's expensive, time-consuming, dangerous, and most important, the thing at the center of it—the victim—can't be willing. That takes the fun out of it. So the two of them start a second, secret business."

I twist his nipple one more time for good measure and smile when Bishop yelps through the ball gag. "This new business is called—ah, some of you are probably making the connection now—Sabine. Some of you may have heard of the Rape of the Sabine women. That was their inspiration. Ironically, these two didn't understand that the Sabine women probably weren't raped. They were abducted but not raped to the degree we commonly believe. Nevertheless, they thought Sabine would be a great name considering the focus of their secret project."

Bishop thrashes violently when I wheel over my cart full of tools and implements, his substantial body shaking the table, but it's firmly locked in place. "Oh, calm down. You're not going anywhere, so you might as well relax."

"As we've previously discussed, Harry Weiner was in charge of abducting the victims, staging their assaults, recording the sessions, and distributing the final product. Let me introduce Bishop Oliver, the money man. Bishop's role was to manage the finances and the marketing. You see, Sabine has subscribers. People pay lots of money to get a firsthand seat to watch the goings' on. They'll pay even more to direct goings' on. For example, did your girlfriend dump you? Hire Sabine to grab her and do unspeakable things. Not ready to go that far? They will scour the streets until they find a woman who looks like her, and you can direct what happens to the stand-in, up to and including death. Maybe you don't see yourself as a murderer. You're just into little girls—or boys, no discrimination here! But you don't want a street kid who sells themselves to survive. You want someone 'clean.' Pure. Innocent. All sorts of things can be arranged for the right price. Just talk to Bishop Oliver. He's your man."

I point a gloved finger to a cardboard banker's box on a nearby folding table. "That box will be here for the police when they arrive, containing forty years of evidence. Receipts, notes, diary entries, photographs, and audio recordings that may or may not have been made with both parties' consent."

I clap and rub my hands together. "Let's get this show on the road! Honestly, I thought long and hard about what would be an appropriate end for this horrendous piece of human trash, and there wasn't anything I could think of that was sufficiently painful. This will be relatively quick and easy. For me. I'm not sure what it will feel like for Bishop."

I hold up a tool and turn it on. "This is a cranial drill. What might I do with something like this, you're wondering? Actually, Bishop inspired me. I've seen videos where Bishop plays Russian roulette' with some of his victims. He'll load a gun with a single bullet. He hands it to the victim. They can take their chances between three outcomes: shoot him, shoot themselves, or land on an empty chamber for no result other than to intensify their despair. Can you imagine? You've been raped and tortured for days, and you're given this opportunity. What would you do? Point it at your attacker or yourself? You think about that for a moment while I get everything ready."

I swap out a drill bit, then move close to the table. "Hey, there, Bishop. Ready to play Russian Roulette, my version? Here's how it's going to go. I am going to drill random holes into your brain. Sometimes it will hurt, and sometimes you won't feel a thing. It depends on where the drill goes. But eventually, I promise, one of those holes will kill you. Hopefully, not too quickly, because this needs to be fun for everyone. Isn't that how you keep your Sabine viewers happy, Bishop? Are you ready? Let's go!"

STASIA

We're almost done, thank God. I'm so tired. I'm tired of the hate, and anger Sabine has created in me. All the bravado I've built up to get through this is starting to dissipate. I can't let myself think about the 'after' yet, not until it's done. All I know is that, once this is over, I'm looking forward to a nice quiet life on a South Pacific island somewhere.

I glance at my partner, and hold up a gloved hand. I have something I need to say to David James Ellington before he's moved from the cage to the surgical table. I drag over the only chair in the room, remove the fabric covering his eyes, and sit so that I can look him in the face. "I've spent almost half my life helping people, healing them. I took a vow to do no harm. But I've intentionally thrown all that away to stop you. I'll never be the same. I don't know if I can return to the emergency room after this. Hell, I may check into a religious order and spend the rest of my life sequestered in silence. I don't know. I know this isn't me; this isn't who I was or who I wanted to be. I've had to step out of myself to do this. The only thing that kept me going was knowing that, finally, your victims were getting some justice. And there will be no future victims, at least not your future victims."

David James Ellington doesn't reply. At least he has the guts to look me in the eye. But there's no emotion on his face. I don't know whether he thinks if he doesn't engage, I'll change my mind, or if he's accepted his fate. Who cares. I continue. "What I do know is, you can't do this anymore. You can't hurt anyone else like you've hurt so many people. For money. For lust. You've caused so much pain. You've destroyed families. Even your own."

That brings a tiny flinch, but it's gone quickly.

There's a new item on the desk by the table. It's a sound box. A small audio player sits next to it. I nod to my partner. "Get him on the table."

David James Ellington doesn't resist as he's half-dragged, half-carried to the surgical table. He doesn't react to being put in the same place two of his associates recently occupied. When he's sufficiently strapped down, I adjust my surgical attire and carry the remote to the table. I nod for the cameras to be restarted.

THE SURGEON

"David James University pushes the boundaries, but it's legal, and none of its 'students' are forced to participate. While you may disagree with its mission, that business has nothing to do with Sabine. David James Ellington loves little girls. That's a badly-kept secret. The DJU girls are too old to hold his interest. That's what started Sabine in the first place."

I hold my finger above the play button on the remote. "I'm going to play a compilation of audio from some of the recordings David James Ellington, Bishop Oliver, and Harold 'Kodak' Weiner have made over the years. I'd warn you that they're graphic, but if you're here in the first place, you're probably not easily offended."

The room is filled with the sounds of begging, screaming, crying voices. Pleas for mommy and daddy. Shouts to stop; it hurts. Sobs of terror and pain. The sound echoes on the stone walls of the factory space, bouncing everywhere, a horrible circle of hell. I've heard the full version, compiled by the team that gathered all the evidence against Sabine. I let it run for three agonizing minutes before I hit stop and turn to Ellington. "Will you confess? There's not any point in denying it. There are boxes of physical evidence, including videos, phone recordings, financial records, photographs, and DNA. At least if you admit to what you've done, you can give some closure to families that deserve to know."

I pull out the ball gag. He stares at me for a long time. I realize he can shout something that will blow my cover. He doesn't know me, but he could yell that the Surgeon is a woman. It's a chance I'm willing to take. All the way through there have been risks, and this is the biggest one, but also the most important one. I have no idea whether he'll go to his death silently, or proclaiming his innocence, or confessing.

I, and millions of witnesses, wait with bated breath.

Finally, he says, "It's true. All of it. Every word you've said, and probably much more."

I slip my scalpel across his throat. It's done.

***

This is the last bit, and I'm more than ready for it to be over. I turn to the camera, David James Ellington's body limp behind me.

"You've finally found a red room. The idea that you couldn't wait to watch is exactly why I've taken these actions over the past week. People like David James Ellington, Bishop Oliver, and Harold 'Kodak' Weiner had the same gruesome interest and the money and means to make it happen. They were in a position to do more than just fantasize. That same money and means protect them from consequences in our modern world. Only the poor are held accountable for their crimes.

"Sabine is a private group founded by David James Ellington and Bishop Oliver forty years ago to meet the twisted needs of these men and their 'friends.' These people are so cynical, so jaded; they need more than regular sex to be turned on. They need to cause or watch pain being inflicted. They believe their desire is more important than another person's right to life.

"When I first learned what Sabine was doing, I thought about taking my findings to the police. But we've seen, time and again, how that turns out. Money and connections allow evil-doers like these people to control the narrative and, eventually, escape consequences. That can't happen any longer.

"Red rooms are primarily an urban legend, but there are people who make and share torture porn and even snuff films. They just don't do it online. Now you've met these people.

"A yellow envelope was left at the front desk of the Fredericksburg police headquarters two minutes ago. Inside are instructions to find this location. The bad news is, I'll be gone by the time law enforcement arrives. The good news is that Elspeth Bridges is here in this very building. She's alive. She's got a long, tough road ahead of her, but I trust people are waiting to help her get through it."

"Please take this as a warning if you do nothing else. The evil-doers have been allowed to get away with too much for too long. Some of us are unwilling to let that continue. Some of us are willing to act. I hope with all my heart and soul I never have to do this again.

"Sabine is stopped. I am done."

STASIA

Realizing we would not have a lot of time, my partner and I developed the exit strategy this morning. He is in charge of whisking away my tools, the cages, the cameras and lights—everything except the bodies and boxes of evidence. All I need to do is get myself and the Surgeon's costume gone.

Later, I'll think this whole experience was surreal. I'm pretty sure I have an existential crisis coming in my not-too-distant future. Now that I'm done being a serial killing vigilante, I have to find a way to redeem myself, reclaim myself.

For now, there's still work ahead. A lot of work.

I leave the gloves on as I strip off the Surgeon's getup: cap, shield, mask, scrub shirt, pants, apron, and finally, the five-inch platform boots I've been wearing. Now that I've finally gotten used to moving around in them, I won't ever wear them again. That's fine by me. I've had more than enough darkness. The disease has been cured. At least this outbreak. I put each piece into a large black trash bag kept just for this purpose and throw the gloves on top. My tools and everything except the bodies have already been whisked away by my partner. His to-do list is longer and more complex than mine.

I don't bother looking back at the carnage. No point. Time to go.

As I make my way through the twists and turns of the factory's interior, I pull the phone out of my backpack. The magical phone that has made the last week possible. Soon I won't need it. But I can't toss it in the garbage with the rest of the gear. It will require a deeper level of destruction.

I'm surprised to see there's a voicemail. Then I realize it was forwarded from my iPhone, which is in my CRV somewhere in the Pacific Northwest. The message is recent. It wasn't there the last time I checked, only a couple of hours ago.

The voicemail makes me want to vomit, but I get control of myself. If I've made it through everything else in the last week, I'm not going to let the FBI be the ones who finally get me to lose my shit. It's going to be okay. We've got a plan. Not for this, but we're agile; we didn't get this far to have everything fall apart.

I open a new message and type, "FBI has 'requested' to meet with me in Spokane first thing in the morning."

There's a pause, then "Plane will be ready in one hour."

I look at my watch. It's 3 a.m. The plane will be ready at four, and a quick Google search tells me it's another five hours to get to Spokane, even in a private jet. The FBI thinks I'm there already, so 'first thing in the morning' probably means 8 a.m., nine if I'm lucky. *Shit, shit, shit.* The hotel is conveniently located near the airport because the plan always was for me to fly into Spokane and complete my trip to Seattle. But will I be able to keep them at bay for a couple of hours? And will I be able to sneak in without them spotting me?

My gut heaves with stress. I don't have time to be weak-bellied. Right now, I need to get to the airport. The plan was always to be far from the factory before the cops arrive, which is still a priority. Now I also have to find a ride to the airport. I will stick with the original first leg of the plan, and then I'll adjust. I need to put my ass in gear.

The backpack is much lighter once I remove my roller blades. If our calculations are correct, I have ten minutes before the police start arriving in this general area. No time to waste. I lean against a low brick wall and put the skates on. My hands are shaking, which slows me down as I try to tie the laces. Finally, I get them secured and stand. *Deep breaths, deep breaths. You've made it this far. You can get the rest of the way.* And even if you don't, it doesn't matter. If the police somehow catch me, I'll live with the consequences. The bastards are dead. They won't hurt another girl. And Elspeth is safe.

I put my arms through the pack's straps and hug the black trash bag against my belly. I'll dispose of it when I dump the roller blades. Time to go.

I skate north and west, out of the quiet industrial area toward parts of town where life is still happening. I move fast, pretending I'm participating in a race.

My heart threatens to stop as multiple police cars race toward the industrial area I'm skating away from. If they think it's strange that a woman is rollerblading in the early morning hours, they don't stop to talk about it. *Thank God.*

Six minutes later, I've gone nearly two miles and see the familiar welcoming sign of a twenty-four-hour McDonald's. There's a large green dumpster at the edge of the parking lot, where employees park. Perfect. I dump the bag, take off my rollerblades, and toss them into the large green bin. I use a stick from a nearby tree to poke and push until the bag and blades are buried deep under empty food packaging. I slip on flip-flops from my backpack and head into the restaurant.

Inside, I get a cup of coffee and order a Lyft. I have thirty-seven minutes to get to the airport.

STASIA

I sleep for most of the five-hour flight, curled up with a blanket wrapped tightly around me. It's the first solid sleep I've had all week, with no dreams at all. When I wake, we're close to landing in Spokane. My body feels sluggish, and my head aches like I'm coming down with something. It reminds me of what I came to think of as adrenaline flu in med school. After days of running on lots of stress and little sleep, when the body finally gets a chance to rest, it is overwhelmed. That's how I feel now.

But I don't have time to feel that.

It's 9:16 a.m. when we land. It takes twenty minutes to get out of the airport. Fortunately, I don't have to deal with baggage claims or the main terminal. An Uber is waiting out front with a sign that reads 'Natasha'.

I slip into the back and my nerves jack up. I pull a puffer vest out of my backpack and slip into it, then cover it with a navy blue suit jacket that's a couple of sizes too large. Both are loaners from the flight attendant on the plane.

"Hotel is ten minutes away, easy peasy," the driver tells me. He reaches his hand back and offers a hotel key card. I slip it into my pocket. "At our friend's request, I've checked out the hotel parking lot. One obvious Fed car, a black Charger, parked close to your CRV. We'll take a lap around the lot, and if things look good, I'll drop you on the back side, and you can go up the stairs. Your room is #2840 on the second floor."

"Thanks." So close to done. So freaking close.

While the driver circles the lot, I duck down. He's confident the Charger is the only FBI presence, and I agree, not that I'm an expert. I hop out per the plan and enter the hotel through the back door. As I enter the door, a dark-haired woman comes out. Our hands touch as we pass. The woman slips into a waiting car, and it pulls away.

My room is down a hallway and on the left. The bed linens are messy, a wet towel on the floor. I risk peeking out the window and spot the Charger exactly where the driver described.

It's 9:45 a.m. My hard-sided suitcase is already open on the luggage rack, and something about seeing my things makes me want to cry. The FBI agents can wait a couple more minutes. I need a shower to wash the filth off.

NICK

Elspeth Bridges is currently in a private hospital suite with her family. There'll be lots of time for questions later, but I won't be involved in that. That's not my job. I am going home to my family later today. Right now, I'm just killing time. And making inquiries I have no right or obligation to ask.

Yesterday I contacted good old Wayne Jameson at the FBI and shared my suspicions about Stasia King. He got in touch with the Spokane office and sent agents to contact Stasia King this morning.

I've been given access to this morning's video feed around the hotel in Spokane, where she was staying. In the recording, her blue CRV is parked on the west side of the hotel. I know it's hers because it's got New York plates. The agents found it and parked a row away in their black Dodge. The security recording says it's 9 a.m. Spokane time. My sources tell me Stasia asked to meet at ten because she got in late the night before and woke with a terrible headache. Reception confirmed Stasia King checked in just after midnight.

I check the video from other angles. Nothing interesting. A few people are checking out, throwing bags into cars or Ubers, and heading off. A family in a minivan pulls in, and a load of kids and mom pour out. At 9:38 a.m., what is easily identified as a paid car pulls up to the side door at the same time a pale blue sedan arrives and pulls in behind it. A thick woman gets out of the Lyft and crosses the grassy area that runs the length of the sidewalk along the building to a side door. The door opens and another woman comes out. She's petite, wearing cargo pants, a pink hoodie, and a baseball cap over her brown hair, which is either short or tucked into the cap. Oversized sunglasses hide her eyes and obscure the upper part of her face. A duffel and handbag are slung over her shoulder. She slides into the car's passenger seat. The camera angle is pointed right into the vehicle, but the cast of the sun is reflecting off the glass, making it hard to see inside. All I see of him is a reddish beard. I can make out her upper body and general features, but not enough to recognize her.

The car pulls away, and I freeze the frame to get the plate number. I scribble down the info and use my not entirely legal resources to see who it's registered to. A rental. I call the team at Komorebi and ask them to track down the person who rented the car. It takes less than thirty minutes. Someone named Brandee, with a registered address of Los Angeles, California.

The agents met with Stasia in the hotel lobby at 10:12 a.m. They confirmed she looked as if she wasn't feeling well, but she answered their questions honestly and openly. Neither got the impression she wasn't being forthcoming. After forty minutes of discussion, they left her to care for her head. They remained in their car outside the hotel until just after noon to be safe. Stasia did not leave while they watched. She'd told them she would be checking out at three and heading to Seattle, her final destination.

The agents who interviewed her reported she seemed to be telling the truth and had documentation of her whereabouts for the last ten days in receipts from restaurants and hotels and even an auto mechanic shop where she had to repair a flat tire.

I'm not sure what I was expecting or hoping for. Despite what the evidence says, I believe Stasia King is involved in the destruction of Sabine and the rescue of Elspeth Bridges.

Wayne told me about the boxes of evidence against Sabine left at the factory. As the Surgeon said, there were videos, photos, and financial records. Multiple handwritten notebooks looked to match David James Ellington's printing. Bishop Oliver's ego was bigger than his sense of preservation; investigators found his personal porn collection at his home, much of it featuring wealthy friends who did not appear to know they were being recorded.

People all over the globe are speaking with legal counsel in anticipation of being called in to explain the contents of those boxes.

Maybe if Stasia King was smart enough to pull off this magic trick, she deserves to be left alone.

Chapter 13

THE AFTERMATH

STASIA

I understand why Palm Springs is a haven for Angelenos. There's something very freeing about the vibe here. The Airbnb is its own little oasis in the middle of a very glamorous desert.

I arrange fruit, cheeses and meats on a platter, and think about my future. My old life, the life where I held my breath as I waited for *something*, is gone. It feels good that I was able to help so many people for so many years. I'm proud of that. But now I'm ready for a change. A life created by me, for me, with each part, big or small, chosen, intentional.

I hear the front door open and retrieve a bottle of champagne from the fridge. Glasses are on the marble island, waiting.

Hendrix slips onto one of the bar stools and pops a berry into his mouth. "They're coming."

More footsteps in the entry hall. A giggle. A grunt.

Jamie enters first, with Ava—oh, wait, she's going by Willow again—hugging him from behind. They're teenagers high on life and possibility. When she sees me, Willow woops and lets go of Jamie to catch me in a tight hug. I squeeze back. It feels so good to touch this woman who has been part of my life for twenty years, even though this is the first time we've been in the same room since that day long ago in a Virginia high school.

A motorcycle engine revs and then stops in front of the house. Our little gang is complete as Xander saunters in, looking relaxed and happy for the first time since I met him at fourteen. He winks at me and leans on the island.

Xander opens the bottle and fills each glass. We're silent for a long moment, studying each other, thinking—at least I am—about everything that happened then and in the days since.

Finally, Willow says, "To the Surgeon and the end of Sabine."

We raise our glasses and touch them together, each of us, the five parts of the Surgeon. Hendrix, who kept an eye on people who needed to be kept track of, moved what needed to be moved and protected us all with his technological knowledge. Jamie providing the money, the physical logistics, and the mountains of evidence he and Hendrix discovered in the safe in the office David James and Bishop shared. Jamie was also a lure, asking Kodak to take photos of his friend. Willow, the sleight of hand artist, the heart and soul of the operation, and the one who thought to have Brandee, Hendrix's girlfriend, play me on the road trip. Xander, the red herring, who was willing to risk his own freedom if that's what it took. And me, the scalpel. StopSabine would not have been possible without each of us. We worked together to complete a mission born twenty years ago, and ended a monstrosity before more innocents could be hurt.

"To the end of Sabine." We toast again. It's time to step into the lives we deserve.

STASIA

Will she be angry? Disappointed? Will her sense of right and wrong force her to turn me in? I honestly don't know. The only thing I know for sure is that Mama will understand.

She doesn't seem surprised that I'm coming down so soon. When she meets me at the door, there's a question in her dark eyes, but she's patient. She fills me in on Elspeth while she dishes up cabbage rolls and pours wine. "She's doing well. She's been to a lot of doctors. Most of her physical injuries will heal with time but of course the mental damage is significant. Patrick and Anna are doing their best. Nick Winston's Komorebi group is doing a lot." She looks a little defensive when she says, "I've been going to some of their online events, too. I hope, someday, you'll consider it."

"Maybe I will," I agree, and this time I'm not saying it just to put her off. I push away my plate. My gut is rumbling, knowing what's coming. "Mama, I have to tell you something."

She silently refills both of our glasses. *Can she somehow know what I'm going to say? Is it possible?*

"Do you remember Xander and Willow Williams? Homer Williams' kids."

Mama nods and her eyes narrow slightly. Otherwise, her expression is unreadable.

"Do you remember back in high school when Willow and I had that huge fight? She disappeared not long after." I breathe in, giving myself one last moment to change my mind. But no. I have to do this. "Before she left, we talked. She was convinced her father had nothing to do with Tasha's death. She made a compelling case."

Mama's face remains the same. It's making me nervous. Alicia appears out of nowhere, jumping from the floor to a chair to the table. She plops down between us, front and back paws stretched out to make her look twice as long. Surprisingly, Mama doesn't tell her to get down.

"She was right."

Mama's eyes are darker than usual when she interrupts. "Anastasia, are you somehow connected to the Surgeon?"

I swallow half my glass of wine. No going back now. "I *am* the Surgeon."

If I was expecting shock, or horror, or disbelief, I would be disappointed. I don't know what I did expect, but it wasn't this complete lack of reaction. Mama keeps her eyes on me, tips her chin up, opens her mouth slightly, then closes it. She presses her lips together. Finally, she says, "Continue."

"All those years ago, when Willow and I had our conversation, we made a deal. If we ever found out who had killed Tasha, and had caused Homer to be murdered, we would be sure they were brought to justice. They would face the consequences for both Tasha's death and Homer's. We didn't know what it would look like, or how we would do it, but we made a pact.

"Willow had heard stories about David James Ellington and his 'school' for girls. She'd also heard a rumor that some of the things he did were very, very bad. So Willow went away, and turned herself into someone who would get his attention. She came back as Ava. She got invited to the school. Because she's smart, and very beautiful, it wasn't hard to become part of the system. Everything went according to her plan, except one thing: she accidentally fell in love with Jamie, who is David James' son."

Mama hasn't touched her wine. She isn't moving. Just staring. I imagine she's wondering who this woman in front of her is, this woman who looks like her daughter but can't possibly be the girl she raised.

I push on, my eyes on the cat as I rub her silky ear. "Willow—Ava—and I have stayed in touch over the years. We originally thought she would try to find evidence to prove that David James Ellington and Bishop Oliver were heinous people, and when the time was right, we'd come forward together—me mostly for moral support—and take everything to the police. When you told me about

Elspeth, and where she was when she went missing, I knew in my gut it was the people called 'Sabine', and it was time. I called Ava before I came down, and we stayed up all night working out a plan."

I pause, because here's where things went from thinking, to doing. "After the Jeffrey Epstein case, we knew there was a good chance Ellington and Bishop would never spend a minute in jail, or, at best, they'd go to a country club prison for a few years. Then they'd get out and be able to do it all again. With their resources, they might even be able to continue their terrible deeds from prison."

Still Mama doesn't speak.

I want to get this over with, but I can't hurry the telling. She needs to know everything, to understand. "Like I said, Ava fell in love with Jamie Ellington, who is truly a good guy. Jamie's best friend is Hendrix. Hendrix spent two decades in a special unit in the military that deals with technology, so he's really good with computers, phones, all that. Since he left the Army, he's been in charge of security for a lot of the Ellington assets. That gave him access to some of Sabine's dirty secrets, although I don't think the Sabine people realized that. With Jamie's access to his father, Ava's access to DJU, and Hendrix's skill, they were able to get a lot more information about what David James Ellington and Bishop Oliver were doing."

Alicia gets up and stretches, then walks across the table and rubs her head against Mama's bent arm. Still Mama doesn't make her get down.

I continue. "When Ava and I developed the new plan, Hendrix set up a private network of phones for just the five of us—"

"Five?" Mama interrupts.

"Me, Ava, Jamie, Hendrix, and Ava's brother, Xander." I drain my glass and Mama pours more wine without me asking. I wish she would give me some indication of her thoughts, but she's the queen of stoicism. "We had to move fast, and we had to be careful or it could all go to hell. Or worse, David James and Bishop Oliver would find out we were onto them and kill us."

That gets a reaction. Her eyes are big and her mouth forms an O. *I'm an ass.* At no point during all of this did I consider what would happen to Mama if I was found out and imprisoned, or worse, killed. I'm going to spend the rest of my life making it up to her. She pulls Alicia into the crook of her arm and hugs her. I don't think she realizes she's doing it.

"From what we've discovered, killing people isn't even a hard day at the office for them. And we knew Elspeth didn't have much time. So, I came here, and the ball got rolling." I wasn't going to go into what that entailed unless she asked questions.

"But—the trip. You went to Seattle. You were driving across the country. I saw your photos, your car, and you." Mama doesn't sound angry, just confused. She frowns as she thinks about it—did she really see me? She points at the turquoise cuff around my wrist. "How could you be here, doing those things?"

"Yes, we made it look that way. The person you saw was Brandee, Hendrix's girlfriend. She's a bit taller, and thinner, but we look similar enough that she could take photos along the way and post them to my Instagram. She drove my car and took the route I'd planned out. She paid for everything with my credit card in case someone checked. It worked out great, until your friend Nick Winston set the FBI after me."

Mama wrinkles her nose and looks down at the cat. "That might have been my fault. It wasn't like you to misidentify the gravesites of Truman and Atchison. You would never make an error like that. I made an off-hand comment to Nick while we were looking at your photos."

"That was an unfortunate oopsie. I corrected it once I saw it, but that was a few days after it was posted. Brandee didn't know enough to realize the mistake. Oddly, not everyone is an expert on presidential gravesite locations." The joke falls flat. I sip more wine, appreciating the warmth, and the sense of calm it's giving me. I'm not sure what to make of Mama's continued lack of emotion. I wouldn't object if Alicia came to comfort me, but I suppose she's gone to the person she feels needs her most.

"Was Xander Williams actually involved in the attacks?" Mama asks. "The police seemed to think so."

I shake my head. "His role was to be the decoy, to distract the police. He has a history of angry outbursts, unfortunately, so that made him a good red-herring for us. He wrote the emails and sent a card and the letter to the editor, but he never got physically close to any of the men. I won't call them victims, Mama. I won't."

She doesn't object so I continue. "There was no way he could actually be tied to any of the attacks. We made sure of that. It would have been too cruel for two generations of King men to be punished for crimes they did not commit."

"You were very busy girls." Mama says, and it's not a compliment. Alicia gives her a look of mild irritation; I think Mama might have stroked her a bit too hard.

Busy is an understatement, but I don't say that out loud. "The FBI wanted to meet me the Sunday before the conference, when I was supposed to be in Spokane. But I was still in Virginia, handling—the last bits. I had to get across the country, fast. Jamie Ellington has access to a number of private planes so I didn't have to wait for a commercial flight. Brandee and I literally passed each other as she left the hotel through a side door and I snuck in. The FBI was thorough in their questioning but..." I shrug weakly.

Mama is staring at me as if she's not sure who I am, and my heart squeezes painfully. "David James Ellington's own son was involved with this plot? Wasn't he in an accident trying to stop the people who took his father?"

"He was. Jamie and Ava knew Bishop and David James would be taken, but were intentionally left out of the plan as to when or how, so they could react authentically. Jamie had no idea Hendrix would force the accident."

"It must have been painful for Jamie to know his father was involved in such things. We want to believe our parents are good people." Mama says. I wonder if she's thinking about George, my own father.

"Jamie loved his father, but he hated him as a man. When he and Hendrix were young, they came across a video..." I swallow hard, and the rest comes out in a whisper "...a video that might have been of Tasha. They didn't understand what it was at the time, just that it was very bad, if it was real. That's when Jamie came to understand his father and Bishop Oliver were doing horrible things."

"How did they know it was Tasha?" Mama whispers, the blood draining from her face.

"They didn't, at first. Not until just recently, in fact."

Mama is confused.

"The girl in the video had a pink watch on." I don't add that's all she had on. "Bernard McNeill had a framed photo of his daughter wearing the same style and color watch. And when Tasha was found...I heard you and Dad," it hurts me to call him that, in ways I can't explain, "talking about how Tasha was found with a pink watch, even though she didn't have a pink watch."

"Why didn't any of you go to the police?" Mama demands, finally showing emotion. Anger. Frustration. Alicia gets up and retreats to the middle of the table.

"We all agreed that if we went to the police, Ellington and Oliver would use their money and their influence and their power to get out of it. They'd frame someone, like they did Homer. Or they'd move out of the reach of American law enforcement. Or they'd spend years manipulating the legal system and continue doing what they were doing. None of that was okay. And Elspeth would likely have been killed immediately."

She doesn't argue.

"Jamie and Hendrix had been collecting evidence since Hendrix left the military. Bishop thought he was good at tech security, but Hendrix is better. None of the evidence is perfect on its own, which is why we—I—got David James Ellington to confess before I killed him." It's the first time I've said the words out loud. Somewhere inside she probably was hoping I was lying about being the Surgeon.

Mama doesn't acknowledge it, though. Instead, she's chewing on her lip. "Why were you easier on him than the others? I wondered that."

"Because he was still Jamie's father. That, and I wanted to be able to get Elspeth to safety as soon as possible. Once we figured out she was in that very same warehouse, everything sped up. The original plan was to space out the men's deaths, similarly to the way we'd done with the attorneys. But none of us wanted to delay getting Elspeth home."

Mama doesn't point out that we could have simply taken Elspeth to the police. We talked about it. They would have asked how we found her. They would have asked lots of things. And the bastards would have had time to run. We needed to finish the plan. It needed to end. We made a decision and now we all have to live with the consequences.

I run a finger around the stem of my wine glass, empty again, and Alicia is attracted by the musical sound it creates. She pokes at it with a black paw. "The other thing is, there are hundreds of men and women who paid Sabine to watch, or even participate, in the terrible things they did. Those people need to be held accountable. The evidence we collected, and the confession, should help."

For a very long time, Mama is utterly silent, the only sound the occasional car driving past the house. Eventually, she taps her index finger on the table—once, twice, three times. "Thank you for telling me. I understand why you did what you did. It pains me that my sweet, loving daughter felt she had no choice but to become a killer, and make no mistake, that is what you are. The saving grace is that I know you are not a killer in your soul. And, part of me is overjoyed that the bastards who did that to Natasha have paid a price." She takes in a deep breath and looks me in the eye. "Doctors put bodies back together. Butchers take them apart. My daughter is a doctor, not a butcher. We will not speak of this, ever again. Never."

We sit in silence, each reflecting on what I've shared, and, in my case, what the future holds. She reaches for Alicia. I reach for the ballerina around my neck and stroke it.

I have one more confession to make.

STASIA

Your gravesite is simple and neatly kept. Mama and I sometimes come here and have a picnic, with your favorite carrot cake, and read you silly stories from *People* magazine, although as the years have passed, it's gotten harder to find gossip about people whose names you'd recognize.

I drop onto the damp grass and sit cross-legged. I don't care if anyone sees me talking to a headstone. I'm sure lots of people do it in cemeteries.

Hiya. I know, it's not your birthday, but it's just as important, to me.

It's weird to think you've been dead more than twice as many years as you got to be alive. Almost two-thirds of my life. You've missed a lot of cool stuff. There are cars that run on electricity; some even drive themselves, but they don't fly like they would in Back To The Future. *There are websites called social media where people chat with their friends, and argue with complete strangers. It's pretty weird. Some people are obsessed with sharing photos of themselves that show everyday life stuff, like what they ate for lunch or what they're wearing. That's weird, too. Now we take pictures with our phones, believe it or not, and everyone has their own phone number, even kids. We can listen to books and podcasts—podcasts are audio stories—on the phone, too. True crime is one of the most popular podcast topics. Your case has been discussed on quite a few of them, but they will never know the real story.*

Tasha, sister that I miss so much, love so much, I need you to know vengeance has been had, justice served, and the bastards will never hurt anyone again.

I dig out a narrow band of soil at the base of the headstone, a few inches long, three or four inches deep. I slip off the ballerina pendant, press it to my lips, and tuck it into the hole.

I'm sorry I broke your ballerina.

XANDER

"Join us for a two-hour special this Sunday as we investigate the case of Homer Williams. Even though this homeless vet had no motive and no opportunity, he was quickly accused and convicted of the rape and death of fourteen-year-old Natasha King. Attorneys, police, and even a judge conspired against this man who had already given so much to his country. Before he could file his first appeal, Williams was found dead in his cell of an apparent suicide. Authorities now say Homer Williams was murdered. With the revelations unearthed in the headline-grabbing Surgeon case, we are learning there is so much more to this story. Join us as we go deeper into the story of a homeless man, a fourteen-year-old girl, and a dark web of rape and abuse, and how they came together to bring a terrible conclusion to a terrible case."

STASIA

Mama and the Bridges family have all joined Komorebi. I'm still sort of convinced it's a cult, but at least it's a good cult. Mama says she's been able to talk about things there she never could speak of before. I see lots of positive changes in her. Whatever is bringing that about is fine by me.

Elspeth is getting help to deal with what happened to her when she was gone.

I've spoken with Margot a couple of times. She's met people who are siblings of other survivors, who understand what it's like to live with that shadow, good and bad. She seems to be doing okay, and I'm really glad for her.

I appreciate the value of Komorebi, but I'm not ready to join. With time, I've convinced myself Nick Winston correctly believes I was involved in the StopSabine activities. I'm trying to move away from that time in my life and find a new normal. Maybe someday I'll get to a headspace where I can put everything in a neat little box somewhere, but I'm not there yet. So I'll keep my distance and be happy that Mama is finding peace she's never had before.

Jamie has taken over full control of the David James Group and renamed it the James Group. Jamie and Hendrix relocated the James Group to the west coast to get a fresh start. The University closed after David James Ellington's death. Ava vanished. At first, Jamie took her disappearance hard, but he and Willow Williams will be married in a few weeks. Her mother and brother will give her away.

I'm the maid of honor.

THE END

Want more Komorebi?

Here's the first chapter of That Carver Girl, that latest entry in the Komorebi serial killers world. Coming June 18, 2026

THAT CARVER GIRL

PROLOGUE

The best hiding spots were near the creek where the hickory trees grew thick enough to make tunnels. She had been playing in these woods as long as she could remember, back when Ryan still played with her instead of going off with his friends all the time, back when everything felt safe and simple and every day was an adventure.

She was six and three-quarters, which was almost seven, which meant she was old enough to go pretty far on her own as long as she stayed on the property. Gram had said so just that morning.

Gram was a little distracted lately. Grandpa had gone to Jesus just a few weeks ago and Lucy sometimes found Gram crying quietly on the front porch of the big house they all lived in.

The Karst Valley Nursery stretched for acres and acres, full of nursery rows and wild patches and secret places that seemed to belong only to her.

Afternoon sun filtered through the canopy in gold streaks, making patterns on the forest floor. Somewhere above, a cardinal was singing. Lucy had her stick, a good one she'd found last week, perfectly smooth and just the right length for a sword or a magic wand depending on what the game required. Today it was a sword because she was hunting dragons.

She'd been tracking one (a particularly mean-looking root system whose tendrils squiggled and wove through the soil) for at least ten minutes when she heard something that didn't belong to the usual forest sounds.

It sounded like something being pulled across leaves and undergrowth.

Lucy froze, suddenly very much aware that she was alone and far from the house. Mom's voice echoed in her head. "Stay where people can hear you in case you need to yell." But this was still their property. Still safe.

It was probably one of the workers or Daddy moving equipment or seed.

She crept toward the sound, curiosity overriding caution the way it always did. Mom liked to remind her, "Curiosity killed the cat."

And then Gram, forever her champion, would add with a wink, "And satisfaction brought it back!"

A small clearing at the edge of the hill came into view through the trees. And there was Daddy, dragging a very large bag. Soil, maybe, but why would he bring dirt to a hill that was nothing *but* dirt?

Lucy's brain tried to make it make sense. Maybe it was a deer?

Then the bag moved. By itself. Twisted. And it made a sound that wasn't a deer sound or a bag sound but something small and in pain and scary.

And there was red. Dark red on the beige canvas.

Lucy took a step closer, branches crackling under her feet.

Daddy turned his head. The thing in the bag thrashed and the canvas shifted. A shape came out through the opening. Long dark hair was matted with dirt and something else. Lucy could see now. It wasn't an animal. It was a woman.

The woman turned her head just enough for their eyes to meet.

Brown eyes, wide and pleading and full of something Lucy didn't have words for yet but would remember for the rest of her life. She was trying to say something, but her mouth was covered. The sounds she made turned Lucy's insides watery.

"Daddy?" Lucy's voice was a whisper.

He turned and looked at her. First he looked surprised, then angry.

And then he laughed.

Daddy loved his jokes, and he laughed like she'd told him a good one. Not a mean laugh or a scary laugh, but something almost delighted.

Lucy's sword-stick fell from her hand, and she ran.

ACKNOWLEDGMENTS

To Kirsten, Noelle, Mariëtte and Adri for helping me work through the process.

To my beta crew, especially Daniel McBreakneck and Lesley Lloyd, who gave excellent feedback early on.

To all the people who are willing to answer my "What if" and "How would you" questions. It's amazing all the weird stuff people know! And it's amazing how many weird people I know!

And thanks, most of all, to the people who encourage me to keep writing. You have no idea how much your kind reviews and stars and private notes asking "When's the next book coming out?" mean. They're pretty much everything.

ABOUT THE AUTHOR

People who know her well think some of the details from Sara's real life would make a fascinating story, but Sara says the stuff she writes is much more believable and a lot less traumatic. She is a fan of good tequila, travel, cooking, and animals, not in that order. Sara was born in Santa Monica, California, but moved on purpose and with intent to Des Moines, Iowa. She's owned a pet food company, co-founded an animal & human welfare nonprofit, and is on the board of her city's library foundation. She lives with her blind canine personal assistant Charlie, who edits her newsletter, and Charlie's seeing-eye cat Eartha Kitta who used one of her nine lives with FIP and lived to tell the tale. (If your cat has FIP, look for FIP Warriors 5.0 on Facebook. There's hope.)

Visit and be the first to know when the next book is coming out. You can also sign up for Charlie's newsletter, and enter to win a free books and goodies.

One of the best compliments an author is if you like a book, tell people about it. If you enjoyed *Little Doves* please leave a review wherever you bought the book—and thank you!

Sara is on Goodreads, Facebook, and Instagram and would love to connect.

www.ingramcontent.com/pod-product-compliance
Lightning Source LLC
Chambersburg PA
CBHW051333250626
47155CB00007B/2585